Broadcasting Disruption

Thomas Brant

CHAPTER 1 - A (Court) Date to Remember

Monday 13th October 2025

The newlyweds were sat in the Smith family living room, tension crackling in the air like static before a storm. James Smith leaned forward on the edge of the worn leather sofa, his hands clasped tightly together, knuckles white with strain. Beside him, Lyra Nott—now Lyra Smith—rested a reassuring hand on his shoulder, her gaze steady despite the knot of nerves tightening in her chest.

They had just received a letter in the post, four really, each one which was a court summons date for R v Cody Lane, one for R v Chloe Smith, James's sister having divorced her husband, Cody, shortly after their manipulations and scandals had begun to unravel, one for R v Kylie Morgan, all three as witnesses for the prosecution in the upcoming trial set to expose the corruption and abuse that had festered within the walls of Manic Radio Group for years. The fourth summons was for R v Manic Radio Group Ltd, Manic Vibes Ltd, Manic Ventures Ltd and Manic Properties Ltd, representing the company as a whole. Each case was set to reveal a different layer of the toxic culture, manipulation, and outright criminality that had defined the organisation James once called his workplace. The trials, all interlinked, would be a pivotal moment for both justice and the broadcasting industry.

James turned the letter over in his hands, the weight of it seeming heavier than the paper it was printed on. "It's finally happening," he murmured, his voice low and filled with a mix of relief and trepidation. "They're actually going to face consequences."

Lyra squeezed his shoulder gently. "And so will Manic. This is our chance to make sure they don't get away with it anymore. Unless..."

James looked at Lyra, his brow furrowing. "Unless what?"

Lyra hesitated, glancing at the stack of papers on the coffee table. Among the legal jargon and court schedules lay a recent tabloid clipping, headlined "Radio's Fallen Stars: The Trials That Could Sink Manic". The media frenzy had already begun, with headlines speculating not just on the outcome of the trials but on the lives of the individuals involved.

Looking at his MacBook, the one that he had had a few months earlier as a replacement for the one that was being used as evidence for the case against Chloe, Cody and Kylie, James noticed that the podcast that he and Lyra had done, a 6 part series titled Broadcasting Boundaries: Inside the Manic Meltdown, had garnered yet another influx of downloads overnight. The podcast, once a cathartic outlet for their experiences, had evolved into a cultural touchstone, exposing the grim realities of corporate radio culture and galvanising public support for accountability.

James sighed deeply and shut the laptop. "The world's watching this, isn't it? They're not just looking at them; they're looking at us too."

"Let them watch," Pete Smith interjected as he walked into the room, carrying a tray with three mugs of tea. The elder Smith's voice carried the gravitas of decades spent behind a microphone, a tone of reassurance amidst the chaos. He placed the tray on the table, careful not to disturb the precarious stack of legal documents. "This isn't just about you, James. It's about every presenter, producer, and staffer who was ever chewed up and spat out by that machine."

James took a mug and cradled it, letting the warmth seep into his hands. "Do you think the trials will really change anything, Dad? I mean, Manic Vibes is still broadcasting like nothing happened. They're even hyping up House of Manic Live. Care to guess who they've got hosting it this year for Brum's one?"

Pete's expression darkened as he sank into the armchair opposite his son. He didn't need to guess—he already knew. "Chloe," he said grimly.

James nodded, his jaw tightening. "Yep, she's got the main opt-outs, as well as Toni Green... and someone who's returning to Manic after they resigned last November."

Pete raised an eyebrow, his curiosity piqued. "Returning? After all this? Who's desperate enough—or daft enough—for that?"

"Al Crozier," James said, and Lyra laughed. James knew that for half of 2022, the whole of 2023 and most of 2024, she and Al had shared a drive show on what was now Manic Vibes Stoke and Cheshire, before he resigned following an on-air incident he had where he, along with Toni Green, had swore live on air on a Sunday evening network show, the two having been covering for Smitty, a 26 year old Manic DJ who'd been ill that weekend and couldn't host Sunday Sessions. Al's resignation had been framed as a "mutual decision," but everyone at Manic knew the truth—it was a PR stunt to cover up the station's inability to control its increasingly chaotic roster of presenters. Now, his return felt like another chapter in the never-ending circus that was Manic Vibes.

Lyra shook her head, her laughter tinged with disbelief. "Of course, they'd bring him back. He's exactly what they need—a wildcard to keep people talking. And Toni? She'll lean into the drama for the airtime. It's all about the numbers."

Pete sipped his tea thoughtfully. "It's always been about the numbers. But numbers don't keep the lights on forever. Public trust does. And right now, Manic's is hanging by a thread."

The room fell silent for a moment, the weight of Pete's words settling over them. The trials weren't just a chance to bring down Cody, Chloe, Kylie, and the Manic hierarchy—they were an opportunity to force the industry to confront its failings. But that weight wasn't easy to carry.

As James got up to get himself a drink, the doorbell rang, echoing through the quiet Smith household. Everyone exchanged a glance, their nerves already taut from the day's developments. Pete rose to his feet, placing his tea on the table, and moved towards the door.

"Who could that be at this hour?" he muttered, more to himself than anyone else.

James followed him into the hallway, a knot of unease forming in his stomach. Lyra remained in the living room, her eyes darting to the stack of summonses, her thoughts racing. Pete opened the door cautiously, revealing a tall man in his seventies, who Pete knew was someone he had worked for back in the Dudley FM days, and now aired DJ Strangelove shows on his network of community radio stations across the Midlands. It was Woody Bones, a legendary figure in local radio circles, and a man who had earned his reputation as a fierce advocate for authenticity in broadcasting. He stood there, his signature leather jacket slightly weathered, and a grin that had seen better days but still carried the warmth of a bygone era.

"Pete," Woody said, his voice rich with the nostalgia of a time when radio was personal and local, "I was in the area, chatting to some pals over at Black Country Radio, and they mentioned they'd been called up as a witness in a criminal case against Manic. The first people to ever subpoena a community radio station for evidence in a case this big. Thought I'd stop by, see if you needed anything."

James knew that both his parents often talked to Woody, as his mum, Sarah, the owner of a production company that supplied shows to community and independent radio stations, frequently collaborated with Woody's network. But to see him here, unannounced, stirred something unexpected—a sense of solidarity amidst the chaos.

Pete stepped aside, letting Woody in. "Come on in, Woody. We could use a friendly face right now."

James then noticed someone following Woody, a woman in her mid-30s who screamed radio station management, and he assumed it was one of the managers of the various Bones owned stations across the Midlands. She was dressed sharply in a tailored blazer, carrying a leather-bound planner and an air of no-nonsense authority. As she stepped into the hallway, her heels clicked against the hardwood floor.

"Pete," Woody began, gesturing towards the woman, "you know Emma Wright, my station manager at Three Towns Radio, right?"

James watched as his dad chuckled. Three Towns Radio, James knew, was the station Bones owned that covered Kidderminster, Bewdley and Stourport, not far from the Pensnett home of the Smith family. Pete extended his hand, his smile warm despite the lingering tension. "Of

5

course, I know Emma. I've done a few Teams meetings with her about the DJ Strangelove show, as well as the podcast Sarah and I did for Three Towns about the old Wolverhampton FM and Dudley FM rivalry, as well as that retrospective we did about the 42 years since Wyvern FM came on the air." Pete's smile widened as he shook Emma's hand, noting her firm, professional grip.

Emma nodded, a polite but focused expression on her face. "Good to meet you in person, Pete. And James," she added, glancing towards him with a faint smile. "I've heard quite a lot about you, especially after Broadcasting Boundaries. Stirring up the industry, eh?"

James gave a half-smile, his hands still tucked into his hoodie pockets. "Not sure stirring up is the right word. More like airing the laundry no one wanted to touch."

Woody chuckled, the sound deep and rich. "Well, somebody had to do it. And it couldn't have come at a better time. Manic's days of sweeping things under the rug are over. But that's why we're here—we're in need of a new programme director for the network, and your presenting contract with Manic is up at the end of the month, Pete. You'd be working with Emma, Taz, Paul, Yousif, Abdul and the other 8 station managers in the network, making sure that the networked slots and the local shows strike the right balance between professionalism and the authenticity community radio thrives on. You'd be based at the Tettenhall studios of South Staffs Radio, and you'd still get to do your DJ Strangelove show. Sarah did mention you were planning on leaving Manic Goldies drive anyway."

Pete froze for a moment, processing Woody's unexpected offer. He glanced at James and Lyra, who both looked equally surprised. The room felt suddenly smaller, the weight of the day's events magnified by the enormity of the opportunity Woody had just placed before him.

"Programme director for the Bones network," Pete said slowly, as though testing the words in his mouth. He leaned back slightly, crossing his arms, his expression a mix of intrigue and caution. "That's... not a small role, Woody. What brought this on?"

Woody shrugged, the leather of his jacket creaking faintly. "You've got the experience, Pete. The industry needs people like you now more than ever—people who understand what radio should be, not what these corporate machines have turned it into. Manic is falling apart, but the community radio sector? It's thriving. And we want to keep it that way. Your name came up more than once when Emma and I started talking about what we need for the future. That and you have a Business degree from the Poly."

James chuckled, as he knew his dad was a Wolverhampton Polytechnic graduate before it became Wolverhampton University, and that while he had worked for Woody Bones from the age of 13, being a child mascot of Dudley FM, then a tea boy, a runner and production assistant before, after graduating from Wolverhampton Polytechnic in the early 90s as one of the last cohorts before it became a university, finally becoming a presenter at the station that had formed the backbone of his career.

Pete exhaled slowly, his eyes shifting between Woody, Emma, and his family. "It's a big ask, Woody. And you know as well as I do that taking this on would mean not just leaving Manic Goldies but stepping into a role that's going to be scrutinised. Especially now, with everything going on."

Emma, ever the pragmatic professional, interjected. "That's exactly why we need you, Pete. The Bones network prides itself on being what radio used to be— authentic, community-driven, and transparent. With what's happening at Manic, people are going to look to us as an alternative. Having someone like you on board sends a message. It says we're serious about raising the standard."

"Anyway, Dad," James said, grinning. "Mum spends most of her time either here recording shows for Reeves Radio to sell to stations like the Bones network, or working with Taz over at Tettenhall studios for South Staffs Radio. Seems like it'd be the perfect fit. Plus, I bet she'd enjoy having you around more during the day."

Pete chuckled softly, shaking his head. "You're both terrible at subtlety, you know that?" He glanced over at Lyra, who offered a supportive smile. "What do you think?"

Lyra shrugged lightly, her tone warm but firm. "I think you've got an opportunity here to do something meaningful. You've always said radio should be about people, not algorithms or egos. This could be your chance to put that into practice."

Woody leaned in slightly, his voice dropping to a more serious tone. "Pete, I know this is a lot to consider, but the trials are going to shine a spotlight on everything wrong with the industry. If you step into this role, you could help shape what comes next—be part of the solution instead of just watching the fallout. Think about it."

Pete nodded, his mind already spinning with the possibilities. The allure of returning to community-focused radio, combined with the chance to help rebuild trust in the industry, was undeniable. But the weight of the trials, the ongoing chaos with Manic, and his family's own challenges made the decision far from straightforward.

"I'll need some time to think it over," he finally said, his voice steady but thoughtful. "This isn't the kind of decision you make lightly."

Emma smiled, a hint of relief in her expression. "Of course. Take your time, but don't take too long. The industry's moving fast, and we'd like to have you on board before the end of the year if possible."

Woody clapped Pete on the shoulder, his grin returning. "We'll leave you to it, then. But remember, Pete—radio's always been about connection. And right now, you're in a position to make a hell of a lot of them."

As Woody and Emma departed, the Smith family settled back into the living room, the weight of the offer hanging in the air. Pete glanced at James and Lyra, his expression softening as he considered everything they'd been through.

"I've spent my whole life in this industry," he said quietly, more to himself than anyone else. "Maybe it's time to do it on my terms."

James nodded, his respect for his father clear. "Whatever you decide, Dad, we've got your back."

And for the first time in what felt like an eternity, Pete felt a glimmer of hope—hope that amidst the chaos, there was still a chance to rebuild, to make things right, and to leave a legacy worth being proud of.

****

CHAPTER 2 - First Appearance at the Magistrates' Court
Tuesday 14th October 2025

The witness room at Wolverhampton Magistrates' Court was packed to the gunnels. James, Lyra, and Pete sat together, their expressions ranging from tense to resigned. Around them, a cacophony of voices filled the air— executives, producers, and presenters from Manic Radio mingled uneasily with staff from community stations. Woody Bones, wearing his signature leather jacket, stood near the corner, chatting with a young solicitor who was scribbling notes with the fervour of someone preparing for their first major case, and another solicitor who was, James assumed, someone who was more experienced than the younger one.

James noticed his own solicitor, Theodore Nott, Lyra's brother, talking to another solicitor, who James assumed was from the same firm as Theodore—sharp-suited and exuding an air of quiet confidence—gestured subtly towards James, catching his eye. James nodded in acknowledgment, his stomach knotting at the gravity of what was to come. Theodore stepped away from his conversation and approached, his demeanour calm but purposeful.

"James, Lyra," Theodore began, addressing them both but keeping his voice low. "It's a procedural hearing today. No surprises, but they'll read out the charges, and the magistrates will decide if the cases are too complex for their jurisdiction—which, given the nature of these allegations, they will be. I was originally slated to be one of the Magistrates for this case, as I'm a Justice of the Peace in this region, but as I'm acting as your solicitor, I've naturally recused myself. The cases will be referred to the Crown Court, likely Birmingham Crown Court, due to its capacity to handle high-profile trials. This is just the beginning, so prepare yourselves—it's a long road ahead."

James nodded, swallowing hard. "And Chloe? Cody? Kylie? Will they be here?"

Theodore glanced at his watch. "Yes, they're required to attend. They'll be brought in for their individual cases, which will proceed one by one. You'll likely see them in the courtroom, but don't engage. Let the process speak for itself."

Lyra squeezed James's hand. "We'll get through this," she said softly, her voice steady despite the unease flickering in her eyes. "One step at a time."

It was then that three people walked in that James recognised - Rory Carter, Kyler Thompson, and Penny Lane—all from the Manic Radio fold. James gulped when he saw the trio walk in, as Kyler and Rory had been two of his abusers, and Penny had been complicit in the degradation he had endured. The sight of them, laughing amongst themselves as if they were at a social gathering rather than a legal hearing, sent a chill through James's body.

"They don't seem too worried," James muttered under his breath, his voice tinged with bitterness.

"They're likely witnesses for the defence," Theodore replied, his tone cautious. "We won't get a formal list until pre-trial proceedings in the Crown Court, but I'd wager Manic's defence will lean on them to back up their narrative. People like Rory, Kyler, and Penny are complicit enough to try and defend the indefensible, even if it unravels under cross-examination."

"But why would they be called now and not at the Crown Court?" James asked, trying to keep his voice steady despite the anger bubbling beneath the surface. "I know on The Bill and Law and Order UK that-"

Theodore chuckled and James wondered why Theodore chuckled softly, his serious demeanour momentarily lightened by James's reference. "James, real life isn't quite like The Bill or Law and Order: UK. This is a procedural hearing, not a trial. Rory, Kyler, and Penny are likely here because they've been subpoenaed for their roles in the events. Their presence could mean they're under investigation as well. The CPS might decide their involvement warrants charges, or they could be used later as witnesses for the defence—or even the prosecution. But for now, no one will be giving testimony. Today is just about setting the stage for the cases to move forward."

"Will there be press, like radio or the papers?" James asked, worried that the presence of journalists might escalate the stress of the day. He didn't want his story splashed across tabloids or dissected by the same industry that had already chewed him up and spit him out.

A woman who Theodore had been talking to stepped across and nodded. "Yes, James, there may be some members of the press present, but restrictions will be in place. The magistrates can impose reporting restrictions, especially since this case involves allegations of abuse, manipulation, and workplace misconduct. Given the potential impact on your mental health and the ongoing investigations, I'll request that the court enforce those restrictions. The focus today isn't on the details of the case but on deciding jurisdiction. That limits what can be reported for now."

"Oh, I forgot to introduce you," Theodore said, chuckling as he held hands with the woman. "Lyra knows who this is, but James, this is Ellie Nott, my wife and a fellow solicitor. She works for Nott Solicitors as a Criminal and Employment Law specialist. She couldn't attend your wedding to my dear sister because she was defending someone down in London the same day that you two had that registry office ceremony. She's here to assist me with your case, as we're dealing with multiple angles: the criminal charges against Chloe, Cody, and Kylie, and the potential employment tribunal claims against Manic Radio for fostering a toxic culture."

James nodded awkwardly, feeling the weight of both the family and professional dynamic at play. "Thank you for helping," he managed to say, though his voice cracked slightly.

Ellie gave a reassuring smile. "We'll do everything we can. Just remember, today is about process, not outcomes. Keep calm and let us handle the heavy lifting."

"Oi, slut!" James heard the voice of Kyler Thompson cutting through the murmurs of the room like a blade. "You just had to ruin the special times that we had, didn't you? Couldn't keep your mouth shut. Now look where we all are." His sneering voice carried across the witness room, drawing startled glances from others present.

James froze, his body stiffening as memories of Kyler's abuse flooded back. Lyra immediately stood, placing herself slightly in front of James, her gaze piercing and protective. "Say one more word, Kyler, and you'll be explaining it to the magistrates," she said coldly.

Before Kyler could respond, Theodore stepped forward, his calm professionalism masking a quiet fury. "Mr Thompson, I advise you to refrain from speaking to my client or his family. Any further comments could be construed as witness intimidation, which carries severe consequences."

James watched as Kyler's smirk faltered briefly under Theodore's sharp words. However, his bravado quickly returned as he muttered, "Witness intimidation, my arse." He turned away, pretending to lose interest, though his body language suggested he was still spoiling for a fight.

Ellie, ever composed, stepped beside Theodore. "James, Lyra, let's take a step back. Remember, we're here to follow the process, not to get drawn into petty provocations. Kyler and his ilk thrive on that."

James nodded reluctantly, his hands clenched tightly into fists. Pete placed a steadying hand on his shoulder, leaning in to whisper, "You've already won by being here today. Don't give him anything to use against you."

"Now, what gets me," Theodore said with a chuckle, "is why the defence may have called for certain individuals like Kyler to attend today's hearing. Normally, Section 51 hearings, ones where cases are referred from the Magistrates' Court to the Crown Court, don't involve character witnesses or anything resembling testimony. Either Manic are trying to intimidate the prosecution, or they're testing the waters to see how much support they can muster for their defence. Either way, it's highly unorthodox, and if they step out of line, we'll be quick to point it out."

The room settled into a tense quiet as the ushers began calling names for the first case to be heard: R v Cody Lane. James and Lyra exchanged a glance as Cody was led into the courtroom, his demeanour calm, almost casual, as though he were immune to the gravity of the situation. Chloe followed shortly after, her expression cold and aloof, though her eyes darted nervously around the room. Kylie Morgan, the third defendant for the day, entered moments later, her appearance calculated to project poise, but the faint sneer on her lips betrayed her confidence.

"Typical," Pete muttered under his breath as the three filed into the dock. "They think they're untouchable."

The magistrates entered the courtroom, their robes neat and expressions neutral. The lead magistrate, a woman with a firm but fair reputation, addressed the court. "This is a Section 51 hearing for the cases of R v Cody Lane, R v Chloe Smith, R v Kylie Morgan, and R v Manic Radio Group and associated entities. Due to the complexity and seriousness of the allegations, this court will consider whether the cases should be referred to the Crown Court."

As the charges were read out—ranging from coercion and harassment to workplace misconduct, fraud, and conspiracy—the gravity of the situation became palpable. Each charge felt like a stone dropped into the still waters of the room, the ripples touching everyone present.

"What they'll do," Ellie said to James, as Theodore, who was on the other side of Pete and Lyra, nodded in agreement, "is lay out the key accusations and evidence summaries to justify why this case is outside the Magistrates' jurisdiction. Given the nature of these allegations—fraud, coercion, systemic abuse—it's almost certain the magistrates will agree to send this to Crown Court. Now, I can tell there's at least 3 members of the press here, but they're all tame ones."

James was confused why there would be tame members of the press present, and Ellie seemed to pick up on his expression. She leaned in slightly, keeping her voice low but clear.

"By 'tame,' I mean ones that work for Woody Bones's community radio network or other independent outlets known for ethical reporting. They're likely here to ensure the story is told without sensationalism. Given Woody's connections, it's no surprise he'd have his trusted people present. It's better than having the tabloid vultures circling. Jayden Brooks, the young bloke in the Nike jacket, he works for South Birmingham Community Radio as a presenter, one of the few that Woody Bones hasn't got under his network. He's known for straight-talking and fair coverage. Jason Hall, the lanky lad next to him, is one of the Three Towns hosts, so he's on Bones's network. The older woman in the corner, that's Pat Whitaker—she's an investigative journalist who's been covering workplace misconduct in the broadcasting industry for years. She's freelance but has a solid reputation for accuracy and fairness. They're not here to stir up drama; they're here to get the facts right."

James nodded slowly, taking in the information. The presence of ethical journalists was a small comfort amidst the tension of the day. He could only hope their reporting would shed light on the truth without twisting it into sensational headlines.

The lead magistrate's voice cut through the room once again. "Given the scope of these cases, and the evidence presented in the pre-trial dossier, it is the decision of this court that all matters be referred to the Crown Court. The next hearing will take place at Birmingham Crown Court on the 18th of November 2025."

James looked at Lyra, whose hand tightened around his. The date was over a month away—time to prepare, but also time to endure the weight of anticipation. He caught Pete's eye, his father giving him a small, reassuring nod. They had crossed the first hurdle, but the road ahead still stretched long and uncertain.

As the magistrates exited the room, the tension in the witness area eased slightly. Theodore leaned in, his voice calm but firm. "This is what we expected. Now, the real work begins. We'll have a formal pre-trial review at the Crown Court, where both sides will outline their key arguments. It's not like the TV shows go, where the prosecution and defence dramatically clash from the outset, there's no surprise evidence that either side whip out in a chance to go 'Gotcha', there's no barristers sleeping with the Judge in order to secure a favourable ruling... yes, they tried that storyline in Judge John Deed, but trust me, that's not how it works. The public are allowed to sit in the courtroom, but with these allegations, we'll likely see restricted seating or additional security measures in place. Now, I bet you've either watched Suits or Bull, yes?"

"Bull, isn't he that guy who is based on Dr Phil, the talk show host? And yes, I'm guilty of boxsetting Suits... especially as the Dutchess of Sussex starred in it." James allowed himself a slight smile at the mention of Suits. "I've also seen on Netflix The Lincoln Lawyer," James said, trailing off as Theodore chuckled and nodded.

"Ah, The Lincoln Lawyer. Ellie hates that with a passion, same with Law and Order UK, and how they portray court cases as one grand theatrical event. Real life isn't quite so glamorous or dramatic. Don't expect a 'gotcha' moment or fiery speeches in the courtroom. Instead, it's methodical, evidence-driven, and often painfully slow. But that's what ensures fairness and justice. And trust me, there's no jury gasping over new revelations the way TV makes you believe."

Ellie chimed in, a wry smile on her face. "Dick Wolf and his bloody series have done more to misrepresent the legal system than anything else. I mean, yes, Bradley Walsh and Jamie Bamber made Law & Order: UK compelling to watch, but the reality of the English courts is far less Hollywood." She adjusted the files in her hands and continued, "The CPS will present their evidence meticulously, and the defence will counter every point they can. It's a battle of patience and detail, not theatrics. And let's not forget the timelines. On TV, trials happen in days, maybe weeks. In real life? We're talking months, if not years, especially with a case as complex as this one. I wouldn't be surprised, as there's 3 human defendants and a quartet of body corporates, companies in other words, which are in the dock, then Christmas next year is spent talking about what happened during these trials. Complex cases like this tend to stretch well beyond what Hollywood—or even British dramas—would have you believe. But that's why we're here. Our job is to keep everything on track and make sure the truth is heard, even if it takes time."

James exhaled slowly, absorbing the gravity of Ellie's words. The road ahead was daunting, but knowing that Theodore and Ellie were guiding the way provided a sliver of reassurance. Lyra leaned into him slightly, her presence grounding him amidst the chaotic swirl of thoughts.

As the Smith family, Theodore, and Ellie made their way out of the witness room, James caught sight of Chloe lingering by the courtroom entrance, her expression as cold and sharp as a winter morning. She made no move to speak but her gaze lingered on him, a mix of defiance and something else—fear, perhaps? He couldn't tell, and he wasn't sure he wanted to. Pete, ever the steady presence, gently nudged James forward, steering him away from the silent standoff.

Outside, the crisp October air was a welcome reprieve from the tension-filled courtroom. As the group walked over to Queens Square, James noticed his dad chuckling as they saw the former Beatties department store, now a shadow of its former self, with posters for Wolverhampton University.

"You know, I need to get my coursework done soon," James said with a wry smile, breaking the tension slightly. "It's funny, really. Had I not joined Manic last October, I'd be at home right now, or at Hits or Capital maybe, my degree in Film and Media Studies having been completed, being able to say that Wolverhampton Uni was the place where my life began to take shape." His voice carried a bittersweet edge, reflecting on how drastically his life had shifted since he entered the chaos of Manic Radio. "You know, I need to thank Theo in a way for getting his paralegal to have words with the Dean of Wolverhampton, to get them to let me do my final year again after I left at the end of December because of that bloody contract Chloe made me sign to become the hub cum dump."

Lyra gave James's hand a reassuring squeeze, her voice soft yet firm. "You've come a long way since then, James. And this"—she gestured back towards the courthouse— "is part of reclaiming your life. Whatever Manic threw at you, they didn't break you. You're here, standing up to them."

Pete, walking a few steps ahead, turned back with a chuckle. "And who knows, James? Maybe in a year or two, you'll be recording a podcast about how to juggle a degree and taking on a corrupt company. Call it Broadcasting Back to Uni."

James couldn't help but laugh, the levity easing the knot in his chest. "I might have to run that one past Lyra first. She's the creative brains in this operation."

As the group made their way towards a café on Queen Square, Woody Bones and Emma Wright caught up with them. Woody's leather jacket creaked slightly as he gestured animatedly. "Pete, I couldn't help overhearing about James and Wolverhampton Uni. You know, the Poly gave you a pretty solid foundation back in the day. Maybe it's time we started looking at how to bring more students into community radio. They need real experience, not just corporate internships where they're fetching coffee and running errands."

Emma nodded in agreement. "Woody's right. With all the backlash against Manic and its toxic culture, there's an opportunity here to create something better. James, you've already shown how important authenticity is to the industry. Maybe you could use your experience to mentor others—help them avoid the traps you fell into."

James hesitated, caught off guard by the suggestion. "Mentor? Me? I'm barely figuring out my own life right now."

Lyra nudged him gently. "You underestimate yourself, James. Look at what we've accomplished with Broadcasting Boundaries. You've already helped people by sharing your story. This could be the next step."

Pete chimed in, his tone encouraging. "They're right, son. And if you ever need a co-host for that podcast about balancing uni and radio, I'm your man. I'll even bring vinyls for the theme music."

****

CHAPTER 3 - The Waiting Game
Thursday 30th October 2025

The days between the procedural hearing and the upcoming Crown Court trial seemed to stretch endlessly. For James Smith, each passing hour was weighed down by a relentless churn of anxiety. The knot in his stomach had become a constant presence, a reminder of the monumental task ahead.

James was sat on the sofa in the Smith family home, a bowl of cereal in front of him that was left abandoned, the want of food not exactly his main concern. His MacBook, which was in front of him as well, had a completed essay that he had done the previous year, which the course guide had stated as a chance to select and research in depth a specific topic in the field of Media and Cultural Studies, Media and Communication Studies, Broadcast Journalism or Public Relations.

Looking at it, James remembered how he had originally wrote about radio in general, and how contemporary hit radio stations like Capital, Hits Radio and the Manic network had become increasingly focused on branding, social media, and scripted interactions rather than authentic broadcasting.

Part of it, however, had been rewritten to reflect his personal experiences at Manic Radio.

"In the early days of commercial radio, stations often cultivated unique identities that reflected the local communities they served. Stations like Birmingham's BRMB or Manchester's Piccadilly Radio built loyal audiences by weaving local culture, news, and personalities into their programming. However, the consolidation of radio ownership in the 1990s and 2000s ushered in an era where brand consistency took

precedence over local flavour. Networks like Global and Bauer, as well as newer entrants like the Manic Radio Group, rebranded local stations under umbrella identities such as Capital and Hits, creating a homogenised listening experience across the UK.

Branding in CHR now extends far beyond station jingles and logos. It infiltrates every aspect of the listener's journey, from the tone of voice used by presenters to the selection of music and even the station's presence on social media platforms. This shift prioritises the "brand message" over individual expression, with presenters often required to adhere to strict guidelines about how they speak, interact, and even dress. For example, Capital FM's "Capital Breakfast" hosts are marketed less as radio presenters and more as multimedia personalities, blending their on-air personas with curated Instagram feeds and TikTok challenges.

While this approach creates a cohesive identity that is easily recognisable to audiences, it often comes at the expense of spontaneity and authenticity. Presenters are no longer valued solely for their ability to connect with listeners but are also expected to act as brand ambassadors, selling not just a playlist but a lifestyle.

At Manic Radio, a subculture of extreme branding emerged, where presenters became interchangeable cogs in a larger corporate machine. The emphasis shifted from genuine on-air connection to a rigid adherence to scripted banter, pre-approved playlists, and social media metrics. The 'Manic Way' demanded that authenticity be sacrificed for virality, turning what was once a platform for creativity into a factory line for disposable content.

Furthermore, the cocaine and alcohol culture among presenters at Manic Radio, while unofficially acknowledged, became a toxic undercurrent of the network's drive for high-energy, relentless performance. The combination of intense branding pressures and this culture not only eroded the mental health of its staff but also created an environment where misconduct could thrive unchecked. This environment, fuelled by the pursuit of numbers and virality, prioritised short-term gain over long-term integrity, both for the station and its employees.

One thing, however, that is hidden inside Manic is the Hum Cum Dump-"

James paused, his fingers hovering over the keyboard. His thoughts were swirling. That last sentence—"One thing, however, that is hidden inside Manic is the Hub Cum Dump"—was a line he had initially typed in anger when drafting this rewritten version of his essay. It was raw and honest but also something he wasn't ready to publish. It was a scar too fresh, too personal, to expose fully.

Deleting that segment, and replacing it, James continued.

"The Big Weekenders, an internal staff tradition at Manic Radio, epitomised the network's focus on excess and spectacle. These events were less about team bonding and more about pushing employees to embody the high-octane, hedonistic lifestyle that the brand projected. From sharing multiple partners for sexual intercourse with protection against STDs discouraged to ensure "trust," to widespread drug use, the culture fostered an environment of debauchery disguised as camaraderie. For many employees, including myself, participation felt less like a choice and more like a tacit expectation. To decline was to risk being labelled as not fitting the 'Manic Way.'

That is not to say that all radio stations in the CHR space have succumbed entirely to this approach. Manic is the exception to the rule, with both Bauer Radio's Heat and Hits networks, as well as Global's Capital continuing with more relatable and balanced approaches to maintaining their CHR identities. Both networks demonstrate that it is possible to merge branding with authentic listener connections, albeit with varying degrees of success. Hits Radio, for example, balances its national appeal with regional opt-outs for localised content, the breakfast shows and regional news being the only remaining aspects of local radio that remain, which many listeners still find relatable. Capital, on the other hand, relies heavily on its 'star power'—a mix of celebrity interviews and cutting-edge pop music to maintain its dominance in the CHR market, with Drivetime and regional news its sole localised offerings.

Despite these differences, what stands out is that both Hits Radio and Capital have retained a sense of balance that Manic Radio has abandoned. Manic's approach has created a uniquely toxic culture that prioritises shock value and social media virality over the very qualities that once made radio a trusted and personal medium. As a former employee, I witnessed firsthand how this relentless drive for branding at all costs can degrade the integrity of a station and harm those working within it."

James leaned back, rereading the final paragraphs. His essay wasn't just an academic exercise anymore—it was part therapy, part manifesto. It was his way of processing what had happened to him and taking the first steps towards reclaiming his identity from the chaos of the past year.

Lyra appeared in the doorway, a cup of tea in hand. "Still at it?" she asked gently, setting the cup down on the table in front of him.

James gave a half-smile. "Yeah. Just finishing up this essay. You know, I wrote it back in October last year, before I joined Manic, and it was almost a love letter to them, painting Bauer and Global as the bad guys in the industry. Ly, what do you think would be the best sources I could use to cite some of the various points I made? I've already used both The Guardian, OFCOM reports, as well as Radio Today as some of the most reliable sources I could think of. I also used some of Bauer's press releases, when they rebranded Free Radio, Signal 1 and the various heritage brands into Hits Radio."

Lyra pulled up a chair and sat next to him, glancing at the screen. "Those are solid choices, but you could also consider adding some academic references. Media studies journals like The Radio Journal or Convergence: The International Journal of Research into New Media Technologies often have peer-reviewed articles on the evolution of radio broadcasting. And don't forget books—there's The Radio Handbook by Carole Fleming, which has some great insights into commercial radio's history and trends. It could give your essay that extra academic edge. I noticed you mentioned Heat Radio. In a way, that's not a traditional CHR station, but more of a niche brand under Bauer's umbrella. You might want to compare that to how Manic has completely shed any pretence of variety or depth in its programming."

"True, but Heat plays similar tracks to Hits, and they are sister stations, even though for advertising it comes under Kiss and the Magic Networks, so I thought it was relevant to mention in passing," James replied, taking a sip of the tea Lyra had brought him. "If you look at the playlist, they push Groovejet, No Doubt's It's My Life, Anne-Marie's 2002, Fifth Harmony's Work From Home, and similar tracks. I could have added BBC Radio 1, couldn't I?"

Lyra nodded thoughtfully, brushing a strand of hair behind her ear as she scanned James's essay. "You absolutely could add Radio 1. It's a strong comparison point—especially since it's public service broadcasting and doesn't have the same commercial pressures as Manic, Bauer, or Global. They still manage to engage younger audiences while balancing authenticity and branding. Mentioning their Live Lounge sessions or the way they curate new music could highlight how a CHR-style station can still offer depth."

James considered her words, tapping the edge of his laptop. "That's a good angle. Radio 1 has its quirks, but it's leagues ahead of the 'Manic Way.' They manage to connect with listeners without forcing their presenters to act like walking hashtags or…" He trailed off, his jaw tightening as memories of Manic's toxic culture resurfaced.

Lyra placed a hand on his arm, her voice gentle but firm. "You're not there anymore, James. Remember that. This essay isn't just an assignment—it's your chance to speak your truth. You're reclaiming the narrative."

James exhaled slowly, nodding. "You're right. It's just… some days it feels like I'm still stuck in their shadow, you know? Like everything I do is about them."

"That's normal," Lyra reassured him. "But every word you write, every step forward, is a step away from their control. You're creating something honest, something real. They can't take that away from you."

James smiled faintly, her words offering a sliver of comfort. "Thanks, Ly. I think I'll include that comparison to Radio 1. Maybe something about their balance between playlisting and presenter individuality. It'll round things out."

Typing on his MacBook, James knew that Lyra's point in addressing BBC Radio 1's aspect of being a public service broadcaster added a new dimension to his argument. Unlike the commercial giants, Radio 1 had the unique advantage of being funded by the licence fee, allowing it to focus on its remit to inform, educate, and entertain without the relentless pressure of advertising revenue.

In addition, he felt he needed to add a paragraph or two about Heat Radio, while being classed as a CHR station, took some of its format from the magazine of the same name and its celebrity and pop culture focus, giving it a distinct niche in the competitive CHR market. This was in stark contrast to Manic Radio's approach, which prioritised shock value and viral trends over any attempt to cater to a specific listener base with depth or variety.

James carefully worded his new paragraphs:

"Heat Radio, while being classed by most as a contemporary hit radio station, playing mainly throwbacks and popular culture songs, such as No Doubt's "It's My Life" and Fifth Harmony's "Work From Home," takes its identity from the magazine of the same name, focusing on celebrity gossip, pop culture, and a lighter, more accessible tone. Unlike Manic Radio's chaotic and often toxic approach to engagement, Heat Radio maintains a sense of cohesion and purpose, leveraging its niche to build a loyal audience. This alignment between content and brand identity demonstrates how CHR stations can carve out a unique space in the market without resorting to sensationalism or compromising workplace integrity.

In stark contrast, Manic Radio's reliance on shock value, sensational stunts, and a superficial focus on social media metrics has alienated both its audience and its employees. The network's unwillingness to invest in meaningful content or foster a positive workplace culture exemplifies the worst aspects of commercial radio's evolution.

Furthermore, the state funded public service addition of BBC Radio 1 to the essay gave me an insight to consider that, unlike its commercial competitors, it has consistently managed to evolve and stay relevant in the CHR space without losing its public service ethos. The network supports new and emerging artists, provides a platform for diverse voices, and balances its playlists with unique segments like the Live Lounge, where artists perform stripped-down versions of their tracks or unexpected covers. Radio 1's ability to remain authentic while engaging a younger audience stands in stark contrast to Manic Radio's over-reliance on virality and gimmicks.

Other aspects of the BBC network include BBC Introducing, where new and emerging artists gain exposure on a national stage, showcasing music that might otherwise be overlooked by commercial stations driven by rigid playlists. This platform fosters a genuine connection with listeners by offering something fresh and meaningful, a stark departure from the formulaic predictability of Manic Radio.

Moreover, Radio 1's presenters are given space to develop their own on-air personas, encouraging authenticity and individuality. This approach not only strengthens the bond with listeners but also creates a healthier work environment for staff—a sharp contrast to the scripted, high-pressure environment that defined my experience at Manic Radio. The contrast between the two highlights the potential for CHR stations to prioritise substance over style while still maintaining broad appeal.

With the advent in the 2010s of streaming services such as Spotify and Apple Music, CHR stations faced new competition for listeners' attention. These platforms allowed audiences to curate their own playlists, removing the need to rely on radio for music discovery. In response, successful broadcasters like BBC Radio 1 adapted by emphasising unique content that could not be replicated by an algorithm. Features like the Live Lounge or segments focused on emerging music offered added value to listeners, demonstrating a commitment to creativity and innovation within the CHR format.

In contrast, Manic Radio's strategy leaned heavily on the superficial allure of virality, hoping that social media stunts and shock tactics would fill the gap left by declining listener engagement. This shortsighted approach neglected the deeper connections that radio could foster, both with its audience and its staff. Instead of adapting to the new landscape with substance, Manic Radio doubled down on style—often to its own detriment."

James saved his updated essay, satisfied that he had captured the essence of his argument. It wasn't just an academic critique anymore; it was a personal reclamation of the radio industry he once loved. Adding comparisons to Radio 1, Hits Radio, and Heat Radio had given the piece a well-rounded perspective, illustrating how CHR could thrive without sacrificing integrity or humanity.

Lyra smiled as she read over his shoulder. "It's strong, James. You've nailed the balance between critique and constructive analysis. And your voice comes through—this isn't just theory; it's lived experience."

James leaned back, exhaling deeply. "Thanks, Ly. It feels like I'm finally starting to take control of the narrative. Manic doesn't get to define my story anymore."

Lyra gave his shoulder a reassuring squeeze. "Exactly. And when the Crown Court case begins, you'll have more than just words—you'll have the truth on your side. Now, eat, as its eleven, and you've been up since seven."

James chuckled, as he looked at the bowl of cornflakes and chuckled, as he knew that he and Lyra had an appointment at twelve at Russells Hall Hospital, as it was 6 months since he and Lyra had conceived a baby, and therefore their routine antenatal check-up was due. Lyra was insistent they didn't miss it, despite the whirlwind of court dates and media attention surrounding their lives. She glanced at her watch.

"We've got just under an hour before we need to head out. Finish those cornflakes, James, or you'll be starving halfway through the scan."

James nodded, pushing himself upright and picking up his spoon. "I'll try, but honestly, I'm more nervous about this appointment than the essay or the court case. It's weird, isn't it? This tiny person is coming into all this chaos."

Lyra smiled warmly, resting her hand on her small but noticeable bump. "They're coming into a world where their parents are fighting for something better. That's what matters."

As James ate, Pete walked into the room, holding his phone. "Just got off the phone with Woody Bones," he said, settling into his favourite armchair. "He's been talking to Emma Wright about expanding their mentoring programme. Apparently, your podcast and what you've been through have inspired them to create workshops for media students. They want to use it as a case study."

James froze mid-bite, looking both surprised and uncertain. "Workshops? As in… me teaching?"

"Not just you," Pete clarified. "They're bringing in people from different stations—Hits, Capital, even BBC Radio 1. They want to show students the spectrum of what radio can be and the pitfalls to avoid. You'd just be sharing your story as part of a broader programme. No pressure."

Lyra grinned, nudging James playfully. "See? You're already making a difference. That's what this is about—showing the next generation that there's more to radio than the Manic way."

James exhaled, his mind spinning at the idea. "I'll think about it. Right now, I just want to get through today."

Pete nodded. "One step at a time. Speaking of which, I've been thinking about Woody's offer for me to join his network as Programme Director. The more I think about it, the more it feels like the right move. But I don't want to overshadow what you're doing, James. This is your fight, and I don't want to take the spotlight."

James shook his head, his expression firm. "Dad, this isn't about me. It's about fixing what's broken. If you think joining Woody's network is the right thing to do, then do it. We're in this together. Anyway, your contract renewal meeting with Manic is next week, isn't it?"

Pete nodded, setting his phone down on the armrest. "It is, but I've already made up my mind. I'm not renewing. They'll want to keep me on Goldies Drive, but I can't pretend everything's fine while the whole organisation is imploding. Woody's offer to join his network feels like a chance to actually make a difference. At least there, I won't be a puppet on someone else's string. I'm the only one of the Dudley hub that's still at One Snow Hill on Goldies after tomorrow. It's Tim's last day."

The mention of Pete's looming departure from Manic Goldies cast a brief silence over the room. Pete had been a staple of first Dudley FM, then Midlands Manic, then the West Midlands Manic Goldies station, carrying a legacy that few others could claim. His decision to leave wasn't just a career move; it was a stand against the chaos that had consumed the industry he loved.

James broke the silence, his tone thoughtful. "Tim's leaving too? That's... kind of the end of an era, isn't it? You two were some of the last real radio voices there."

Pete nodded, a flicker of sadness in his expression. "Tim's heading to Boom Radio. He had been planning to go back in May, but Manic wouldn't release him from his contract early. He's ready for something with more heart, and honestly, so am I. It's strange, though, isn't it? Watching the people who built radio's soul scatter to the winds, while what's left behind becomes unrecognisable."

****

CHAPTER 4 - A Father's Worry
Friday 31st October 2025

The Smith household was unusually quiet for a Friday morning. Pete, James, and Lyra were gathered in the kitchen, sipping their respective drinks—tea for Pete, coffee for James, and herbal tea for Lyra. Outside, the crisp autumn air carried the faint scent of damp leaves, and a grey sky loomed overhead. Halloween decorations were sparse this year, with only a lone pumpkin sitting on the windowsill, its carved face more melancholic than menacing.

James was scrolling through his emails, his face set in concentration when suddenly he saw one which made him worried.

From*: codester00@hotmail.co.uk*

To*: jamie3443snetta@yahoo.co.uk*

Subject*: Final Warning*

James,

You think you can just walk away and ruin my life? Think again. This isn't over. You've always been a weak little boy, hiding behind your daddy and your girlfriend. But the tables are turning. Watch your back.

Happy Halloween,

Cody

James froze as he read the email's subject line: Final Warning. His heart began to race, his coffee momentarily forgotten. The email address, codester00@hotmail.co.uk, sent a shiver down his spine. Cody Lane. The alias was unmistakable, and the timing was far from coincidental.

James's stomach twisted as he reread the email, each word dripping with malice. His hands trembled slightly as he pushed the laptop away, staring blankly at the screen. Lyra noticed his sudden change in demeanour and set her tea down.

"James? What's wrong?" she asked, her voice laced with concern.

He gestured weakly to the laptop, unable to find the words. Lyra slid the computer towards her and read the email, her expression shifting from confusion to anger.

"Is this... Cody?" she asked, her voice low and steady, though her eyes flashed with fury.

James nodded, his voice barely above a whisper. "He's threatening me. Again."

"Again?" Sarah asked as she walked into the living room, her voice laced with worry. She paused when she saw James's pale face and the laptop in front of Lyra. "What's happened?"

Lyra handed her the laptop. "Cody. He's sent James a threatening email. It's not even subtle. Do you think Chloe told Cody all of James's fears and vulnerabilities?" Lyra finished, her tone sharp with anger and protectiveness.

Pete, who had just entered the room with a steaming mug of tea, set it down carefully. His face hardened as he read the email over Sarah's shoulder. "What the bloody hell is he playing at now?" he muttered, his usual calm demeanour slipping into visible frustration. "This isn't just a nasty email—it's intimidation. And with the trial coming up, this needs to be reported immediately."

"You know, I was thinking," James then said. "The courts are dragging their backsides on the custody cases too, aren't they? I mean, about Chloe's baby, your grandson and my nephew, and Kylie's baby... my... child. I mean, Cory is 3 months old, my child, and she's still in foster care as Kylie dumped her on Social Services, and Chloe's insisting that her baby, Owen, stays with her. I mean, what's Chloe going to do if she goes into prison? Is she going to drag Owen into a prison cell with her?" James continued, his voice tinged with frustration · and exhaustion. "How's that fair to him? And what about Cory? She's innocent in all this mess, but she's already caught up in the fallout of what Kylie did. I mean, the foster family won't let me even see Cory, so I'm missing out on being there for her during her first months. It's all so twisted. And then... well, we've found out for certain what the gender of Lyra and my baby is. Dad... you're going to have another grandson."

Pete's expression softened at the news, the tension momentarily melting from his face. "Another grandson?" he said, his voice breaking into a small, warm smile. "Well, that's something worth holding onto amidst all this madness. Congratulations, son, Lyra."

Lyra smiled faintly, her hand resting on her bump. "Thank you, Pete. It's been one of the few things keeping us grounded."

James, however, couldn't hold onto the joy for long. "But what kind of world is he coming into? A world where his sister's been abandoned by her mum, his half-brother, Alfie, up in Liverpool with his mum, who again won't let me see him, and his cousin who might end up being raised in a prison nursery? It's not fair. None of this is fair."

Pete sighed deeply, sitting down at the table and looking at his son with a mixture of pride and sorrow. "James, the world's always going to throw curveballs at us. But what matters is how we handle them. You're doing everything you can for Cory, Alfie, and the new baby. Anyway, as Theo said the other day, when you asked him, it all depends on if Kylie or Penny put you on the birth certificate as the father depends on the rights over Cory and Alfie. If you're not listed, it complicates everything. But if you are, you have legal grounds to fight for custody of Cory and access to Alfie. It might take time, but it's not impossible. You've got Theo and Ellie on your side, and they're bloody good at what they do."

"Yeah, but if you remember Dad, the GDPR request I did a few months ago when the whole thing started which Theo recommended I do, and then got the ICO to intervene and compel Manic Radio to release my employee records, showed that my DNA matched the DNA of the foetus at the time they did a paternity test as part of their unethical 'baby bonus' scheme. That's how we know for sure that Cory is mine. Kylie might have signed away her parental rights when she left Cory with Social Services, but this shouldn't be so complicated if the records clearly state I'm her father. And Alfie, the same tests Manic did show that he's mine too. At least with this little one," he said, rubbing Lyra's bump gently, "there's no ambiguity. Lyra and I are together, and we'll raise him in a stable, loving home. And if the social have concerns because 6 months ago, I was still on cocaine, then you and Mum are here to help, so that should count for something." James's voice cracked slightly, and he looked down, his hand still resting on Lyra's bump. "I just want to do right by my kids."

Lyra leaned closer, placing her hand over James's. "And you will, James. You've already come so far. We'll fight for Cory and Alfie, and this baby will grow up surrounded by love, no matter what happens with the rest of it."

Pete nodded, his face lined with concern but also determination. "We'll get through this, James. Together. But for now, we need to focus on what's in front of us. That email from Cody? We're not letting it slide. It's intimidation, plain and simple, and it's against the law. Theo and Ellie need to know about this immediately."

Sarah spoke up, her voice steady and practical. "I'll forward the email to Theo. He can liaise with the police and make sure this is documented. Cody's trying to rattle you before the trial, but we won't let him. He's probably hoping you'll react in a way that gives him an edge in court."

"Right," Pete agreed. "Stay calm, James. Don't engage with Cody or anyone else trying to provoke you. Focus on the things you can control—your essay, the baby, and getting ready for court. The rest, we'll handle."

James sighed, his hands gripping his coffee mug tightly. "I'm trying, Dad. But it feels like everything is spinning out of control. One minute I'm writing about the radio industry, and the next I'm dealing with threats from a guy who should be locked up. I don't even know how to balance all this."

"You don't have to do it alone," Pete said firmly. "You've got us, James. And you've got Theo and Ellie. This fight isn't just yours—it's all of ours."

Sarah added, "And don't forget, you've already taken the hardest steps. You've exposed the truth about Manic, you've taken responsibility for your mistakes, and you're doing everything you can to be a good father. That counts for something, James. It counts for a lot."

Lyra reached over and squeezed James's hand. "Listen to them, James. We've faced worse, and we've come out stronger. Cody's threats are just noise. They don't define who you are or what kind of father you'll be."

James nodded slowly, his grip on the mug loosening. "Thanks, everyone. I needed to hear that. I just... I want to believe it'll all work out. You know, I need to get out of here for an hour, I need to get some fresh air. I might jump on a 2 up to Dudley, nip into... oh, yeah, the Council shut their drop-in centre, didn't they?"

"Yeah, they shut that centre a while back," Pete replied, his tone tinged with frustration. "Another cutback in the name of 'efficiency'. Why? What was you going to do?"

"I was going to see if I could... well, apply for a council house for Lyra, me and our baby to move into after he's born," James replied. "It might not be much, but it's a start, isn't it? Somewhere to build a fresh beginning for all of us without the memories of everything that's happened here."

Lyra smiled softly. "That's a good idea, James. Somewhere stable, where we can focus on us and the baby without all the noise from... well, everything else."

Pete nodded approvingly. "It's a practical move. But you're right—Dudley Council's cutbacks have made things tougher. You'll probably have to apply online or make an appointment through their housing team. I can help you look into it if you'd like."

"Yeah, let's do that later," James said, his voice a little lighter now. "It feels like the right thing to do. I'll check what the process is when I get back."

Pete stood and grabbed his coat. "Tell you what, I'll walk with you to the bus stop. A bit of fresh air wouldn't hurt me either, and we can chat on the way. Sound good?"

James nodded, finishing his coffee and standing up. "Yeah, that sounds good. Thanks, Dad."

****

As the two men walked along Bird Street onto Tennyson Street, where the 2 and 2A, the buses from Merry Hill to Dudley and the Wrens Nest estates, stopped, Pete glanced sideways at James. His son's shoulders were hunched against the crisp autumn breeze, and his hands were stuffed into the pockets of his jacket. Pete could see the weight James was carrying, even in the way he walked.

"You know, James," Pete began, breaking the silence, "you're doing the right thing by Lyra. Not just by marrying her, but by sticking by her and the baby you two are bringing into this world. That kind of commitment isn't easy, especially with everything else going on. Do you know why I never talked to your Uncle Nigel, my brother, before he killed himself, even though your cousins on the Smith side of the family seem to think I should have?"

James looked at his dad, puzzled by the sudden shift in topic. "No, not really. You've never mentioned much about Uncle Nigel. Why didn't you talk to him?"

Pete sighed deeply, his breath visible in the chilly air. He knew his brother was a bit of a sore point in his mind, as, unlike Pete, Nigel had struggled immensely with the pressures of life. Pete and Nigel had chosen drastically different paths, and while Pete had found solace and identity in his radio career, Nigel had been consumed by his demons.

"Nigel and I were close when we were younger," Pete began, his voice tinged with regret. "He was always the funnier one, the life of the party. Your granddad, my dad, and your great-uncle, my uncle, owned a construction company over in Kingswinford, a family owned business. They always wanted both of us to join and take over someday. But Nigel… he couldn't handle the pressure. He tried, but it wasn't for him. And I… well, I got a weekend job when I was 13 working for Woody Bones as a mascot, then as a tea boy, then a runner and production assistant at Dudley FM. You see, Ed Doolan, Les Ross, Malcolm Boyden, they were idols of mine back in the late '80s, early 90s. They were the voices of my teens on the radio, on BRMB, Beacon and the other local stations. I used to listen to them, learn how to present myself, how to connect with people just by talking. I knew from a young age that I wanted to be in radio. So, when I started working for Woody, it felt like I found my place. But Nigel... he stayed in the family business because he thought that was what he was supposed to do."

Pete paused, his gaze distant as they waited at the bus stop. "Nigel was never happy. He struggled with depression for years, but back then, people didn't talk about it. They just told him to 'man up,' keep going, and not let anyone see him falter. And then your cousins, Troy, Alex and Rachel, came along, and instead of stepping up and being a father to them, he walked out on your aunt Maggie, walked out and disappeared for months at a time. When he came back, he'd make promises, say he'd get his act together, but it never lasted. It was like he couldn't face the reality of being a dad or a husband. He was ashamed of himself, James, and that shame ate away at him."

Pete paused again, his voice faltering slightly as he continued, "I tried to reach out to him, you know? But every time I did, he'd brush me off. He'd tell me I didn't understand, that I was too busy with my career and didn't know what it was like to feel trapped. And maybe he was right. Maybe I didn't understand. But I loved him, James. I wanted to help him, but he wouldn't let me in. And then things came to a head, and I told him that if he didn't go back to Maggie and the kids, if he didn't make an effort to be there for them, then he was no longer my brother. That he was excommunicated from the family. Your granddad and great-uncle backed me, they said that Nigel needed to step up or step out completely. It wasn't fair to Maggie or the kids to have him drift in and out of their lives, making promises he couldn't keep. But I'll tell you something, James..." Pete's voice cracked slightly, and he looked down at the pavement as the bus approached in the distance. "I regret those words every single day."

James frowned, his confusion evident. "Why? It sounds like you were trying to help Aunt Maggie and the kids. You gave him a clear choice."

Pete nodded, but his expression was heavy with guilt. "I was trying to protect them, yes. But I didn't realise just how far gone Nigel was. I thought I was giving him tough love, the kind of push he needed to get his act together. But instead, I pushed him away completely. He disappeared for good after that. He'd faked his death... or so we thought."

The bus came to a halt, and Pete gestured for James to board. As they sat down, Pete continued, his voice softer now. "We thought he was gone for years. No one heard from him. We even held a memorial service for him after the police found a body they thought was him. But then, out of the blue, in 2008, when you were seven, the police found his body... in a construction site... funnily enough when they were digging up part of the freshly laid car park at Russells Hall Hospital."

The bus pulled off, and Pete couldn't help but fell the irony, as, in 3 stops time, the bus terminal for Russells Hall Hospital would be their destination. Pete sighed deeply, rubbing his temples as he gathered his thoughts. James sat beside him, silent but visibly processing what his father had just revealed.

"Russells Hall," Pete continued, his voice tinged with irony. "Of all places. They found him in a shallow grave beneath what was supposed to be a car park extension. The forensic team said he'd been there for at least five years, when the grass and landscaping had been completed over the original car park surface. It turned out he had been murdered—likely by someone he got mixed up with during one of his disappearances. The police never figured out who did it. And, James... I realised then that my 'tough love' approach might have driven him into the arms of the wrong people."

James stared at his father, a mixture of shock and sorrow on his face. "Dad... I never knew. Why didn't you tell me sooner?"

Pete sighed, his eyes focused on the passing scenery outside the bus window. "Because it's not an easy story to tell, son. I failed Nigel in a way I'll always regret. I thought cutting him off would make him step up, but instead, it pushed him over the edge. And now, every time I see you struggling—dealing with Manic, with Cody, with everything—I think about him. About how I might've done things differently if I'd understood more back then."

James nodded slowly, the weight of his father's confession sinking in. "I don't blame you, Dad. You were trying to do what you thought was right. But I guess... it's a reminder that we need to talk about this stuff, even when it's hard. Especially when it's hard."

Pete placed a hand on James's shoulder, his grip firm and reassuring. "Exactly, James. That's why I'm here now. I don't want to make the same mistakes with you. If you ever feel like things are too much, if it feels like the walls are closing in, you come to me or your mum, or even Theo and Ellie. We're here for you. Always."

The bus pulled into the Russells Hall Hospital terminal, and the two men knew that they had another 20 minutes on the bus until they arrived in Dudley. "You know, I remember when this bus was ran by Travel Merry Hill, back in the late 90s, early 00s," Pete said, chuckling. "They were owned by National Express, but they used to sponsor some of the shows on Dudley FM as we were the closest radio station to their Merry Hill, then Pensnett Trading estate depot. The ads used to have this catchy jingle: 'Travel Merry Hill, we'll get you there still!' Not the best grammar, but it stuck in your head. I remember doing a live remote broadcast on one of their double-deckers for a charity event, the old 264, going round Ashwood Park, Kingswinford, Bromley Lane, Russells Hall, up to Dudley, through Holly Hall into Merry Hill and then through Hawbush and Wordsley back to Ashwood Park again. It was to raise money for the maternity ward at Wordsley Hospital, we'd been sponsored to do an entire shift live from the bus. Can you believe it? A whole breakfast show while rattling around on the roads. I remember one passenger, he was a bus spotter, saying that it was ironic that a 'Yam Yam radio station was broadcasting from a Washwood Heath built bus' as the bus model we were on was a Metrobus Mark 1 built by MCW in Washwood Heath in Birmingham. They don't make buses like that anymore. Solid, a bit noisy, but reliable."

James chuckled, appreciating the shift in tone. "A breakfast show on a moving bus? I didn't know they made buses in Brum?"

Pete smiled, a nostalgic glint in his eyes. "Oh, they did, lad. MCW—Metro Cammell Weymann—used to make buses in Washwood Heath. Back in the day, their Metrobuses were everywhere. Solid machines, built to last. I remember that broadcast like it was yesterday. We'd hired the top deck of the bus so we could do the live links, had a diesel generator on the seats by the stairs, me on the front seats presenting while the rest of the crew managed the equipment and sound checks."

James watched as his dad then chuckled. "Passengers would come upstairs thinking there were seats on the top deck, as it was one of the peak runs into Dudley which went onto a 243, if I remember right, as we did a loop of the Timbertree estate and then back to Dudley. The 243, James, was what the 18 is now, that Diamond route that goes between Merry Hill and Timbertree, but back then, it only did the Dudley to Timbertree section, linking the estate with Dudley town centre. Anyway, those passengers would get quite the surprise finding a full radio setup instead. Some of them even stayed for a quick chat on air. That's the kind of stuff we used to do—real engagement, connecting with people in ways that made them smile. It wasn't just about numbers or metrics back then. It was about the community."

James laughed, picturing his dad on a bumpy bus with a microphone in hand. "Sounds chaotic, but fun. You don't get that kind of thing now, do you? Everything's too polished, too controlled. The spontaneity's gone."

Pete nodded, his expression thoughtful. "You're right, James. That's what's missing from radio today—authenticity. It's all about playlists, brand alignment, and viral moments now. But people crave real connection. That's why Woody's network feels like a lifeline. They're trying to bring back what made radio special in the first place."

The bus slowed as it approached Dudley town centre. James glanced out of the window, taking in the familiar sights. "I guess that's what I'm trying to do with the podcast. Bring some of that authenticity back, even if it's just by telling the truth about what happened at Manic."

Pete smiled, a glimmer of pride in his eyes. "And you're doing it, son. You're helping people see what's behind the curtain, showing them that radio can be more than just noise. You're making a difference."

As the bus pulled into Dudley, Pete noticed that the bus station, which was meant to open with the first phase of the Metro line between Wednesbury and Brierley Hill, was still closed, but unlike 6 months earlier, it was more closer to being completed, having closed fully in January 2024 when Phase one construction ramped up. The skeletal structure now resembled the renders shown in local papers, though the endless delays had left residents frustrated. Pete sighed, looking at the shiny yet still unusable facility. "Well, they've made progress, at least. But you know, this Metro line was supposed to be done years ago. You know, in Brierley Hill library, there's some plans which have it as being done and dusted by 2010."

"2010? You mean that they've been working on this since I was nine?" James asked, his voice tinged with disbelief as the bus pulled to a stop near Dudley Market. The father and son stepped off, greeted by the cool breeze carrying the unmistakable scent of warm pasties from Greggs nearby.

Pete chuckled dryly. "It's a proper Black Country saga, isn't it? Every few years, there's a new plan, new promises, but it's always 'delays due to unforeseen circumstances.' If they'd spent half as much effort on actually building the Metro as they did on announcing it, we'd have been riding it by now."

As they walked toward the High Street, James gestured toward the boarded-up shops that peppered the area. "It's not just the Metro, though, is it? Dudley feels like it's been stuck in limbo for as long as I can remember. Every time they try to 'regenerate' it, they seem to take two steps back. Even Wilkie's shut a couple of years ago when they went bust. I remember going there as a kid with Mum to get school shoes. Now, it's just another empty shell."

Wilkies, or Wilkinsons, was a major hardware and homeware retailer that had been a staple of many UK high streets for decades. Its closure left a gap not just in Dudley but in towns across the country. Pete nodded, his expression sombre as they passed by the boarded-up storefront that once housed the store.

"Yeah, Wilkies going was a big loss," Pete said. "It's not just the practical stuff you miss—it's the feeling of normality it brought to the town. People knew they could pop in for anything from paintbrushes to plant pots. Now it's just another Poundshop clone with poor stock and overpriced tat. Dudley used to have character, James, real character. Now, it's like they're trying to sand it all down into something generic that doesn't quite work."

James sighed, glancing at the few market stalls that remained, their tarpaulin covers flapping in the breeze. "It's a shame, really. Dudley could be so much more. But it feels like every time they start something, they run out of steam halfway through. At least Sofi's is still on Castle Street. She's had 3 buses crash into her chippy, but she still rebuilt every time. Sofi's is like a metaphor for Dudley itself—resilient, battered, but still standing."

Pete chuckled, as he knew that Sofi's, one of two chip shops in Dudley town centre, the other being the Birdcage Grill where Trindle Road, Hall Street, King Street and the former Birmingham Street met up was, sold battered chips, a Black Country delicacy that had stood the test of time, much like the town's spirit. "Aye, Sofi's is a proper institution. Once we've nipped into Home Bargains, we'll nip into Sofi's and sit in the grounds of Bottom Church to eat them. It's about time we supported the local legends, eh?" Pete's tone was lighter, but his words carried an undertone of the pride and nostalgia he felt for his roots.

James grinned, the prospect of greasy chips wrapped in paper lifting his spirits slightly. "Sounds like a plan, Dad. Let's do it."

****

CHAPTER 5 - Procedures Must Be Flashed Back
Friday 7th November 2025

James looked at the notification on his phone from Theo, who had sent him a message marked "Urgent." His thumb hovered over the screen before he opened it.

Theodore Nott: *James, the Crown have laid further charges against others from Manic which you'll need to give evidence for. I'll call shortly to go through the details. Stay calm.*

The phrase "further charges" echoed in his mind. He had barely come to terms with the original charges and the prospect of testifying in court. Now, the idea of new accusations and additional defendants felt like another mountain to climb.

Lyra, sitting across the kitchen table with a mug of herbal tea in hand, noticed the shift in James's expression. "What's wrong?" she asked, setting her mug down.

James handed her the phone, unable to find the words. Lyra read the message quickly, her brow furrowing. "More charges? Against who? Cody, Chloe, Kylie… or someone else?"

"I don't know," James replied, his voice heavy with frustration. "Theo didn't say. He's going to call soon. I thought we were starting to get a handle on all this, and now this."

Pete entered the kitchen, his presence as steadying as ever. "What's all this about?" he asked, glancing between James and Lyra.

Lyra handed Pete the phone, and he read the message. His jaw tightened, but his tone remained calm. "Right. Let's not panic until we know the details. Theo will explain everything."

As if on cue, James's phone buzzed. Theo's name appeared on the screen. James took a deep breath and answered.

"Hi, Theo. What's going on?"

Theo's voice was calm but firm, a tone James had come to associate with difficult news. "James, I won't sugar-coat this. Rory Carter, Kyler Thompson and a few others are being charged with raping you, following your initial disclosures and the evidence uncovered in the investigation. Detective Inspector Williams called me this morning to confirm that the Crown Prosecution Service is moving forward with those charges, alongside new allegations of workplace harassment and misconduct against senior executives at Manic Radio, including Rory and Kyler."

James felt his stomach drop. The word rape hit him like a sledgehammer, despite having known deep down that this was the inevitable outcome of the investigation. Saying it out loud in court, testifying to what had happened, felt like exposing a wound that had barely begun to heal.

Theo continued, his tone softening slightly. "I know this is a lot to take in, James. These charges are significant, and they strengthen the case against Manic's culture of abuse. But I need to prepare you—this will mean more time in court, more scrutiny, and possibly more attempts by the defence to discredit you."

Lyra reached across the table, taking James's free hand in hers. He nodded silently, his throat too tight to respond.

After a moment, he managed to find his voice. "Will I have to face them in court? Rory, Kyler... the others?"

Wednesday 16th April 2025

"You know, James," Kylie said with a smirk as she sauntered into Chloe and Cody's Central Birmingham apartment. The flat was bustling with preparations for one of Manic's infamous parties, with Chloe organising things as part of her university break. It was 8 p.m., just after Kylie's Manic Vibes West Midlands show, and James knew from experience that this was when Kylie would be at her most abrasive.

She held a glass of wine in one hand and gestured dramatically with the other. "You really are the perfect party piece. Everyone's talking about you, Reevesy. You've become... indispensable." Her tone dripped with mockery, and James felt his stomach churn.

"Indispensable for what, Kylie?" James asked, trying to keep his voice steady, though the knot in his chest betrayed his growing anxiety.

"For keeping everyone entertained," Kylie replied with a cruel grin. She stepped closer, lowering her voice. "Do you really think you have any value beyond that? Let's not kid ourselves. You're a toy, James. And tonight, you're going to put on your best show yet. We've got some of the Stratford and Speke crew, including your favourite cock, Kyler Thompson, coming over. You're going to give them the kind of entertainment they'll never forget."

James's breath hitched. The insinuation was clear, and it wasn't the first time he'd heard it. He clenched his fists, forcing himself not to react. Showing fear or defiance would only make things worse, he'd learned that the hard way. Kylie thrived on power, and resistance only fuelled her.

"I'm not your puppet," he said quietly, his voice barely audible over the thrum of party preparations in the background.

Kylie's laughter was sharp and cruel. "Oh, but you are, Reevesy. That's what makes you so special. You keep playing the victim, but we both know you'll do whatever I say. You've got no choice. Or did you think you did?"

James stared at her, the words burning in his chest. She was right in so many ways, but something inside him recoiled at the thought of surrendering completely. He didn't want to be her puppet, to be reduced to a tool for her amusement, but Kylie's control over him had been insidious and relentless. Every move, every whisper, every touch had chipped away at his dignity.

The fact that he had almost, the previous day, managed to escape the hell that he was in, when Lyra tried to force his dad, Pete, to allow him back in the family home, now seemed like a distant dream.

Suddenly Cody came towards him, his jeans opened, the Head of News for the Central region's erection at full attention as he grinned maliciously. James felt his breath hitch as Cody leaned in closer, his tone dripping with mockery. "Reevesy, you know the rules," Cody sneered. "If you want to keep playing the big-time DJ, you've got to play nice with the team. You're part of the Manic Way, after all. And tonight's no different."

James froze, his body rigid with dread. The knot in his chest tightened until it felt like he could barely breathe. He had heard these words before, but tonight, with Kylie smirking in the background and Cody's cruel presence looming over him, the suffocating weight of his circumstances felt unbearable.

"Just leave me alone," James muttered, his voice barely audible.

Cody laughed darkly, his face inches from James's. "Oh, that's cute. But you know how this works, Reevesy. You're our entertainment. And you'll do exactly as you're told, or we'll make sure you don't have a career left to go back to."

Kylie's voice cut through the tension like a blade. "Cody, don't scare him too much. We need him to perform. Poor little Reevesy doesn't handle pressure well, do you?" She tilted her head, her faux-concern masking the venom in her words.

James felt like a trapped animal, his mind racing with desperation. He knew that resistance would only escalate the situation, but the thought of giving in made his skin crawl. He wanted to scream, to fight back, to run—but every avenue felt blocked by the oppressive walls of control they had built around him.

Friday 7th November 2025

James blinked back to the present, his chest heaving as he struggled to pull himself out of the memories. Lyra squeezed his hand tighter, her voice steady and grounding. "James, you're not there anymore. You're here, with us. They can't hurt you."

"They... they're... still there, Ly... still in my mind," James stammered, his voice cracking under the weight of the memory. "I... I still remember Kyler's cock... raping... me... how he made me feel like a whore... how I was nothing but his... cock sleeve, my mouth with his..."

Wednesday 16th April 2025

It was twenty past 8, and James saw Kyler walk into the apartment, the Manic Vibes South Coast breakfast host in a McFly t-shirt, ripped denim shorts and trainers that squeaked faintly on the polished wooden floor. Kyler carried a case of beer in one hand, his cocky grin spreading as he took in the chaos of the party preparations.

"Evening, legends!" Kyler called out, his Mancunian twang cutting through the noise. "Looks like the party's shaping up nicely. Chloe, babe, you've outdone yourself! I've got beer... not that piss weak lager you lot keep drinking!" He dropped the case on the counter, spinning a bottle deftly before cracking it open with a flourish.

James stood stiffly in the corner of the room, his shoulders hunched as he tried to blend into the background. He felt Kyler's eyes on him almost immediately, the confident swagger in the man's gait making James's stomach churn. The tension in the room shifted subtly as Kyler approached, his grin widening into something more predatory.

"Well, well, if it isn't our resident superstar," Kyler said, clapping James on the back with enough force to make him stumble slightly. "Kylie, have you got the needle ready so we can make this whore feel a bit more... cooperative tonight?" Kyler's words, dripping with cruelty and arrogance, sent a cold shiver down James's spine. His pulse quickened as the room seemed to close in on him. He knew what was coming. It always came, no matter how much he wished it wouldn't.

Kylie smirked from her spot on the couch, lazily swirling the wine in her glass. "Oh, don't worry, Kyler. Our boy Reevesy here is always ready to put on a show, aren't you, sweetheart?" She shot James a look that was both mocking and venomous, her words a clear reminder of the control she held over him.

James didn't respond. His throat felt like it was closing up, and his mind was racing. He could hear the dull thrum of the party preparations in the background—the sound of bottles clinking, laughter, and the muffled bass of a playlist someone had started. But it all felt distant, like it was happening in another world.

Kyler leaned in closer, his grin turning sinister. "Come on, Reevesy. Don't be shy. Everyone's here for a good time. Don't tell me you're going to be a buzzkill."

The room erupted in laughter at Kyler's words, the sound grating in James's ears. He clenched his fists at his sides, his nails digging into his palms. He wanted to fight back, to shout, to run—but every instinct told him it would only make things worse. He felt trapped, caught in a web of manipulation and cruelty that seemed impossible to escape.

James then noticed Chloe pass Kyler a needle that was attached to a syringe, and he knew what was in it, cocaine, a drug that, yes, he was addicted to, but normally he didn't inject, instead snorted or smoked. His chest tightened as he realised what was about to happen, the familiar sense of dread washing over him like a tidal wave. Chloe smirked, the syringe glinting under the overhead lights as she handed it to Kyler.

"Time to loosen up, Reevesy," Chloe said, her tone laced with mock cheerfulness. "You'll thank us later."

Kyler held up the syringe like a trophy, his grin widening. "This'll make you the life of the party, mate. Trust me, you'll love it."

James tried to back away, but his legs felt like lead. He was cornered, with Kyler towering over him and Chloe blocking his only path to the door. The laughter and casual chatter of the others in the room carried on, oblivious or indifferent to the scene unfolding in the corner.

"I don't... I don't want it," James stammered, his voice barely audible. His heart pounded in his chest, the fight-or-flight response kicking in, but there was nowhere to go.

Kyler rolled his eyes, his grin never faltering. "Don't be such a killjoy, Reevesy. We all know you need a little help to get into the spirit of things." He grabbed James's arm with surprising force, pulling him closer.

James struggled weakly, but his resistance only seemed to amuse Kyler. Chloe leaned in, her expression one of mock concern. "Oh, come on, James. Don't make a scene. We're all friends here, aren't we?"

The words felt like a slap in the face. Friends? These people were anything but. James's mind raced, searching for a way out, but the room seemed to close in around him. Kyler was already preparing the syringe, and Chloe's presence loomed like a shadow.

"Hold still," Kyler said, his tone hardening. "This'll be over before you know it."

James's pulse roared in his ears as Kyler grabbed his arm, roughly pulling up the sleeve of his shirt. He felt the cold metal of the needle press against his skin, and then the sharp sting as it pierced the flesh. His body tensed, every instinct screaming for him to run, but he was paralysed by fear and the oppressive weight of their control.

As the drug entered his system, a wave of dizziness and nausea washed over him. His vision blurred, and the sounds of the room grew distant and distorted. The laughter, the music, the clinking of glasses—it all faded into a surreal, nightmarish haze.

Then a second syringe, one that James didn't recognise. As Kyler brandished the second syringe, James's blurred vision caught the unmistakable glint of malice in his tormentor's eyes. This one wasn't the usual cocaine hit he dreaded. The liquid inside shimmered slightly under the harsh light, its clarity unsettling. James's heart thudded violently against his ribs as panic overtook him.

"What... what is that?" James stammered, his voice slurring as the first injection began to take hold, sending an icy fire through his veins.

"To help you remain constantly erect, big bro!" Chloe said with the sound of someone who was relishing every second of her own cruelty. She leaned closer, her voice softening mockingly. "Don't worry, Reevesy. This is just so you're ready for the main event. You know, you've got to keep the fans entertained." Her laughter rang out like nails on a chalkboard.

James's protests became incoherent as the drugs already in his system dulled his ability to resist or even fully comprehend what was happening. He felt the second needle pierce his arm, the unfamiliar substance spreading through his body like liquid fire. His muscles twitched involuntarily, and his head swam with a sickening combination of nausea and arousal that felt foreign and deeply wrong.

Kyler's smug grin widened as he leaned in closer, his breath hot against James's ear. "There we go, Reevesy.

You're all set. The night's just getting started, mate. Try to keep up."

The room erupted into laughter and crude commentary, the distorted, surreal sound blending into the pounding bassline of the playlist playing in the background. James felt himself slipping further away, retreating into the furthest corners of his mind where he could block out the horror unfolding around him. His body betrayed him, reacting to the chemical assault, and he was powerless to stop it.

Friday 7th November 2025

James sat frozen in the kitchen chair, his body rigid as the memories clawed their way to the forefront of his mind. The flashbacks gripped him like a vice, each image sharper, more vivid than the last. He could still hear their mocking laughter, feel the needle piercing his skin, and the sickening helplessness that followed.

Lyra's steady voice cut through the fog. "James," she said softly, leaning closer. "You're not there anymore. You're safe now. Whatever they did to you, it doesn't define you. It's over."

James shook his head, his voice trembling. "It's not over, Ly. They're still out there. And now... now I have to stand in court and relive it all. Tell the whole world what they did to me." His words faltered, the weight of the truth pressing down on him.

Pete, who had been listening in silence, stepped forward and placed a reassuring hand on James's shoulder. "You don't have to do this alone, son. We're with you, every step of the way. You've got Theo, Lyra, and me. And the truth is on your side."

James looked up at his father, his eyes glistening with tears. "What if it's not enough? What if they twist everything around? They'll have lawyers, money... power. And I'm just me."

Pete crouched down so he was eye level with his son. "Listen to me, James. What they did to you was monstrous, and no amount of lawyers or money can change that. The truth has a way of shining through, even in the darkest places. You've survived this long, and you'll get through this too. But you don't have to carry the burden alone. Anyway, I've got to get to work... I'm meant to be doing my annual contract renewal today... but I'm not going to accept it - today is going to be my last day on air... but I'm not going to tell Cal that it is... until I go on air."

James stared at Pete, his father's unwavering determination a stark contrast to the chaos swirling in his own mind. He swallowed hard, trying to find strength in Pete's words. His father's decision to walk away from Manic Radio, to reclaim his own integrity after years in a system that had chewed him up and spat him out, resonated deeply. If Pete could stand up to them, then perhaps he could too.

"You're really leaving, Dad?" James asked, his voice quieter now, almost childlike.

Pete nodded, a flicker of sadness crossing his face. "I've given everything to this industry, James. But it's not the industry I fell in love with anymore. It's taken more than it's given, and I'm done pretending it hasn't. Woody Bones has offered me a role at his community network. It's not glamorous, but it's honest. It's real. That's what I need now."

James nodded slowly. "Real. Honest." The words felt foreign on his tongue, so far removed from everything he'd experienced over the past few years. But they also felt like a lifeline—something to cling to amidst the storm.

Theo's voice crackled through the phone, breaking the moment. "James, I know this is overwhelming, but I promise we'll be prepared. We'll go over everything before you take the stand. Every word you say will be the truth, and no amount of legal manoeuvring can erase that."

James took a deep breath, the weight of the flashbacks still heavy on his chest but beginning to ease under Theo's calm reassurance. "What happens next?" he asked, his voice steadier now.

Theo hesitated for a moment, then continued. "The CPS has listed the charges for a preliminary hearing next week. The court will determine the timeline for the trial. In the meantime, you'll need to work with me to prepare your testimony. We'll rehearse it, so you feel confident. And remember, James, you're not just telling your story for yourself. You're paving the way for justice—for others who've suffered at their hands."

James nodded, his resolve hardening. He wasn't just fighting for himself anymore. He was fighting for everyone who'd been chewed up and spat out by Manic Radio's toxic culture, for everyone who'd been silenced.

Pete stood and clapped James on the shoulder, his grip firm and reassuring. "You've got this, son. And no matter what happens, we'll be here for you."

Lyra leaned in, her voice soft but filled with determination. "We'll get through this, James. Together."

James looked between them, the people who had stood by him through everything, and for the first time in a long time, he felt a flicker of hope. It was faint, barely more than a spark, but it was there. And that was enough—for now.

As Pete grabbed his coat and prepared to leave for what would be his final day at Manic Goldies, James called out to him. "Dad, when you go on air today… make it count."

Pete turned back, his eyes glinting with a mix of pride and mischief. "Don't worry, James. I intend to."

****

CHAPTER 6 - Last Day on Air
Friday 7th November 2025

The day was bittersweet for Pete as he walked into the One Snow Hill studios. In theory, it was his contract renewal day, but instead, he had decided to step away from Manic Goldies. After three decades in broadcasting, Pete felt he could no longer ignore the erosion of the industry he had once loved. Walking through the sleek, impersonal lobby of One Snow Hill, Pete reflected on how far things had shifted from the local, community-driven radio he had started in. The warm hum of excitement and camaraderie had long been replaced by cold branding and rigid corporate structures.

Heading towards the lifts, Pete knew that the building, shared with KMPG, a renowned accountancy firm, symbolised everything about the transformation of radio into a corporate machine. Polished floors, endless glass panels, and muted grey decor spoke of efficiency, not creativity. It felt more like entering a bank than a radio station. He scanned his pass, the little green light confirming his access for the last time and stepped into the lift.

As the lift ascended, Pete thought about the day ahead. He had his regular drive-time show to host, but this wouldn't be just another broadcast. This would be his swan song—a chance to say goodbye on his own terms and remind listeners of what radio could truly be.

It was 2pm, and Pete knew that he had 2 hours to prep and reflect on his journey before going on air at 4pm. His producer, Rachael Powell, who Pete knew was leaving herself, as she had been poached by Global for their Smooth 80's breakfast show, presented by someone Pete knew, a former GWR, GCap and current Global employee, Nigel "Fresh" Freshman, who had hosted regional shows on various stations over the years, greeted him with a knowing smile.

"Afternoon, Pete," Rachael said, setting her headset down on the desk in the small but polished studio. "You ready for the big one?"

Pete grinned, though his heart was heavy. "As ready as I'll ever be. You know, Rach, it feels strange. I've been doing this for decades, but today... it feels different."

Rachael nodded, her expression softening. "You've got every right to feel that way. You're one of the good ones, Pete. They don't make presenters like you anymore— people who genuinely care about the audience, not just the metrics."

Heading to the Goldies Lounge, the breakroom where the hosts of the three regional Goldies shows, Manic Goldies West Midlands, Manic Goldies East Midlands and Manic Goldies Oxfordshire South Midlands, a recent move from the Olympic Park hub to Snow Hill, often gathered, Pete found himself greeted by some familiar faces. Tim Young, his East Midlands counterpart, who, like him, had come to Manic from Woody Bones's original local network, which in 2010 had been brought by Breeze Media before its eventual acquisition by Manic, raised a cup of tea in salute. "Afternoon, Pete. Isn't it your contract renewal day?"

Pete chuckled as he poured himself a cup of tea. "It is, Tim. But this year, I'm renewing my life instead of my contract. Today's my last day."

Tim nearly choked on his tea. "You're kidding. Your last day? I thought you were a lifer like me—well, until today. It's my last day too. Headed to Boom Radio on Monday. Decided it's time to go somewhere with a bit more soul. Where you going?"

"Woody's poached me," Pete said with a grin. "He wants me to be Programme Director at his community network. It's back to basics, Tim. Real community-focused radio, no playlists handed down from some corporate office 200 miles away. It feels like coming home."

"That bloody rascal! You know Kira from Vibes London is rejoining him too?" Tim said, chuckling, and Pete sighed as Kira Walsh, a 42 year old woman who had done the mid-afternoon show on Brum's Best, one of the past Woody Bones local stations before Breeze Media's takeover in 2010, had been a standout personality who connected deeply with her audience. Knowing she was also heading back to Woody Bones's network made Pete's decision feel even more like the right move.

"Yeah, he's getting her for a mid-morning slot on his new Solihull licence, Heart of England Sounds. He asked me if it was worth her taking the job, and I told him absolutely. Kira's the real deal, Tim—one of the few people in this business who still gets what radio's about: connection. Not hashtags, not metrics. Just real, human connection. You know he's got a slot for you if you want it between your Boom shows, one for your old haunts of Mickleover?"

Tim's eyes lit up at Pete's mention of Mickleover, as Pete knew that, before his move to the Midlands when Manic moved their East Midlands station, East Midlands Vibes, to the old Dudley hub, Tim would do a daily commute from Mickleover, where he lived, to the then Broadmarsh studios of the station that is now Manic Vibes East Midlands. Pete knew that it had been a straight shot from Derby to Nottingham on the A52 via car, but the move to Dudley had complicated Tim's commute.

Tim nodded with a wistful smile. "You know, I've thought about it. Woody's network is tempting. It's everything radio used to be—local, meaningful, and authentic. Maybe I'll give him a call once I've settled into Boom. I reckon the listeners in Mickleover would appreciate a familiar voice again."

Pete raised his cup. "Here's to going back to where we belong, Tim. It's time to give people what they deserve— real radio."

Fiona Blanchard, the Manic Goldies Oxford South Midlands host, who Pete was still a bit cautious about as, despite the scandals and happenings, was a management suck-up, reporting everything to Cal Ellington, the Central Regional Director for Manic, entered the Goldies Lounge at that moment, her perfectly coiffed hair and polished smile giving her the air of someone who never missed an opportunity to align herself with authority.

"Afternoon, Pete, Tim," Fiona said brightly, her tone betraying none of the undercurrent of tension Pete often felt in her presence. "So, big renewal day for both of you, I hear. I trust you'll be signing on for another year?"

Pete met her gaze evenly, taking a slow sip of his tea before replying. "Not this time, Fiona. Today's my last day."

Fiona's smile faltered for just a moment, though she quickly recovered. "Oh? Well, that's… unexpected. I'm sure Cal will want a word with you about that. Leaving on renewal day isn't exactly… standard protocol."

Pete shrugged, his expression calm. "I'll speak to Cal when the time comes. Right now, I've got a show to prepare for. And don't worry—I'll make sure my departure doesn't leave any loose ends. You know me, Fiona, I'm nothing if not professional."

Tim chuckled into his tea, clearly enjoying the exchange. Fiona, sensing she wasn't going to get much more out of Pete, excused herself with a tight smile and left the lounge.

"She'll be reporting that straight to Cal, you know," Tim said, grinning. "Probably spinning it like you're abandoning ship in the middle of a storm."

Pete shrugged again. "Let her. I'm not leaving Manic in the lurch—I'm leaving it to its own devices. They've made it clear over the years that people like us are interchangeable cogs in their machine. They'll spin my exit however they want, but I know the truth. And so do the listeners."

Tim raised his cup again. "Here's to that, mate. Now, go knock 'em dead on air. Give your listeners something to remember."

****

At 4pm, Pete sat behind the microphone in Studio A1, the Manic Goldies West Midlands studio, the familiar sound of the jingle fading into silence as he prepared to speak. He took a deep breath, the weight of the moment settling on his shoulders.

"Driving home with the greatest hits of the '60s, '70s, '80s and '90s—this is Goldies Drivetime with Pete Smith, on FM, on DAB, online and ad-free on the Manic Prime app."

Pete let the music bed fade out, leaving just enough silence to command attention. His voice, as familiar to his audience as an old friend, was steady but carried an undertone of emotion that hinted at the significance of the day.

"Good afternoon, everyone. It's Friday, the 7th of November 2025, and it's me, Pete Smith, live on Manic Goldies across the West Midlands, Herefordshire, Worcestershire, Shropshire, Telford and the Wrekin, Staffordshire and the County of the Bard himself, Warwickshire. We've got a track from 1976 coming up for you, but first, it's the news across the Central region with Mia Cartwright."

The upbeat jingle of the news intro filled the studio as Pete leaned back in his chair. He knew that Mia was on the floor below, the floor Manic Vibes, which had, since July, employed a whole new roster of young, inexperienced presenters after the fallout from the scandals surrounding James, Chloe, and the others who had been embroiled in the toxic culture. The news segment was short and professional, with Mia's confident voice delivering the headlines—local traffic updates, a new exhibition at Birmingham's art gallery, and, of course, the ongoing saga of the Metro extension. Pete smiled faintly; even on his last day, some things never changed.

Looking at his screens, one with Zetta, a radio automation software displaying the carefully curated playlist, another with GSelector, the sister software to Zetta that was responsible for programming the day's music schedule, Pete felt a pang of nostalgia. The software was efficient, reliable, and soulless—another symbol of how radio had shifted from spontaneous, human connection to algorithm-driven precision. But today, Pete was determined to inject some soul back into the airwaves.

As the news finished and the jingle signalled the end of the segment, Pete leaned back into the microphone.

"Thank you, Mia. Always keeping us up to date with what's going on in the region. And now, as promised, let's rewind the clock to 1976 with an absolute classic. But before we do, I want to take a moment to talk directly to you, our listeners."

Pete let the silence linger just long enough to capture attention, a trick he'd perfected over the years.

"You know, when I started in radio, it was all about connection. About sitting in a little studio and talking to you, wherever you were—whether you were driving home, making tea, or just looking for a friendly voice to keep you company. It wasn't about algorithms or social media metrics. It was about real, honest communication."

He paused, glancing at the clock. He had carefully planned this speech, knowing he wanted to leave a mark without drawing too much attention from management before his resignation became official.

"I told you a few months ago about my days working for Woody Bones and his small network of Midlands stations, doing various shifts, from the early morning on Dudley FM, to the pan-regional football phone-in on Saturday afternoons. Back then, it was just a small team of us, doing our best to bring you something real, something that felt like it was coming from down the road, not some corporate office miles away."

Pete leaned closer to the microphone, his tone becoming more personal.

"Today, after more than 30 years in this industry, I'm signing off. This is my last day on Manic Goldies, my last show with you all. It's not a decision I've made lightly, but it's the right one. Radio has changed so much over the years, and while change can be good, sometimes it comes at the cost of the very heart of what made something special. For me, that heart has always been about connecting with you—being a voice in the noise, someone you can rely on to share a laugh, a memory, or a story."

He paused again, the weight of his words hanging in the air.

"I'm stepping away because I believe in radio's potential to be more than just playlists and branding. I believe it can still be a force for good, a way to bring people together. And while this chapter is closing for me here at Manic Goldies, it's not the end of my journey. I'll be moving on to something smaller, something that feels more like home. I'm going to be re-joining my old friend, Woody, in his network of community radio stations, where the focus is still on the community, the people, and the stories that matter to them. It's a chance to go back to what I love most about this job—being part of something that feels genuine and real."

Pete's voice softened, a hint of emotion breaking through his usually polished tone. "I want to thank each and every one of you who've tuned in over the years. Whether you've been with me since the Dudley FM days, or you've just discovered Goldies, you've made this journey unforgettable. To the folks who text or phone me daily because they've got no family to talk to, yes, Gladys in Streetly, who's 98, her children and grandchildren living in New Zealand, I'm talking to you... To the girls at Hardwick's Casuals in Kings Norton, the knicker factory where I've been part of your workday for years, and to Dave the lorry driver who always calls in when he's stuck on the M6—thank you. You've been more than an audience. You've been friends."

Pete took a deep breath, glancing at the studio clock. He knew management might be listening, but at this point, he didn't care. "Radio isn't just about the music or the ads or the branding. It's about people. It's about stories. And it's about the connection between us, the presenter, and you, the listener. That's what I've always tried to bring to this job, and that's what I'll carry with me as I move on. You'll still be able to hear me now and again, by going to www.kiddy-"

Pete heard the sudden start of Abba's 1976 hit "Dancing Queen" fill his headphones and he knew that Zetta's automation had already timed down to its next track.

Pete leaned back in his chair, a bittersweet smile playing on his lips. The interruption was fitting in a way— corporate efficiency cutting into the heartfelt moment. It was emblematic of everything he had been talking about: the rigid, impersonal systems that had come to dominate what was once a deeply human medium.

The irony that he had 4 minutes until his next link, a speedlink which he had to backsell, then introduce, the tracks that followed, was not lost on Pete. As the studio filled with the familiar melody of Dancing Queen, Pete leaned back in his chair, watching the clock tick down. The track seemed to mock the reality he was leaving behind—bright and polished on the surface but hollow beneath for those who had experienced the transformation of radio firsthand.

When the song ended, Pete leaned back into the microphone, his tone upbeat but deliberate. "That was Dancing Queen by Abba, taking us back to 1976. Coming up next, we've got more of the greatest hits to keep you company this Friday afternoon."

He transitioned smoothly into the next segment, but his mind was already a step ahead. He had two hours left to craft the perfect send-off—something that wouldn't just fade into the ether like another day's broadcast. He wanted to leave the listeners with a sense of what they were losing, a spark of nostalgia for what radio had been and what it could be again.

As the third track in the trio finished, the Coldplay 1990s hit "Yellow," Pete knew he had to hit the traffic bulletin. He switched effortlessly to his professional tone, delivering updates about congestion on the M6 near Walsall and delays on the A38 through Birmingham. It was routine, but his heart wasn't in it. He was counting down the minutes until his final farewell.

"And finally, the Distressway heading out of city is congested because the contraflow has failed, resulting in 2 lanes in and out of city centre being gridlocked. Take care out there and we'll keep you updated on Goldies Travel."

Pete's tone shifted as he returned to the show. "Now, back to the music. Here's a classic from Fleetwood Mac, 'Go Your Own Way.' It feels rather fitting today."

The opening chords played, and Pete leaned back, reflecting on his career. He thought about the nights he spent in tiny studios, the excitement of live broadcasts, and the connections he had built with his audience. This was more than a job—it was a legacy. Yet, the corporate world had tried to strip away the soul of radio, turning it into a sterile business venture.

While the track played, the studio telephone rang, and Pete could see Rachael pick it up. Looking at the screen on the wall with the clock, he noticed it was quarter to 5, and that it was the usual time Gladys would phone to chat with him live on air. Rachael glanced at Pete and mouthed, "It's Gladys." Pete gave her a thumbs-up, knowing this would be one of the final moments he could connect with listeners who had become like extended family over the years.

As Fleetwood Mac's Go Your Own Way faded out, Pete leaned into the microphone. "And that was Fleetwood

Mac, a song that feels particularly poignant today. Now, I've got someone very special on the line. She's been a regular voice on this show, all the way from when I used to do some network shows on Woody Bones's network and her local station was Walsall Radio, through the current hits programming when it was changed to Midlands Manic, and from April this year, when we changed from Midlands Manic, the hits station, to Manic Goldies, our current greatest hits format. Gladys from Streetly, how are you today?"

The familiar, cheerful voice came through the line, bringing a warmth to the studio. "Oh, Pete, I'm doing alright, love. I couldn't miss your show today, not with all the changes going on. They've not got rid of you, have they? I'd miss our chats."

Pete chuckled, a genuine laugh that lightened the atmosphere. "No, Gladys, they haven't got rid of me— I'm leaving on my own terms. After all these years, it's time for a new adventure. But I'll miss hearing from you. You've been a part of my afternoons for so long."

Gladys's voice softened. "Oh, Pete, you've been such a comfort. You don't know how much it means to hear a friendly voice when the house gets quiet. You're like family to me."

Pete felt his throat tighten. Moments like this were why he had stayed in radio for so long. "That means the world to me, Gladys. And just because I won't be on Goldies anymore doesn't mean I'm disappearing. I'll be moving to Woody Bones's network. Look, have you got a smart speaker?"

Pete knew there was a local stock of smart speakers which were usually for regional competition winners on some of the more fun competitions and quizzes that both Manic

Goldies and Manic Vibes used to run, and he decided he'd make sure Gladys had one, so she could keep in touch with his new station.

Gladys chuckled on the line. "Oh, Pete, you know I wouldn't know how to use one of those gadgets if I had one! I'm a bit old-fashioned, love."

Pete smiled, already making a mental note to arrange delivery of one to her. "Don't worry, Gladys. I'll make sure you're set up. I'll get Rachael to help with the details. You'll be able to find me on Woody's network, and I'll make it easy for you. No technology barriers here—just friendly voices and familiar tunes."

Gladys's voice cracked slightly. "Thank you, Pete. You've always looked out for your listeners. That's what makes you so special."

Pete felt a lump in his throat, but he kept his tone steady. "It's listeners like you who've made this job worthwhile, Gladys. You've been a part of my life as much as I've been part of yours. And that's something I'll never forget. Now, I remember when I first came on air on Walsall Radio back in 2005, when I was asked by Woody Bones to do a joint Dudley-Walsall breakfast show for a week, you phoned up on the last day of my wife, Sarah Reeves, and I were hosting the show, asking if I could play the song you got married to back in 1946, a year after the War, to your late husband Arthur, and I played it."

Pete paused, glancing at the clock. The warm silence in the studio felt like a shared moment between him and his audience, especially Gladys, who had been a constant presence throughout his career. Sending a quick message on the system he and Rachael used, he asked her to override Zetta's automation with a track from the Second World War era, one of Gladys's favourites. The familiarity of the song, Vera Lynn's We'll Meet Again, had always resonated with her and many others, carrying memories of hope and resilience.

Rachael gave Pete a thumbs-up, and he spoke into the microphone with a genuine warmth. "Gladys, let's take a trip down memory lane together. This one's for you, Arthur, and all the wonderful memories you've shared with us over the years."

As the opening notes of We'll Meet Again filled the airwaves, Pete leaned back, letting the music do what radio had always done best—connect people through shared emotions and timeless stories. Gladys's soft "Thank you, Pete" echoed in his headphones before the call ended, leaving a poignant silence in the studio as the song played.

Pete took a moment to gather himself. This was what radio was supposed to be—personal, meaningful, a bridge between the past and present. He looked out over the studio, the sleek equipment and screens a stark contrast to the raw humanity that moments like this brought to the surface.

As the song drew to a close, Pete leaned back into the microphone. "That was Vera Lynn with We'll Meet Again, a song that's carried us through so much, and one that feels particularly fitting today. To all of you listening—thank you for letting me be part of your lives, your afternoons, your stories. It's been an honour. Up now, it's a 90's classic from the Britpop era, one that even I occasionally cry to - Spice Girls with 2 Become 1."

****

CHAPTER 7 - Legal Action and Statements

Saturday 8th November 2025

James had to chuckle at the tweet that Greatest Hits Radio had posted late Friday evening. The cheeky dig at Manic Goldies was subtle yet sharp, clearly targeting Pete's emotional farewell.

@GreatestHitsUK: *While @ManicGoldiesWM scrambles for a replacement, we at GHR just keep delivering the timeless tunes you love with @simonmayo, no matter where in the UK are at drivetime. We'll Meet Again indeed @PeteontheRadio, the holder of RAJAR #1 for Birmingham Drive for a whopping 49 consecutive quarters.*

RAJAR, or the Radio Joint Audience Research, was the trusted standard for radio ratings in the UK, and the graph was a stark reminder of Pete's unmatched popularity. James knew this dig would hit Manic where it hurt most: their pride.

The fact that his dad had been the one at Manic who, on the day the Queen had passed, been responsible for making the network wide announcement, not just on the hit music or classic hits stations, but Rock, Blues, Classical and even Metal stations, because he had been the senior presenter for the Manic network, made the tweet sting even more. Pete Smith wasn't just a presenter; he had been a cornerstone of Manic Radio's identity. Losing him was more than just a personnel change—it was a public relations nightmare.

The way the final song on Pete's show, George Michael's Careless Whisper, faded into silence the previous evening, had resonated far beyond Manic Goldies' usual listenership. Clips of Pete's farewell speech, laced with heartfelt nostalgia and a call for authenticity, had gone viral. Social media was abuzz, with listeners sharing memories of Pete's voice accompanying their commutes, long drives, and quiet afternoons.

But it wasn't just the listeners who were talking. Industry insiders, former Manic employees, and even rival stations weighed in. While Greatest Hits Radio's cheeky tweet grabbed attention, other stations like Boom Radio and BBC Radio 2 subtly acknowledged Pete's departure with messages celebrating his career.

@BoomRadioUK: *Here's to Pete Smith, a voice of the Midlands and a legend of the airwaves. The kind of presenter who reminds us of what radio is all about. #BroadcastingGreats*

@BBCRadio2: *Respect to Pete Smith for 30+ years of incredible broadcasting. A true professional who has inspired so many. #RadioLegend*

James scrolled through the responses, noting how many listeners were openly criticising Manic for letting Pete go.

@ListenerAnne52: *Manic's lost its heart. Pete was the only reason I still tuned in. Guess it's GHR for me now.*

@RadioFanatic88: *Pete Smith leaving Manic Goldies? Proof they've completely lost the plot. #SaveLocalRadio*

The backlash wasn't confined to Twitter. James noticed a trending hashtag: #ManicMeltdown.

James grinned, sipping his tea. It wasn't often that the public turned against Manic with such ferocity. The network, usually so adept at managing its image, was conspicuously silent. No carefully worded statements or PR damage control had surfaced overnight. James guessed they were scrambling to figure out how to spin Pete's departure in their favour—a Herculean task given the circumstances.

"Looks like they're struggling, huh?" Lyra's voice broke through his thoughts as she entered the kitchen, her bump visible under a cosy jumper. She glanced at James's phone screen.

"Struggling is putting it lightly," James replied, turning the screen to show her the tweet from Greatest Hits Radio. "They've got no idea how to handle this. Dad leaving wasn't just a blow—it was a public spectacle. And now every station in the country is capitalising on it. Even Nation Radio's network of stations have been making digs at Manic... and Radio 4 has called it a cultural turning point in modern broadcasting. When Radio 4 starts commenting on the state of commercial radio, you know it's bad for Manic."

Lyra laughed, pouring herself a cup of herbal tea. "Well, your dad didn't just leave quietly, did he? He made it a proper event. That speech, the Vera Lynn dedication, the personal anecdotes—it was all so Pete Smith. It reminded people of what they're losing. Manic can't PR their way out of this one."

"You know what would have pissed Manic off the most... Dad had the remaining 30 smart speakers in the Goldies store cupboard and sent them to listeners he decided deserved them the most. He wanted to make sure that Gladys and the others could tune into Woody Bones's stations without any hassle. It's a genius move, really. Not only did he leave on his terms, but he also took part of the audience with him."

Lyra nearly spilled her tea, laughing. "He's not just a legend—he's a revolutionary! Imagine the look on Cal

Ellington's face when he realises the store cupboard is empty. That's the kind of chaos Manic deserves after everything they've done."

James smirked. "Oh, Cal must be fuming. He always treated Dad like a relic, but now he's the one being left behind. And the fact that Woody is openly courting Dad's audience just adds salt to the wound."

"Oh, Cal never liked me," Pete said, coming down the stairs, as James knew that his dad was recording some DJ Strangelove shows for the various Woody Bones stations that took his syndicated show in his home studio. Pete looked refreshed despite the emotional goodbye the previous day. "Jane Spearmore, the old Regional Director, my old boss before she left in 2023, was from the old school world, of radio. She understood that local connections mattered, even when corporate overlords like Lite and Manic wanted everything streamlined. Cal's different—he's a numbers man, not a radio man. I heard rumours, but I never had them confirmed, that he used to work for the Manchester hub and was a sexual predator, which tallies with how, after he came to Dudley, the Dudley hub joined the hedonistic culture that eventually blew up in Manic's face. There was rumours of him and a young Manchester staff member called Cassie Longton. Gotta be some kind of admin lady or something, as there's never been a presenter with that name. But from the way he acts, I wouldn't be surprised if there's a skeleton or two in his closet." Pete grabbed a mug and poured himself a coffee.

James chuckled. "Dad... Cassie is Toni Green, the same Toni Green who hosted Bee Manic's drivetime show and is now on the Manic evening networked show," James explained, his tone tinged with both amusement and exasperation. "She's the one who had all those public spats with Kyler Thompson before their chaotic breakup.

Remember, she's practically a poster child for how messy things can get at Manic."

Pete paused mid-sip, his eyebrows raising in surprise. "Wait, you're saying that Cassie Longton is Toni Green? The same Toni Green who dated Al Crozier last year? How do you know?"

"Kylie... well... kinda shagged... him," James said, sighing. "I... may have overheard her and Chloe talking once when I was... well, when Cody was using me as his personal cum receptacle. Apparently she's got dirt on half of the bosses."

Pete's hand froze mid-air, his coffee mug hovering just below his chin. The weight of James's words hung heavy in the room, and for a moment, no one spoke. Lyra's eyes widened slightly, her grip tightening on her mug of herbal tea. Pete set his coffee down carefully, his expression a mix of disbelief and quiet fury.

"Let me get this straight," Pete began, his voice low and deliberate. "You're telling me that Kylie and Chloe have been throwing around dirt on executives like it's a party trick, and Toni—formerly Cassie—has enough leverage to keep herself untouchable at Manic?"

James nodded, the tension in his shoulders evident. "Yeah. Toni's been around long enough to know where the bodies are buried—figuratively, of course. And Kylie... well, Kylie's always been good at playing the game. Between her and Chloe, they've got a network of information. That's why they've stayed on top for so long. But it's a mess, Dad. A toxic, festering mess. I did tell Theodore, but he said that it'd be dismissed in court because its classed as hearsay unless corroborated by hard evidence. And let's face it, Manic's legal team would bury it before it ever saw the light of day. Do you want to know what dirt they have on the management?"

Pete rubbed his temples, his expression growing more serious by the second. "James, I'm not sure I want to know, but considering everything we've been through, I think it's better to hear it straight from you. What sort of dirt do Kylie and Chloe have on the management?"

James took a deep breath, clearly uncomfortable but resolute. "Well, for starters, there's the stuff on Cal Ellington. Apparently, he was heavily involved in the toxic culture at the Manchester hub before he was transferred to Dudley. Then there's Felix Morgan, Kylie's cousin, the Deputy Head of Legal... he's... well... let's just say that he, according to Kylie, created the hub cum dump position."

James shuddered as he mentioned that, as he himself had been, between January and April, the Dudley and Birmingham hub cum dump—a dehumanising and exploitative role Manic used to control and manipulate staff, particularly younger presenters. He knew that his dad knew the whole behind the hub cum dump role, so he didn't need to elaborate. Instead, he pressed on. "Then there's the allegations about how they manipulated RAJAR data for the Manchester hub a few years back. Kylie claims Felix Morgan orchestrated some of it to secure higher ratings artificially."

Pete's face darkened, his jaw tightening as he absorbed James's words. "That explains a lot about how quickly the toxic culture spread from Manchester to Dudley. If someone like Felix was pulling strings at a legal level, it's no wonder the rot set in so deeply. And the hub cum dump role... that's beyond disgusting. I still don't understand how Manic's executives thought they could get away with such happenings... or how I ignored it while I was immersed in my own world of drivetime playlists and corporate demands. You know, last night, I realised I enabled the whole thing by being ignorant of the whole thing. I was so focused on surviving in this soulless corporate radio machine, doing my job, and hitting the targets, that I turned a blind eye to what was happening around me. That's on me, James. I know you've been at Manic only a year, but I... I should have been watching what was going on in the hubs more closely. I should have noticed the signs—the cracks in the façade. I failed to protect the younger generation of presenters from the very culture that's now tearing Manic apart."

Pete's voice trembled with a mix of guilt and anger, his words hanging heavy in the air. Lyra placed a reassuring hand on his arm, her tone gentle but firm. "Pete, you can't blame yourself for everything. The toxicity at Manic didn't start with you, and it wouldn't have ended with you staying silent. What matters now is that you're standing up against it—and you're doing something about it. You've inspired people, including James, to fight back."

James nodded, his own expression softening. "Dad, you've done more than you realise. Your farewell speech, the way you handled your departure—it's already making waves. The backlash Manic is facing isn't just about you leaving; it's about everything you stood for, everything they've lost. People are finally waking up to how far they've drifted from what radio should be. You might feel like you enabled it by staying silent, but you've done more to challenge it now than anyone else in your position ever could."

James heard a ping from his dad's mobile as a notification came in. Pete picked up his phone, glancing at the screen. His brows furrowed slightly before a wry smile tugged at the corners of his mouth.

"What is it, Dad?" James asked, curious about what could have elicited such a reaction.

Pete turned the screen towards James and Lyra.

From: *charlotte.mcdonald@manicradio.group*

To: *pete@reevesradioltd.radio*

Subject: *Contract Breach – Employee Payroll Number 71465*

Dear Mr Smith,

It has come to our attention that your actions following your resignation from Manic Goldies, including public statements made during your final broadcast, may constitute a breach of your employment contract with Manic Radio Group including, but not limited to, disparagement clauses and unauthorised use of company property. Furthermore, reports indicate that you have distributed company-owned smart speakers without prior approval, an action that may also breach company property policies.

We kindly request that you refrain from making further public statements about Manic Radio Group and its subsidiaries. Additionally, we require the immediate return of any company property, including any unused smart speakers, and reserve the right to pursue legal action should these matters not be resolved promptly.

Please contact the HR department by 5pm on Monday, 10th November 2025, to discuss the resolution of these issues. Failure to comply may result in further legal proceedings.

Sincerely,

Charlotte McDonald

Head of HR

Manic Radio Group

Pete let out a short laugh, shaking his head. "They're really scraping the bottom of the barrel, aren't they? Disparagement clauses and smart speakers? This isn't a legal warning—it's a tantrum in email form."

James leaned in to read the message more closely, his brow furrowing. "Dad, they can't be serious. They're trying to intimidate you into silence. But you didn't do anything illegal, and the speakers... come on, you sent them to listeners who've supported you for decades. They've lost all sense of perspective."

It was then that James re-read the header, as well as the first line of the email, when he realised that, his dad, as a freelance employee, was not a direct employee of the company and therefore not subject to the same contract restrictions as full-time staff.

James smirked. "Dad, you're not even on their payroll as a full-time employee anymore. You're a freelancer. You've been a contractor since they reclassified your role. The whole email is baseless."

Pete's eyes widened for a moment before a slow grin spread across his face. "You're right, James. I haven't been a direct employee since last year. They reclassified me during that contract renewal, remember? Any so-called 'disparagement clauses' or property policies would have been tied to my old contract, not my freelance agreement. I'm going to need a contract lawyer, aren't I?"

Suddenly the sound of keys entering the front door lock broke the tension in the room as Sarah entered, carrying a bag of groceries. She glanced at the three of them, immediately picking up on the atmosphere.

"What's going on?" Sarah asked, setting the bag down on the counter. Her gaze moved between Pete, James, and Lyra, noting their serious expressions.

James passed Pete's phone to Sarah, letting her read the email. As her eyes scanned the message, her face shifted from curiosity to disbelief. "Are they serious? Disparagement clauses and smart speakers? Pete, this is desperation. They're trying to scare you."

Pete chuckled, his earlier frustration giving way to a sense of bemusement. "That's exactly what we were saying. They don't have a leg to stand on. I'm a freelancer now, and any clauses tied to my old contract are void. They're just grasping at straws. Anyway, with the smart speakers, the SharePoint said that, in the Competition and Gifting Policy, that it was up to the discretion of the presenters and their producers who received a smart speaker, provided it was related to audience engagement and approved under the marketing budget. Since Rachael and I made the decision to send them to listeners who've supported us for years, it's entirely within policy. They're making a fuss over nothing because they know I'm hitting them where it hurts—their reputation."

Sarah placed the phone on the counter and crossed her arms, her voice steady but with an edge of determination. "Pete, they're trying to rattle you, but you've got the upper hand here. You're in the right legally, and morally, you've already won. The public are on your side. Let them send all the intimidating emails they want—it won't change the fact that they've lost their most authentic voice."

Pete smiled at his wife, appreciating her unwavering support. "You're right, love. They can try, but they won't silence me. And if they want to take this further, I'll happily shine a spotlight on their practices. Let's see how much they enjoy the scrutiny."

James grinned, his earlier unease melting into admiration for his dad. "They picked the wrong person to mess with. You've got decades of goodwill with your audience and the industry backing you. Manic's just showing how desperate they are."

Lyra chimed in, her voice calm but firm. "And if they want to take it to court, Theo will tear them apart. They've got no grounds for legal action, and the public backlash will only grow if they try."

Pete nodded, his resolve strengthening. "Then let them come. I'm not backing down. Radio has always been about connecting with people, and that's what I'll keep doing—with or without Manic."

Sarah placed a reassuring hand on Pete's arm. "You're not alone in this, Pete. We've got your back."

As the family rallied around Pete, the weight of Manic's threats seemed to diminish. They knew the battle ahead might be tough, but they also knew Pete's integrity and the support of his audience would carry him through.

A few hours later, the front door bell sounded, and James got up to answer it. Standing on the doorstep was a police officer, one who was an Inspector, accompanied by a duo of plain clothes investigators. The officer's stern expression softened slightly as James opened the door, but his presence was unmistakably official.

"Good evening," the Inspector began, holding up his identification. "I'm Inspector Williams from West Midlands Police. This is Detective Sergeant Allen and

Detective Constable Green. We're here to speak with Mr James Smith. Is he available?"

James stiffened at the sight of the police officers. His initial reaction was panic, a reflex born out of months of stress and paranoia. Lyra appeared behind him, her hand resting lightly on his shoulder, grounding him in the moment.

"I'm James Smith," he said, his voice steadying despite the knot forming in his stomach. "What's this about?"

"DC Green and I are from the unit that deal with... certain unsavoury acts..." DS Allen said with a slight hesitation, glancing between James and the rest of the family who had gathered at the door. "We're here to get a further statement with regards to the case of Mr Kyler Thompson, Rory Carter, and others involved in the charges laid against them. Recent developments, including corroborative testimony from a former employee of Manic Radio, have brought new evidence to light. We need to ensure all your statements align with the updated facts for the ongoing investigation."

****

CHAPTER 8 - First Custody Hearing
Monday 10th November 2025

James knew that finding a decent shirt and tie in his wardrobe was like finding a needle in a haystack. Most of his clothes were more suited to his days as a student and not as a father standing in an initial custody hearing in court, fighting for his children. With Lyra's help, he managed to pull together a simple, respectable outfit: a navy-blue shirt and a grey tie that didn't scream "radio DJ" but rather "responsible adult."

The courtroom, located in Birmingham's Civil Justice Centre, was a far cry from the image of dramatic trials on television. It was utilitarian, with muted tones and a functional layout designed more for efficiency than grandeur. The atmosphere was heavy, the stakes palpable. James could feel the weight of every glance, every shuffle of paper.

Lyra sat beside him, her presence a steadying force. Despite being heavily pregnant, she exuded calm and determination. Theodore Nott, James's solicitor, was already seated, his polished demeanour and meticulous preparation giving James a much-needed boost of confidence.

Across the room sat Kylie Morgan, dressed to the nines in a sharp suit that screamed professionalism, though her carefully constructed image couldn't completely mask the disdain in her eyes. Beside her was Penny O'Rourke, her demeanour more subdued but no less calculating. Both women had come armed, not just with legal representation but also with arguments aimed squarely at discrediting James.

James's own legal representative, Dr Miriam Patel, a doctor of law from Cambridge and close friend of

Theodore Nott, sat beside him, flipping through her notes with the precision and calm of someone who had seen far more contentious custody battles. Dr Patel's reputation as a fierce advocate for fathers in family court was well-earned, and James felt reassured knowing she would be presenting his case.

The magistrate entered, a middle-aged woman with a no-nonsense air and a glance that seemed to pierce through any façade. As everyone rose and then sat, the hearing began with procedural formalities.

The magistrate, Mrs Justice Harrington, addressed the court. "This is a preliminary hearing to assess the custodial arrangements for the children Cory Smith and Alfie O'Rourke. We will hear submissions from the respective parties before determining interim arrangements pending further hearings."

It was then that James remembered that Kylie, as a single mother and not on speaking terms with her own family, ever since her third year at Wolverhampton University when she had loaned £20,000 for a luxury car she promptly crashed, had no real support network. Penny, on the other hand, came from a large and close-knit family in Liverpool, who had rallied around her since Alfie's birth, but, as it was half past 9, her husband, Weston O'Rourke, would be at work, as he was a producer at the new Belfast studios of Manic Radio, their hub for the Northern Ireland and Republic of Ireland Manic Vibes and Manic Goldies station, and that she had had to fly from Belfast International at the crack of dawn to attend the hearing. James suspected Penny's large support network might work against him, but he also hoped that her husband's absence might highlight a point in his favour—he was here, ready to fight for his children, no matter the cost.

"Objection, ma'am. My client would like to object to the name given by yourself to her child, Cory Morgan."

James looked at Kylie's legal representative, who had interrupted the magistrate with a tone of sharp professionalism. The solicitor, Ms Rachel Greaves, adjusted her glasses and continued, "The name 'Cory Smith' implies paternity has been legally established, which, as of this hearing, is a matter of contention. My client requests that the court refer to the child as 'Cory Morgan' until paternity is definitively resolved."

James felt a surge of indignation but forced himself to remain calm. He glanced at Dr Patel, who gave him a reassuring nod before addressing the magistrate.

"Your Honour," Dr Patel said, rising gracefully, "my client does not dispute the need for clarity on this matter. However, I must point out that substantial evidence, including a DNA test conducted by Manic Radio as part of its internal policies, has already established Mr Smith as the biological father of Cory."

"With all due respect, Dr Patel," Kylie's solicitor, Ms Greaves, interjected smoothly, "the DNA test in question was conducted under questionable circumstances and without the oversight of a certified third-party agency. As such, it cannot be deemed conclusive in this court."

"Your Honour, I would like to admit-"

"Enough." the magistrate interjected, her voice calm yet firm, cutting through the growing tension. Mrs Justice Harrington adjusted her glasses and fixed both solicitors with a piercing gaze. "This is not the time for tit-for-tat arguments. This hearing is about determining interim arrangements in the best interest of the child. Paternity can and will be addressed separately if necessary, but for now, I will allow the child to be referred to as Cory Morgan for

93

procedural neutrality. However, I expect both parties to focus on the welfare of the children rather than procedural disputes."

James exhaled slowly, grateful for the magistrate's firm hand. Dr Patel gave him a small nod of reassurance before sitting down. Across the room, Kylie smirked slightly, as if she had won a minor battle. James clenched his fists under the table but kept his composure, determined not to let her get under his skin.

The magistrate gestured for Ms Greaves to proceed. "Ms Greaves, you may begin with your submissions."

Ms Greaves rose, her tone smooth and professional. "Your Honour, my client, Ms Kylie Morgan, has been the sole caregiver for Cory since birth. While the court may be aware of recent difficulties in her personal circumstances, these have not impeded her ability to provide a stable environment for her child. My client acknowledges Mr Smith's desire to be involved, but his recent history—specifically his struggles with substance abuse and the well-documented toxic environment at his previous employer—raises significant concerns about his suitability for custodial responsibilities at this time."

James felt his stomach tighten. Ms Greaves's words, though carefully measured, cut deeply. He glanced at Lyra, who gave his hand a reassuring squeeze under the table.

Dr Patel stood as soon as Ms Greaves sat. "Your Honour, my client does not dispute that he has faced challenges in the past. However, Mr Smith has demonstrated remarkable progress in recent months. He has successfully completed a rehabilitation programme, is actively attending Narcotics Anonymous meetings, and has taken concrete steps to rebuild his life. Furthermore,

Mr Smith has been denied his parental rights as a father to even see Cory, despite his proactive efforts to establish a relationship with her. Denying him interim access based on past issues, when he has taken every available step to address them, would not serve the child's best interests. Additionally, Your Honour, my client is ready and willing to undertake any parental assessment deemed necessary by this court to demonstrate his capability. Finally, I would like to ask if you are aware of R v Kylie Morgan, which is scheduled in the Crown Court on the 18th of November this year?"

James looked at the Magistrate, who was shocked, and he assumed that she was unaware of pending criminal proceedings against Kylie Morgan. Mrs Justice Harrington's expression shifted subtly, a flicker of surprise crossing her face before she regained her composure. She adjusted her glasses and addressed Dr Patel directly.

"Dr Patel, I was not aware of any pending criminal charges against Ms Morgan. Kindly elaborate, keeping it brief and relevant to today's hearing."

Dr Patel nodded. "Your Honour, Ms Morgan is due to appear at Birmingham Crown Court on the 18th of November, facing charges relating to coercive control, rape, theft, drugging, as well as other related offences. These charges stem from her alleged involvement in activities that have had a direct and profoundly negative impact on Mr Smith and other parties. While I understand this hearing is not the venue to adjudicate those charges, they are relevant insofar as they raise significant concerns about Ms Morgan's ability to provide a safe and stable environment for Cory."

The courtroom fell silent, the weight of Dr Patel's statement hanging heavily in the air. Across the room,

Kylie's composure faltered for a fraction of a second before she recovered, her expression hardening into a mask of defiance.

Mrs Justice Harrington leaned forward slightly, her gaze sharp. "Ms Greaves, is your client prepared to respond to these allegations, given their potential relevance to the welfare of the child?"

Ms Greaves stood, her expression measured but tense. "Your Honour, my client strongly denies the charges and maintains her presumption of innocence, as is her legal right. The upcoming trial should not prejudice the court against her ability to parent effectively. Furthermore, I would remind the court that Mr Smith's own legal and personal history, including allegations of substance abuse and his participation in the toxic culture at his former workplace, must also be weighed carefully."

James felt a surge of anger at the implication, but Dr Patel placed a calming hand on his arm before responding. "Your Honour, my client acknowledges his past struggles, which were exacerbated by the environment at his previous workplace. However, unlike Ms Morgan, Mr Smith has faced no criminal charges, and is in fact King's evidence to support investigations into systemic issues at his former employer. He has shown a willingness to confront his past and actively improve his circumstances. The same cannot be said of Ms Morgan, who is currently under investigation and awaiting trial for serious offences. Furthermore, Ms Morgan is a single lady with no family support network or co-parent to assist her, whereas Mr Smith has a stable partner, Ms Lyra Smith, who is present today and who has expressed her commitment to supporting him in raising Cory. He resides at his parents' house, and so has the support and guidance of his family, ensuring a stable, multi-generational environment for Cory."

"Bet he's still a cokehead," James heard Kylie mutter and he knew that she had let her composure slip. Her words were low, but in the quiet of the courtroom, they carried enough weight to reach the magistrate's ears.

Mrs Justice Harrington's gaze snapped toward Kylie with a sharpness that immediately silenced the room. "Ms Morgan," she said, her voice steely, "I would remind you that this is a court of law. Any further outbursts or remarks will not be tolerated."

Kylie's solicitor, Ms Greaves, quickly leaned in, whispering something into Kylie's ear. Kylie crossed her arms but said nothing further, her expression sullen.

Dr Patel rose again, calm and measured. "Your Honour, I believe Ms Morgan's comment speaks to the very concerns we've raised. My client has undergone rigorous testing to confirm he is free of substances and remains committed to maintaining his sobriety. I have here a copy of the most recent toxicology report, which shows that Mr Smith has been clean for six months. Additionally, he has letters of support from his rehabilitation programme and his Narcotics Anonymous sponsor, as well as a character reference from his father, Mr Pete Smith, who is a well-known and respected figure in the broadcasting industry. I also have photographs of Ms Morgan, two days earlier, in Carters Green, West Bromwich, talking to a known drug dealer."

The courtroom fell silent again as Dr Patel placed the documents on the desk in front of her, neatly aligned. The magistrate, Mrs Justice Harrington, glanced at the stack of evidence, her expression unreadable.

"Dr Patel," she said, her tone even, "I will accept the toxicology report and letters of support into evidence. However, I must ask for clarification regarding the photographs you've mentioned. Are you submitting these as evidence of Ms Morgan's association with individuals involved in illegal activities?"

Dr Patel nodded. "Yes, Your Honour. These photographs were taken by a private investigator hired by my client. They depict Ms Morgan engaging in what appears to be a conversation with an individual who is a known drug dealer, according to local police records. While we cannot prove the nature of their interaction without further investigation, the photographs raise serious questions about her judgement and the environment in which Cory is being raised."

Ms Greaves shot to her feet, her voice sharp but controlled. "Your Honour, this is highly prejudicial. The photographs lack context, and their introduction at this stage is an attempt to smear my client. Ms Morgan was in Carters Green on personal business unrelated to the allegations being made here. We request that these photographs be excluded from consideration."

The magistrate raised a hand, silencing further argument. "Ms Greaves, I will determine the relevance of the photographs. For now, they will be admitted on a provisional basis. If necessary, their admissibility will be reviewed at a later stage. Anyway, I turn to the case of Alfie O'Rourke."

As Mrs Justice Harrington shifted her attention to the matter of Alfie O'Rourke, Penny sat up straighter, her expression calm but tinged with unease. James glanced briefly at her, noting the flicker of anxiety in her eyes despite her outward composure. Unlike Kylie, Penny had managed to maintain a professional demeanour, though James suspected the strain was taking its toll.

"Ms Greaves," the magistrate began, "as Ms O'Rourke's solicitor, I invite you to make submissions regarding the custodial arrangements for Alfie O'Rourke."

Penny's solicitor, Mr Adam Pearson, stood, exuding a confidence that suggested he was well-prepared. "Your Honour, my client, Ms Penny O'Rourke, has been Alfie's primary caregiver since birth. While Mr Smith has expressed interest in being involved, it must be noted that Alfie's environment with Ms O'Rourke is stable and supported by her extended family in Liverpool. This familial network provides Alfie with a consistent and loving environment, and any disruption to this arrangement would not be in the child's best interests at this time."

"Where's her husband?" James muttered to Dr Patel, grinning. "Clue, look at the Manic Prime app and Manic Vibes Northern Ireland."

Dr Patel, ever composed, leaned towards James and whispered, "Let's not jump to conclusions in the courtroom. Save your observations for when it counts."

"I'm just suggesting to you that he's at work in Belfast, and Penny's here, so where's Alfie?" James pointed out to her, as he knew that she'd likely make a sharp observation to counter Penny's legal argument effectively. "She and Weston live in Belfast - it says here on the court documents, and her family is in Liverpool, so she'd have either to leave Alfie in Belfast with her husband or bring him to Liverpool while she's here. Either way, it raises questions about who is currently providing care for Alfie."

Dr Patel nodded subtly, the wheels clearly turning in her mind. When her turn came to respond, she rose smoothly, her tone measured but firm.

"Your Honour, while we acknowledge that Ms O'Rourke has been Alfie's primary caregiver, we must address an important point regarding the logistics of her care arrangements. As court documents state, Ms O'Rourke resides in Belfast with her husband, Mr Weston O'Rourke, who is currently employed by Manic Radio in their Belfast hub. Given her presence here in Birmingham for this hearing, I respectfully ask the court to clarify who is currently caring for Alfie. If he has been left in Belfast, this would indicate reliance on third-party care, which raises legitimate concerns about consistency and stability."

Mr Pearson stood, his tone defensive but polite. "Your Honour, Alfie is currently in the care of a trusted family member in Liverpool. My client travelled to Birmingham this morning specifically for this hearing and will return to her son promptly."

Dr Patel pressed forward, her expression calm but resolute. "Your Honour, while I respect Ms O'Rourke's efforts to attend this hearing, her decision to leave Alfie in Liverpool underlines a key issue. Especially as she presents her Manic Vibes Liverpool drivetime show not from Liverpool, but from Belfast, where her husband produces the Manic Vibes Northern Ireland breakfast show. This arrangement raises questions about the practicalities of her caregiving and whether Alfie's environment truly offers the stability and consistency she claims."

The magistrate, Mrs Justice Harrington, looked between the two legal representatives, her expression impassive. "Mr Pearson, can you confirm whether Ms O'Rourke routinely commutes between Belfast and Liverpool for her broadcasting commitments? If so, this court would like to understand how these arrangements align with the stability and continuity of care for Alfie."

"Erm... Your Honour... my client remotely presents her drivetime show from Belfast and travels to Liverpool during her weekends off to spend time with her extended family. This arrangement is manageable and has no adverse effect on Alfie's well-being. During her working hours, her husband, Mr Weston O'Rourke, provides care, supplemented by trusted family members when necessary."

Dr Patel's face remained neutral, but her eyes sparked with quiet determination as she rose again.

"Your Honour, while I appreciate Mr Pearson's clarification, I must point out that the arrangement described indicates a fragmented caregiving setup. The frequent movement between Belfast and Liverpool, combined with Mr O'Rourke's own professional commitments, introduces a degree of inconsistency in Alfie's care. Furthermore, I believe her father-in-law is currently a guest of His Majesty's Prison Service on a murder charge, of which he has a life sentence, her mother-in-law, who lives in Ballymena, is currently a resident under the Mental Health Act, and one of her sisters-in-law are a prostitute."

The courtroom was silent, save for the faint sound of pens scratching notes. Penny's calm facade faltered, her knuckles whitening as she gripped the edge of the table. Across the aisle, James kept his expression neutral, though he felt vindicated by Dr Patel's unrelenting logic. Mrs Justice Harrington took a long, deliberate pause before addressing the court.

"Dr Patel, while your point about the familial circumstances is noted, I must remind all parties that this hearing is focused on the interim custodial arrangements for the children. We will not allow unrelated characterisations to divert attention from the welfare of the children involved. However, I do find the geographical and logistical elements of Alfie's care arrangement relevant and will consider these in my deliberations."

Mr Pearson, visibly flustered, rose to respond. "Your Honour, while Dr Patel has presented a rather unflattering depiction of my client's extended family, I must reiterate that Alfie is currently thriving under Ms O'Rourke's care. Her extended network in Liverpool provides a safe and nurturing environment whenever her professional obligations require her to be away."

Dr Patel quickly followed up. "Your Honour, with respect, my client, Mr Smith, offers a significantly more stable arrangement. Residing in Birmingham with his partner, Ms Lyra Smith, and his parents, he can provide a consistent, supportive environment for Alfie, one that does not require frequent relocation or reliance on extended family members spread across multiple cities."

Mrs Justice Harrington nodded, her gaze shifting to Penny. "Ms O'Rourke, I would like to hear directly from you. Can you elaborate on how you ensure stability for Alfie amid your professional commitments and travel between Belfast and Liverpool?"

Penny's voice was steady, though her words carried a faint edge of defensiveness. "Your Honour, I have always prioritised Alfie's well-being. While my work requires flexibility, my family have always stepped up to support me. Alfie has never lacked care, love, or stability, whether he is with me in Belfast or with my family in Liverpool. I believe it's important for him to grow up knowing both sides of his family and to feel connected to his roots."

Mrs Justice Harrington nodded again, her expression revealing little. "Thank you, Ms O'Rourke. I will take your statement into consideration. Now, I turn back to Mr Smith's legal team for any final submissions regarding both children before I make my interim decision."

Dr Patel stood once more, her voice clear and confident. "Your Honour, in summation, my client seeks interim joint custody arrangements for both Cory Morgan and Alfie O'Rourke. Mr Smith has demonstrated a commitment to his sobriety and personal growth, with a strong support network that includes his partner, his parents, and his extended family. He is not seeking to disrupt the children's lives but rather to provide a stable and loving environment where they can thrive. Denying him access, particularly while serious allegations against Ms Morgan remain unresolved, would not serve the best interests of the children."

As Dr Patel sat, Mrs Justice Harrington leaned back in her chair, her hands folded. Her gaze swept the courtroom before she spoke.

"This is a challenging case, involving complex dynamics and significant allegations. However, my primary responsibility is to the welfare of the children involved. In light of the submissions, I will make the following interim arrangements."

The room seemed to collectively hold its breath.

"For Cory Morgan, I order custody be placed with Mr James Smith in the interim, while Ms Morgan is evaluated by social services in light of the pending criminal charges against her. Ms Morgan will have supervised visitation rights twice a week at a location agreed upon by both parties, under the supervision of a social worker. The safety and well-being of the child must remain paramount. These arrangements will be reviewed at the next hearing following the outcome of the criminal proceedings."

James felt a wave of relief wash over him, though he maintained his composure. Kylie's expression hardened, her carefully constructed facade cracking slightly as she leaned toward Ms Greaves, whispering furiously.

Mrs Justice Harrington continued, turning her attention to Penny. "For Alfie O'Rourke, I find the current caregiving arrangement, involving frequent travel and reliance on extended family, to be less than ideal for maintaining stability. However, as Mr Smith is currently a resident of Dudley and Ms O'Rourke is a Belfast resident, I cannot expect either party to be required to travel significant distances for custody exchanges on an interim basis. Therefore, I order the following.

"Ms O'Rourke will retain custody, however I strongly, and I mean strongly, advise, that at minimum, virtual video calls be arranged between Mr James Smith and Alfie O'Rourke twice a week to maintain their developing relationship. Additionally, Mr Smith will have the right to unannounced visits, should he have the funds and the ability to travel, and shall notify the court prior to any planned travel to Belfast for these visits. Any interference with these arrangements will result in a formal review of custody."

Penny nodded stiffly, her expression calm, though James noted the tension in her posture. He could sense her frustration but also her careful restraint, knowing any reaction would be scrutinised.

Mrs Justice Harrington leaned forward, addressing both parties. "These are interim measures, and I expect full cooperation from all parties involved. The welfare of Cory and Alfie must remain at the forefront of every decision and action taken. Further hearings will assess these arrangements and allow for any adjustments necessary based on the evolving circumstances."

She paused, her gaze sweeping across the room. "This court will reconvene in three months to review progress. In the meantime, I urge both parties to focus on fostering a healthy and supportive environment for the children. This is not about winning or losing—it is about doing what is right for them."

The magistrate rose, signalling the end of the hearing. "Court adjourned."

James let out a breath he hadn't realised he was holding. Lyra squeezed his hand, her eyes filled with pride and relief. Dr Patel leaned over, offering a small but reassuring smile. "Well done, James. This is a strong step forward. Now, let's focus on ensuring you make the most of this opportunity."

Across the courtroom, Kylie and Penny gathered their belongings, their expressions a mix of frustration and resolve. James noticed Kylie's glare as she whispered to Ms Greaves, clearly plotting her next move. Penny, by contrast, maintained a neutral expression, though her tightened jaw betrayed her irritation.

As they stepped outside the courtroom into the crisp November air, James felt a surge of determination. This wasn't the end—it was just the beginning. He had fought for his children today and had been heard. Now, it was time to prove himself as the father they deserved.

****

CHAPTER 9 - Late... or Deliberate?
Friday 14th November 2025

James glanced at his watch for what felt like the hundredth time. It was quarter to five, and Kylie was nowhere to be seen. He sat on the worn leather sofa in his parents' living room, the tension in the air palpable. Lyra sat beside him, her hand resting on her baby bump, offering silent reassurance. Pete, ever the calming presence, stood near the window, peering out into the fading November light as the streetlights flickered to life.

"She's cutting it fine," Pete muttered, his voice tinged with frustration. "If she's not here by five, we'll have grounds to raise this with the court."

James nodded, though the knot in his stomach tightened. He had half-expected Kylie to pull something like this. The magistrate's decision at Monday's hearing had been a clear victory for him, granting him interim custody of Cory. But he knew Kylie too well to think she would hand over their daughter without some kind of drama.

"She's doing this on purpose," James said, his voice low but steady. "She wants to make a scene. Make me look like the unreasonable one."

Lyra squeezed his hand. "Stay calm, James. If she's late, it's on her, not you. We've got the court order. She can't wriggle out of this."

Theodore and Dr Patel, who had come because of their concerns about Kylie's behaviour, sat across the room, reviewing the court documents again. Theodore's sharp suit was slightly rumpled, and Dr Patel's usually calm expression betrayed a flicker of irritation.

"If she doesn't show up by the agreed time," Dr Patel said firmly, "we'll document it and file an incident report with the family court first thing Monday. The court order is explicit: 5 pm drop-off at this address."

James knew that the pacing up and down in the living room wasn't helping, but he couldn't help himself. The anticipation, the worry, and the simmering anger all churned together, threatening to spill over. Pete turned from the window, his expression tight but controlled.

"Five minutes to go," Pete said, glancing at James. "If she's not here, we document everything. No confrontations, no arguments. Just let Dr Patel and Theo handle it."

James nodded, though he couldn't entirely push away the frustration bubbling under his skin. "She's going to twist this, isn't she? Make it look like I'm the bad guy."

"She might try," Theodore said without looking up from the papers in front of him. "But the facts are on your side. The court order is clear, and we have witnesses here. If she's late—or worse, if she doesn't show—it only strengthens your case."

"Alexa, open Big Ben," James said to the Alexa device in the corner of the room, as if hearing the chimes of Big Ben might ground him amidst the storm of emotions. The familiar, resonant tones filled the room, marking the passing of another minute. It was now 4:56.

Pete turned back to the window, his shoulders tense. "Nothing yet," he muttered.

Lyra leaned forward, her voice calm but purposeful. "James, remember, no matter what happens, this isn't about Kylie—it's about Cory. You've done everything right so far. Don't let her get to you."

James took a deep breath, nodding. "I know. I just... Cory's only 3 months old, she doesn't deserve this, being traded like a pawn in someone else's game," James finished, his voice cracking slightly. He clenched his fists, trying to channel the frustration into resolve. "She deserves better than this."

Pete turned away from the window, his jaw tight. "She does, and she's got you fighting for her. That's what matters."

"I've just thought," Sarah said with a look that made James pause mid-step. "Cory is 3 months old, right? She should be on breast milk, so..."

James looked at his mother, clueless as to what she was suggesting. "What do you mean, Mum?" he asked, stopping his pacing to face her.

Sarah folded her arms, her expression one of quiet resolve. "Kylie never mentioned anything about breastfeeding during the hearing, did she? If Cory is on formula, that's one thing, but if Kylie has been breastfeeding, it could complicate things. Your aunt Helen's a GP, and she reminded me once when I was pregnant with you that breastfeeding can impact custody arrangements, especially for very young infants. It's considered in the best interest of the child to maintain that bond, even in shared custody situations."

James blinked, the implications dawning on him. "You're saying Kylie might use breastfeeding as an excuse to withhold Cory?"

"It's possible," Sarah said, her voice steady. "But if she's been switching to formula, or if there's evidence Cory hasn't been exclusively breastfed, it undermines that argument. Either way, the court would want clarity. And... well, Lyra, dear, your breasts are leaking, aren't they?"

Lyra's cheeks flushed a deep red, but she managed a small nod, her hand instinctively moving to her bump. "Yeah, they've started leaking a little," she admitted, her tone tinged with embarrassment. "It's early, but it happens sometimes during pregnancy. What are you suggesting, Sarah?"

"Well, as you're in your third trimester, and you haven't yet had your baby, well... erm... you might not be able to feed Cory just yet," Sarah said gently, glancing at Lyra with a reassuring smile. "I'll get Helen to pop over, give you a check-up and to give Cory a quick assessment when she arrives, just to make sure she's being properly fed and cared for. If Kylie's been neglecting any aspect of Cory's care, it'll come out, and it will give us grounds to act."

James glanced at the clock. 4:58. He let out a deep breath, trying to shake off the growing anxiety. "Let's just hope it doesn't come to that. I want to believe she'll show, even if it's just to keep up appearances."

Theodore stood, smoothing down his suit. "If she doesn't, we proceed by the book. No accusations, no assumptions—just facts. If Cory's welfare is compromised in any way, we'll address it through the proper channels."

As Sarah grabbed her phone, James noticed the clock turn to 4:59, and the Alexa device was starting to announce the upcoming hour. The atmosphere in the room was tense, the seconds ticking by with excruciating slowness. Pete moved to the window one last time, his eyes scanning the quiet street outside.

Bong

Bong

Bong

Bong

Bong

That was it, James knew, it was precisely 5 pm.

James felt his heart sink as the final chime of Big Ben echoed through the room. Pete turned away from the window, shaking his head. "No sign of her. She's officially late."

Dr Patel stood, her expression calm but steely. "Right, let's document everything. James, can you confirm the time and the absence of Kylie Morgan for the record?"

James nodded, his voice steady despite the turmoil churning inside. "It's 5 pm, and Kylie Morgan has not arrived to hand over Cory Morgan as per the court order."

Theodore pulled out his phone, snapping a quick photo of the clock on the wall and making a note in his leather-bound diary. "This is crucial evidence. We'll file an incident report first thing Monday. If she fails to comply with the order entirely, this will reflect very poorly on her in the eyes of the court."

Pete moved to stand beside his son, placing a reassuring hand on his shoulder. "You've done everything you could, James. This is on her now."

James clenched his fists, a wave of anger and helplessness washing over him. "What if something's happened? What if she's using Cory as leverage, or worse, she's in trouble herself?"

Lyra reached for his hand, her touch grounding him. "Let's not jump to conclusions. We don't know why she's late. But we do know you've got witnesses, legal support, and the court order on your side. We'll handle this."

As the clock struck 5:30 pm, the tension in the room was cut by the distant sound of a car engine outside. Pete, still stationed near the window, peered out and immediately turned back to the group.

"She's here," Pete announced, his tone a mixture of relief and exasperation.

James straightened, a wave of emotions crashing over him—relief, anger, and apprehension. Lyra gave his hand one last squeeze before letting go, her calm presence bolstering his resolve. Theodore and Dr Patel exchanged glances before standing, their demeanours professional and composed.

The group moved towards the front door as the car parked in the parking bay outside the Pensnett house. James opened the door to see not Kylie, but his aunt, Helen Carmichael and his cousin, Penelope. It was ironic, James knew, that his cousin's shortened name was Penny, and that Penny O'Rourke's own maiden name was Penny Carmichael, which only added to the tangled web of names and relationships in this custody battle. James exchanged a quick glance with Helen, her expression a mixture of curiosity and concern.

"Hey, James," Penelope said, and he hugged the older woman who he was close to, his mother being her aunt by blood, the Reeves family genes in both James and Penelope evident as she smiled warmly at him. "We thought we'd stop by to support you. Mum said you might need an extra set of eyes and ears if things got heated."

James returned the hug, grateful for their presence. "Thanks, Pen. Thanks, Aunt Helen. It's... it's been tense."

Helen Carmichael, a no-nonsense GP with years of experience handling everything from family squabbles to medical emergencies, placed a reassuring hand on his
112

shoulder. "We're here for you, James. Let's keep things calm and focused on Cory, and I need to check Lyra too. Have you been attending anti-natal classes with her, James?"

"I've been doing my best, especially with going back to Uni and trying to juggle everything," James replied, glancing back at Lyra with an apologetic smile. "I've made it to a few classes, but not as many as I'd like."

Helen gave him an approving nod. "It's good you're trying. Being there for her during this time is just as important as fighting for Cory. Now, let's handle one thing at a time. Where's Kylie?"

Before James could answer, the rumble of a second car pulling into the street drew everyone's attention. Pete stepped outside to get a better look, motioning for James and the others to stay calm. The car—a silver SUV with tinted windows—came to a stop, and after a long pause, the driver's door opened.

"Alright, slut?" the voice of Kyler Thompson said, and James gulped, as he stepped out of the car, his smirk instantly setting James on edge. The fact that he then went to open the passenger door, and helped Kylie out, kissing her made James feel a rush of anger mixed with disgust. James clenched his fists, forcing himself to stay rooted to the spot as Kylie stepped out of the car, her expression one of smug confidence. She was dressed to make an impression—heels clicking against the pavement, her oversized sunglasses hiding most of her face, and her designer coat wrapped around her like a shield.

Kyler leaned casually against the car, his arms crossed as if he was part of some theatrical performance. His presence alone was enough to make James's blood boil, but the kiss—meant to provoke, no doubt—was the final straw.

"Daddy, why is Cory going?" James heard a voice of a 4 year old, a small voice that pierced through the tension like a dagger. James froze, his heart sinking as he realised the child speaking was Kyler's son, Link. The boy peeked out from the back seat, his wide eyes filled with innocent confusion.

James's breath hitched as he stared at the child in the back seat. He hadn't expected Kyler to bring his son, Link, into this already fraught situation. It was typical of Kyler to escalate tension in any way he could, but involving a child felt like a new low.

Pete stepped forward, his calm but commanding presence cutting through the rising tension. "Kylie," he said evenly, "you're late. The court order was for 5 pm, and it's now gone half past."

"Piss off, old man," Kyler said with the grin of someone who knew exactly how to push buttons. "If you want to talk to my fiancée, you go through me first."

James's heart pounded in his chest, as, before April, he and Kylie had been in a relationship, even though it was a coercive and manipulative one. The fact that Kyler had been married to Toni Green, another of Manic Radio's toxic survivors, made the situation even messier, especially as Link was the product of Toni and Kyler's union, meaning that the tangled relationships surrounding everyone felt like an endless spiral. James fought to keep his composure, aware that any outburst would play directly into Kylie and Kyler's hands. He couldn't afford to let emotions override the strategy he and his legal team had carefully planned.

"As a Magistrate, I do-"

But before Theodore could continue, Kylie interrupted him, squealing like a child playing up for attention. "Oh, Theo, you don't need to start on your posh-lawyer act with me. I know the routine. I'm only late because Cory needed feeding, and I didn't want her to be unsettled during the journey."

"That may be," Theodore retorted, and James knew that his brother-in-law was set to give Kylie the legal equivalent of a reaming for her tardiness, "but the court order was explicit. Feeding or not, arrangements must be adhered to. Being late undermines the court's directives and, frankly, casts doubt on your reliability."

Kylie tilted her head, her sunglasses sliding slightly down her nose to reveal a mocking glint in her eyes. "Oh, Theo, darling," she purred, her tone dripping with sarcasm, "I had no idea you were so invested in my punctuality. Surely a few minutes isn't a crime."

Theodore's jaw tightened, but his voice remained calm and measured. "Thirty-five minutes isn't 'a few', Kylie, and it sets a precedent. The court doesn't take kindly to disregard for its orders, especially when a child's welfare is at stake."

James took a step forward, his voice steadier than he felt. "Where's Cory?"

Kylie's smirk faltered slightly, but she quickly regained her composure. "She's in the car with Link," she said, gesturing vaguely towards the backseat. "She's fine, James. Honestly, you act like I'd ever do anything to harm her."

"Daddy... Cory's stinky," Link's voice cut through the tension with an innocent bluntness that only a child could deliver. Pete's stern gaze didn't waver as he turned towards Kylie.

"Then I suggest you get Cory out of the car immediately," Pete said firmly. "If she needs changing, James will take care of it."

Kylie huffed dramatically, clearly annoyed by the lack of indulgence. She turned back to the car and opened the door with a theatrical sigh. As she reached in to retrieve Cory, the baby's small cries began to fill the chilly November air. James's heart twisted at the sound, and he instinctively moved closer, his every nerve screaming to hold his daughter.

Kylie emerged, holding Cory in her arms. The baby was bundled up in a thick pink blanket, her tiny face scrunched up and red from crying. James stepped forward, but Kylie hesitated, her grip tightening slightly.

"She's unsettled," Kylie said with a falsely sweet tone. "Maybe she'd be better off staying with me tonight."

"No." James's voice was resolute, and he extended his arms. "The court order is clear. Hand her over."

For a moment, Kylie's mask slipped, and James saw the flicker of something darker in her eyes. But then she smiled—cold and calculated—and passed Cory to him. James cradled his daughter gently, her cries quieting almost immediately as she nestled into his chest. Relief flooded through him, and he pressed a kiss to her forehead.

"There you go, sweetheart," he murmured softly. "Daddy's got you now."

Lyra stepped closer, her own tears glistening as she reached out to stroke Cory's tiny hand. "She's beautiful, James," Lyra whispered. "You've got her now. She's safe."

"Daddy, I want Cory!" Link said, before crying, and James felt his heart break, as the bond a 4 year old child could make with a baby was something pure and innocent, untainted by the manipulative games of the adults around them. James looked at Link, his small, tear-streaked face pressed against the window of the car, and felt an unexpected pang of sympathy. This child was as much a victim of Kyler and Kylie's chaos as anyone else.

That, of course, set Cory off, and James could see the 3 month old in his arms was in tears, and that the mush from her nappy was leaking onto her blanket. The scent of an overdue nappy change hit James immediately, causing his stomach to twist, though he remained outwardly composed. Lyra moved instinctively, taking a step closer.

"James, let's get her inside," Lyra said gently. "We can clean her up and settle her."

Pete, standing like a sentinel by the doorway, gestured towards the house. "Bring her in, son. Let's get her sorted. Helen can help if needed."

James nodded, holding Cory close as he turned towards the house. "Lyra, grab the baby bag," he called over his shoulder, noticing that Kylie hadn't handed over anything beyond the baby herself.

"Oh, didn't I tell you... I threw it all," Kylie said with a grin, and James knew, secretly, that he was lucky he and Lyra had raided Mothercare in Merry Hill for everything bar the kitchen sink the previous day. "Oh, and she's being breast fed, and you can't feed her, can you, Reevesy... looks like Double F Nott will have to step in and make a special court application for me to come back tomorrow morning to feed her," Kylie finished, her voice dripping with mock concern.

James clenched his jaw, his fists tightening instinctively. Pete's hand on his shoulder stopped him from responding immediately, grounding him in the moment.

"You've made your point, Kylie," Theodore interjected, his voice cutting through the tension like a knife. "But let me remind you: the court order grants James custody as of 5 pm today. If you have concerns about feeding arrangements, they should have been raised during the hearing, not weaponised here. As it stands, James has every right to care for his daughter, and any attempt to undermine that will only weaken your case. As for you disposing of the baby's belongings, that can be interpreted as neglect and further evidence of your disregard for Cory's welfare. I strongly suggest you consider your actions moving forward, Kylie."

Kylie's smirk faltered again, her eyes darting between Theodore, James, and Pete. She clearly hadn't expected Theodore's composed but firm rebuttal. Kyler, however, let out a low chuckle, shaking his head as if this was all a game.

"Relax, Theo," Kyler said, his tone dripping with mockery. "It's not like Cory's going to starve overnight. Besides, I'm sure Reevesy here can handle a little nappy change, can't you, mate?"

As James stepped into the warmth of the living room, he felt a wave of relief wash over him. The sight of his family—Lyra, Pete, Sarah, and now Helen and Penelope—rallying around him gave him a renewed sense of strength. They were here for Cory, for him, and for the fight that lay ahead.

Helen stepped forward, her clinical eye immediately assessing Cory's condition. "James, lay her down on the sofa," she instructed gently. "Let's get her cleaned up and check her over."

"Hang on a second," Pete said, and James knew that his dad was going to head into the bedroom on the ground floor, the one that he and Lyra shared, to grab the nappies and a changing mat that had been brought from Mothercare. Moments later, Pete returned with the supplies, laying them out on the coffee table with an efficiency that spoke volumes about his experience as a parent.

"Here we go," Pete said, handing a packet of baby wipes to Helen. "Let's make sure she's comfortable."

James carefully placed Cory on the sofa, her tiny frame wriggling as her cries quieted slightly. Helen's gentle hands moved with practised precision, unwrapping the blanket and removing Cory's soiled nappy.

"Well, it's nothing unusual for a baby this age," Helen said reassuringly, glancing up at James. "She's healthy, but it's clear she's been left in this nappy for longer than she should have been. That's something we'll document, just in case."

James nodded, his jaw tightening. "Thanks, Aunt Helen. I'll make sure she's never in this state again."

Lyra knelt beside him, her presence calming. "You're doing great, James. She's safe now, and that's what matters."

****

CHAPTER 10 - The Evening Before The Case Opens

Monday 17th November 2025

James had to admit that, as it was the night before the criminal cases that his own sister, Chloe, her former husband, Cody, his ex-girlfriend, Kylie, and the various Manic companies, he was nervous. The fact he was a prosecution witness meant that he knew that he couldn't sit in the public gallery during the trial. Instead, he would be required to wait outside the courtroom until called to give evidence. The weight of it all pressed down on him as he sat at the coffee table in the living room of his parents' house, papers spread out before him.

The fact that Lyra and his dad were also witnesses in the cases, and so they were similarly confined to the witness room before being called to testify, added another layer of tension. James glanced at the clock on the wall. It was nearing 6pm, and the house was quieter than usual, though the atmosphere was thick with unspoken anxieties.

James looked up from his papers, meeting Theodore's calm gaze. Theodore, dressed casually but still managing to exude an air of professionalism, sat across from him at the coffee table. The lawyer was explaining the first day of the trial process, his voice steady and reassuring.

"So, as I was saying," Theodore continued, "the first day is usually procedural. The charges will be formally read out, and the judge will set the tone for the trial. The jury will be selected tomorrow morning, and once that's done, the prosecution will deliver its opening statement. You'll likely be called to give evidence on Wednesday or Thursday, depending on how long the prosecution's initial case presentation takes."

James leaned forward, his brows furrowed in confusion. "But I thought jury selection took ages, and the lawyers fought over it, like they show in The Lincoln Lawyer or Bull. Isn't there supposed to be loads of challenges and strategy about who gets on the jury?"

Theodore allowed himself a small smile, leaning back in his chair. "Not in England and Wales, James. Jury selection here is a much simpler process compared to the theatrics you see in American legal dramas. It's randomised, and barring any valid disqualifications or exemptions, the selected jurors will serve. Lawyers can only challenge jurors in exceptional circumstances, and even then, it's rare."

Lyra, seated beside James and resting a hand on her baby bump, chimed in. "So, no dramatic courtroom battles over the jury?"

Theodore shook his head. "No dramatic battles. The judge will swear in the jurors, and unless there's a compelling reason to object, the trial will proceed with whoever's been selected. It's designed to keep things efficient and impartial."

Pete, who had been quietly listening from his spot near the window, spoke up. "So, what happens tomorrow? Is it just the charges being read out and the jury sworn in?"

"More or less," Theodore replied. "The prosecution will outline their case against Chloe, Cody, Kylie, and the Manic companies. It'll be a broad overview, but it'll set the stage for the evidence and testimonies to come. The defence will reserve their opening statement until later in the trial, as is typical. Now, Dr Carmichael, the Crown will likely call you early in the case given your medical expertise and the role you played in documenting James's condition the day that he finally managed to be removed from Kylie's control," Theodore finished, nodding towards Helen Carmichael, who had just entered the room with a fresh cup of tea. She set it down on the table, her expression both serious and supportive.

"Yes, they've already told me to be prepared," Helen confirmed, taking a seat. "James, just so you know, although I saw you as a GP back then, when you escaped from that toxic situation, my role here is more as a factual witness regarding your physical and psychological state at the time. The clause of medical confidentiality in my line of work doesn't prevent me from testifying in cases where public interest and legal obligations take precedence, particularly when safeguarding or abuse is involved. Everything I say will be based on my professional assessment and documentation from when I saw you here."

James felt confused why his aunt was emphasising her role so much, but he appreciated her reassurance. "Thanks, Aunt Helen," he murmured. "It's just… weird, you know? Thinking of you testifying about me like I'm some sort of case study."

Helen smiled softly. "I understand, James. But what I saw back then, and what I recorded, could make all the difference in holding them accountable for what they did to you. You've been through hell, and this trial is a chance to expose it for what it was—abuse, manipulation, and exploitation."

"Now, the order of witnesses. The CPS have said that James, you will be the last to be called among the key witnesses, as your testimony ties much of the case together," Theodore continued, his tone calm but firm. "Your account is pivotal, as it connects the threads of coercion, manipulation, and abuse perpetrated by Chloe,

Cody, and Kylie. The prosecution wants to ensure the jury has the full context before hearing from you."

James nodded slowly, processing the enormity of the responsibility he bore. "So, I'll have to wait outside the courtroom until then?" he asked.

"I've asked, and as you're not scheduled until Monday 24th, and as you've got parental considerations to manage, the judge has agreed to allow you to remain at home until the day before your testimony," Theodore explained. "It's not standard, but given the sensitive nature of the case and the measures in place to protect witnesses, this is a reasonable accommodation."

James exhaled a breath he hadn't realised he was holding. The thought of sitting in the courthouse for days, stewing in anxiety while waiting to testify, had been gnawing at him. At least this way, he could be in a familiar environment, surrounded by his family and Lyra.

"What about Lyra and Dad?" James asked, glancing at Pete, who was still by the window, and Lyra, who was absently tracing circles on her baby bump.

"As Lyra is pregnant, and she is also nursing Cory, the Judge... oh, I forgot to mention, it's been allocated not to a regular Crown Court judge but a High Court Judge, Sir Thomas Harvey, a Judge of over 20 years' experience," Theodore said, pausing briefly for emphasis. "Given the circumstances, Sir Thomas has granted both Lyra and Pete accommodations similar to yours. Lyra will not need to appear at the courthouse until she is called to testify, and arrangements will be made for breaks if required, considering her pregnancy. Pete, however, will need to be on standby at the courthouse from the second day of the trial onward as his testimony will likely follow Helen's."

Pete let out a low whistle, a mix of respect and apprehension crossing his face. "A High Court Judge, eh? So, this case is being taken very seriously."

Theodore nodded. "Indeed. The charges are severe, and the evidence extensive. This is not a case the Crown Prosecution Service is taking lightly. Chloe, Cody, and Kylie face allegations that extend far beyond your individual experiences, James. The charges are, for Chloe, rape, assault, administering a substance to facilitate sexual activity without consent, coercive control, possession with intent to supply controlled substances, and perverting the course of justice. Cody faces similar charges and so does Kylie."

"Well, that's torpedoed Chloe's future law career," Pete said with a slight chuckle, and James knew that his sister was still balancing her career at Manic and her Law with Criminology degree at the University of Birmingham, hoping to secure a future in legal practice. The irony of her facing such grave criminal charges while pursuing a law degree wasn't lost on anyone in the room.

James gave a dry chuckle, though it was more from disbelief than humour. "Guess she won't be standing in court as a barrister anytime soon."

"No, but she'll have plenty of time to study courtroom procedure from the dock," Theodore said wryly, though his expression quickly sobered. "On a serious note, this trial is going to be gruelling for all of you. The defence is likely to employ aggressive tactics, especially with you, James, given your pivotal role in this case. You need to be prepared for cross-examination. Anyway, the charges in the case of R v Manic Radio Group Ltd, Manic Vibes Ltd, Manic Ventures Ltd and Manic Properties Ltd are particularly complex. They involve corporate negligence, enabling an environment of systemic abuse, failing to safeguard employees, and facilitating criminal activities such as drug distribution and coercion. The Crown is building a strong case to demonstrate that the corporate culture actively contributed to the crimes committed by Chloe, Cody, and Kylie."

"So, what's the defence likely to argue?" James asked hesitantly, his voice tinged with apprehension.

Theodore adjusted his glasses, his expression serious. "For Chloe, Cody, and Kylie, the defence is likely to focus on discrediting the witnesses—particularly you, James, given your history with drug use and the relationships involved. They may argue that your actions were consensual or try to paint you as unreliable and-"

"But how could I consent when half the time since January I was drugged up because of Kylie and Chloe, and how could I even consent to anything when I wasn't in a state to make clear decisions?" James interrupted, his voice rising with a mix of anger and frustration. "They controlled everything—what I did, what I said, even what I thought. Kylie even made me put my pay from Manic into her account, she'd stand over me, watching me, telling me that if I didn't, I'd be forced to service even more people she brought into my life!" James's voice cracked as he recounted the painful memories, his fists clenching at the table. "I was late with my mid-March wages, and she... she made me service Cal and half the regional management, made me their cock sleeve with my arse and mouth... made me... made me act as if I wanted more, act as if I enjoyed being their whore."

James then sighed, as he knew that he was going to say something that he'd never told his dad. "Dad, I... I did try to reach out to you mid-March, to get help from you then... back when Manic was still in the Dudley hub, but when I came to you, you treated me as if I was a stranger, completely blanking me. You said you never wanted to talk to me, that I wasn't your son."

James then sighed, as he knew that he was going to say something that he'd never told his dad. "Dad, I... I did try to reach out to you mid-March, to get help from you then... back when Manic was still in the Dudley hub, but when I came to you, you treated me as if I was a stranger, completely blanking me. You said you never wanted to talk to me, that I wasn't your son. And then a month later, when Lyra found me in the Brum hub, when she interrupted Cody... when she told you the situation and asked if I could come home, you said no. You said I was an adult and needed to deal with my choices. You wouldn't even hear her out. It was only because Lyra put herself at risk the next day, agreeing to be the next cum dump, coming to rescue me at Chloe's flat that I finally got out. Do you want to know what happened at that... when she... when she came?"

The room fell into an uneasy silence, the weight of James's words hanging heavily in the air. Pete's face tightened, the regret and guilt he'd been wrestling with since James's escape evident in his downcast gaze. He didn't respond immediately, the tension stretching as everyone waited for his reaction.

Wednesday 16th April 2025

"Almost there, Reevesy," Cody sneered, his tone dripping with mockery. "You'll be the star of tonight's entertainment. Don't let the crowd down now."

James felt Cody's sperm fill his hole as Harry also moaned in satisfaction, finishing in James's mouth. The room erupted into applause and laughter, the crowd revelling in James's continued degradation. His mind floated somewhere far away, the cocaine and humiliation blending into a numbing haze. He wasn't sure how much more of this he could take, but he had learned by now that resistance only made things worse.

"You know, big brother," Chloe then said, and James looked to see his sister reaching for his cock while Harry still had his arms pinned. "We've got one final guest coming, and this time, instead of her using you like a mechanical bull, you get to use her." Chloe's grin widened, her voice oozing with malice and twisted glee. "Lyra's coming over. She's finally agreed to join the party. And you're going to break her in, big brother. Make sure she remembers this night forever."

James froze, his drug-addled mind struggling to process what his sister had just said. A wave of nausea churned in his stomach, cutting through the cocaine-induced haze. Lyra? No. She couldn't be here. She shouldn't be dragged into this nightmare. The thought of her—strong, kind Lyra—being brought into this hell twisted something deep inside him.

"Chloe, no," James managed to croak, his voice hoarse and barely audible. "Leave her out of this."

Chloe's laughter was sharp and cruel. "Oh, but she's already agreed, Reevesy. She wants to save you, isn't that sweet? She thinks she can take your place, be the new star of our little show. Isn't she just adorable? You know, I can't wait to suck her nipples, to have her eating me out like a whore, to have her begging Cody to stop."

James's mind reeled at Chloe's words, his heart pounding despite the numbing effects of the cocaine. The thought of
128

Lyra, who had shown him kindness when everyone else had treated him as disposable, being thrown into this twisted nightmare filled him with a new kind of dread. She didn't deserve this. No one did—but especially not her.

"Chloe, please," James begged, his voice breaking as tears streamed down his face. "Don't do this to her. She's not like us. She's... better than this."

Chloe tilted her head mockingly, pretending to consider his plea. "Better than us? Oh, big brother, you're so naive. No one's better than anyone here. She made her choice. She agreed to come, so she's already one of us. And if you're lucky, maybe she'll enjoy it. Just like you have."

James clenched his fists, a flicker of defiance sparking within him. For months, he had let them control him, humiliate him, break him down piece by piece. But the thought of Lyra being dragged into this darkness, of her being used and degraded the way he had been, lit a fire he hadn't felt in a long time.

He couldn't let this happen. Not to her.

"Where is she?" James asked, his voice steadier now, though his body still trembled with the aftershocks of his abuse. "Where's Lyra?"

Chloe smirked, clearly enjoying brother his desperation. "She'll be here soon. Don't worry, big. You'll get plenty of time to... welcome her to the family."

James could feel the panic rising, his heart pounding in his chest. Despite the haze of cocaine and exhaustion, a part of him stirred with a desperate need to act. He couldn't let Lyra walk into this trap, couldn't let her become another pawn in Chloe's cruel games. His mind raced, searching for a way to stop what felt inevitable.

"Chloe," James said, his voice trembling but louder now, "if you bring Lyra into this, I swear I'll tell everyone everything. Every last thing you, Cody, and Kylie have done to me. I'll go to the police, I'll go to the press— whatever it takes. I won't let you ruin her."

Chloe froze for a moment, the mockery slipping from her face. For the first time, a flicker of uncertainty crossed her features. But it was quickly replaced with a smirk, her confidence returning as she crossed her arms and leaned closer to him.

"Oh, James," she said sweetly, her tone dripping with false sympathy. "You think you have any power here? You're nothing but a puppet, remember? No one will believe you, especially not now. But by all means, try. See how far you get."

James felt his stomach churn, the weight of her words pressing down on him like a vice. She was right—his credibility was in tatters, his life reduced to a series of humiliations and degradation. But he couldn't give up, not now, not when Lyra was at stake.

The sound of the door opening snapped James out of his spiralling thoughts. He turned his head, his breath hitching as he saw Lyra step into the flat. She was dressed in a crop top, skirt and heels, something that James was surprised Lyra would own, especially as she was more of the blouse and trousers type. The sight of her in such an outfit, likely coerced, sent a pang of anger and desperation coursing through James. She looked visibly uncomfortable, her posture stiff and her expression tense, though she tried to mask it with a brave front.

"Lyra," James croaked, his voice cracking with a mixture of relief and despair. His arms struggled against his restraints, though he knew there was no way to free himself without help.

Lyra's eyes locked onto James, her face softening with a mix of concern and determination. "I'm here to take you home," she said firmly, though her voice wavered slightly under the oppressive atmosphere of the room.

Chloe let out a mocking laugh, clapping her hands together as though this was some grand entertainment. "Oh, isn't this sweet? Lyra to the rescue. But I don't think you understand, darling—you don't get to take him anywhere... yet. Cody, babe, give her some snow to help her loosen up a bit. Let's make her feel at home first." Chloe's words dripped with malice, her smirk widening as Cody approached Lyra with a small packet of cocaine in hand.

Lyra's eyes flicked to Cody, then back to Chloe, her jaw tightening as she took a deliberate step back. "I'm not here to play your games, Chloe," she said, her voice cold and steady. "Let James go, or I'll make sure you regret this. You've gone too far, and you know it."

The tension in the room thickened as Lyra's defiance cut through the cruel laughter. For a brief moment, the power dynamic shifted, the certainty of Chloe's control wavering as Lyra held her ground. James felt a flicker of hope— small, fragile, but enough to remind him that not everyone in his life sought to exploit him.

It was then he noticed that Lyra then accepted the bag, and a rolled up banknote, and his heart sank. But as Lyra brought the note to her nose, she paused, her hand trembling slightly. She turned her gaze to Chloe, her expression resolute.

"I'll play along," Lyra said slowly, her voice even but carrying an undertone of warning, "but only if James is untied and given a choice. If you're so confident in your control, let him decide whether he stays or leaves. Otherwise, this stops right now, and I'll be the one calling the police."

Chloe's smirk faltered briefly, the room suddenly heavy with tension. Cody glanced between the two women, uncertainty flickering in his eyes. It was clear he hadn't expected Lyra to push back with such defiance.

Chloe leaned against the back of the sofa, her mockery replaced by a calculating look. "Alright, Lyra. Shag Reevesy once you've had some of the nice lovely powder," Chloe said, her voice laced with mockery as she tossed the bag of cocaine onto the table. "But you'd better make it worth our while. Let's see if you can live up to the hype."

James looked at Chloe, shocked. He had heard all sorts of things, but he was confused-his own sister encouraging Lyra to join in the depraved scene that had become his life was incomprehensible. He couldn't let Lyra go through with it—not for him, not for any reason. The flicker of hope he'd felt moments ago was being drowned out by a surge of desperation and guilt.

"Lyra, don't," James croaked, his voice trembling with the weight of everything he had endured. His eyes pleaded with her, trying to convey what he couldn't put into words. "You don't have to do this. Please."

"James... I... I've got to... Kylie... she said that if I... you know... in front of everyone, she'd let me take you back to safety. She said it was the only way, and I can't just leave you here." Lyra's voice broke slightly, her composure slipping as she glanced between James and Chloe. "She... she said that if I become the hub cum slut, then you'd be *released from this nightmare and be free to rebuild your life. I can't leave you here, James. I just can't."*

James's heart shattered at Lyra's words. The lengths she was willing to go to for him tore at his already fragile resolve. He couldn't allow her to sacrifice herself for his sake, not when he had endured so much already. His jaw clenched as he tried to gather his thoughts, searching for something—anything—that could prevent this.

Monday 17th November 2025

"Lyra was the only one who put herself at risk to rescue me," James said, his voice trembling as he recounted the harrowing events. "And she did it without hesitation, even knowing what they could do to her. She gave me a chance to escape when no one else would."

The room was silent as James's words hung heavily in the air. Pete looked down, his expression pained, clearly grappling with the guilt of his own inaction. Sarah placed a hand on Pete's arm, offering silent comfort, while Lyra, seated beside James, reached out to squeeze his hand.

"I'm so sorry, James," Pete finally said, his voice thick with emotion. "I let you down when you needed me most. I should have seen what was happening, but I was too caught up in my own world. I... I failed you as a father."

James looked at his dad, the pain of the past etched into his face. "Dad, you did fail me. But what's important now is that you're here, supporting me through this trial, helping me fight for Cory and for justice. That means more than you know."

Pete nodded slowly, his eyes glistening with unshed tears. "I'm here now, son, and I won't let you face this alone. Not again."

Theodore cleared his throat, breaking the heavy silence. "James, I know revisiting these memories is painful, but your testimony will be crucial. It's not just about holding Chloe, Cody, and Kylie accountable—it's about exposing the culture that enabled their actions. The jury needs to see the full picture, and you're the one who can paint it."

James took a deep breath, nodding. "I'll do it. I'll tell them everything. If it means stopping them from doing this to anyone else, then it's worth it."

Lyra leaned her head on his shoulder, her presence a source of strength. "You've got us, James. We'll get through this together."

James sighed, as Lyra held him, but before he could say anything, he heard Cory, who was in a basket next to Sarah, start crying softly. The sound of his daughter's cries snapped James out of his heavy thoughts, grounding him in the present. Getting up, he rounded the living room and gently lifted Cory from her basket, cradling her against his chest. Her cries quieted almost immediately, her tiny hand clutching at his shirt. James felt a wave of calm wash over him as he held her, her warmth and vulnerability reminding him of why he was fighting so hard.

"She's your anchor," Lyra said softly, watching him with a faint smile. "Whenever it feels overwhelming, just remember she's what this is all for."

James nodded, pressing a kiss to Cory's forehead. "I know. She deserves better than the chaos Kylie and Chloe would drag her into. She deserves to grow up safe and loved."

Pete stood, moving closer to James and placing a reassuring hand on his shoulder. "You're doing right by her, James. It's not going to be easy, but you've got all of us backing you. We'll get through this trial, and we'll make sure Cory has the life she deserves."

****

CHAPTER 11 – In The Dock
Tuesday 18th November 2025

Chloe Smith sat in the dock of Birmingham Crown Court, her hands trembling slightly as she clutched the edge of the wooden railing. Despite being granted bail due to her three-month-old son, Nigel Alan, the gravity of the charges weighed heavily on her. She had named her child Nigel Alan Smith, after her late uncle Nigel and her maternal grandfather, Alan Reeves, a nod to her family's legacy. Yet here she was, not as a proud mother, but as a defendant in one of the most significant criminal trials the city had seen in years.

Her solicitor, Oliver Stokes, a young Dublin graduate who had been employed by Manic Radio to represent her, as part of the contract that she was still under with the company, sat beside her in the defendant's bench. Despite his polished suit and confident posture, Oliver's nervous glances at the prosecution table betrayed his own unease.

The Barrister who was representing her and Cody, even though they were in the process of awaiting their decree absolute due to their marriage being less than a year old, was a seasoned advocate named Victoria Hunt. Victoria was renowned for her tenacity in court, and her sharp cross-examinations had earned her the nickname "The Barricade" among her peers. Even so, the weight of the charges against Chloe and Cody presented a formidable challenge, and Victoria's tight smile suggested she knew this case would test every ounce of her skill.

Looking at Kylie, Chloe had to chuckle at how the blonde was more interested in her nails and looking at Kyler Thompson, her new boyfriend, a predator who Chloe knew had all but coercively controlled a young presenter at Manic named Cassie Longton, who had changed her name and had become the infamous Toni Green, a name that had been synonymous with Manic's chaotic and toxic culture. Chloe's chuckle caught Kylie's attention, and the blonde gave her a sharp look before returning her focus to Kyler. It was clear that Kylie wasn't taking the seriousness of the situation to heart, which only served to underline the arrogance and recklessness that had brought her to this point.

As a law student at the University of Birmingham in her third year, Chloe knew that she was acutely aware of the gravity of the charges she faced. Her legal studies had given her an understanding of the judicial process, but being a defendant in a high-profile trial was an entirely different reality. She felt a bitter irony in her predicament—studying to become a solicitor, only to find herself on the opposite side of the courtroom.

"I've changed my mind," Cody muttered, trying to grab the attention of Victoria Hunt, who was busy organising her files for the hearing that was about to begin. Cody Lane, sitting next to Chloe in the dock, looked tense and jittery. His usually smug demeanour had been replaced by a nervous energy, his fingers tapping an erratic rhythm on the bench.

Victoria turned her gaze sharply towards him, her voice a quiet but firm whisper. "Mr Lane, now is not the time for theatrics. Compose yourself."

Cody leaned closer to her, his voice barely audible. "I don't think I can go through with this. I want to change my plea."

Chloe's head snapped towards him, her eyes narrowing. "Are you serious?" she hissed under her breath, her voice laced with disbelief. "You're going to roll over before we've even started?"

Cody looked back at her, his face a mixture of guilt and defiance. "I can't do this, Chloe. The evidence against us is overwhelming, and I'm not going down with you and Kylie if I can cut a deal."

Chloe's lips curled into a sneer, her voice a low hiss. "You coward. Changing your plea now won't save you—it'll just make you look desperate. They'll still throw the book at you, Cody. You think the CPS will just let you off because you're suddenly feeling remorseful?"

"I want to do this," Cody said, and Chloe noticed her husband had a twinkle in his eye, one that was showing that he was scheming something to undermine the others involved in the case. His sudden determination wasn't driven by genuine remorse, Chloe realised, but rather by a calculated attempt to save himself, even at the expense of everyone else.

"If that's the case, Mr Lane," Chloe heard Victoria Hunt interject sharply, her tone low but commanding as she leaned closer to Cody. "You will need to discuss this with your solicitor outside this courtroom. This is not the time or place to make impulsive decisions, especially ones that will impact your defence strategy."

"Screw my defence strategy. I'm willing to name names, give evidence, and tell them everything about the culture at Manic and the roles everyone played. Oh, and Oliver, I no longer want you to represent me. I'll represent myself if I have to, but I want to make a deal with the prosecution." Cody's voice was defiant now, though it carried an undercurrent of panic that betrayed his bravado.

Chloe's face turned red with anger, her knuckles whitening as she gripped the edge of the dock. "You're a spineless traitor, Cody," she hissed, her words venomous.

"If you think throwing me under the bus will save your neck, you've got another thing coming."

Victoria Hunt's expression hardened, her patience clearly wearing thin. She glanced between the two defendants, her voice low and clipped. "Enough. Both of you. This is not the time for infighting. If you want to change your plea, Mr Lane, you will address it with the judge when the court convenes. But understand this—any deals you try to make will come at a cost, and the prosecution will not look kindly on last-minute theatrics."

"I'm serious. I've had enough of the whole of it," Cody said, sighing. "I... I just want to end this nightmare, and if it means throwing every single person involved under the bus, so be it. Manic, Chloe, Kylie... the whole lot. I'm done covering for everyone. Anyway, Chloe, don't forget I've got access to your other OneDrive, the one you hide all your personal files in. I've seen what you've got on there—photos, videos, documents. If I go down, I'm taking you all with me."

Chloe froze, her mouth slightly agape as the implications of Cody's words hit her. Her mind raced as she considered what he could possibly have uncovered. She had always been meticulous about keeping her most incriminating evidence hidden, but if Cody truly had access to her private files, then her carefully constructed defence could unravel before her eyes.

"You wouldn't dare," Chloe whispered harshly, her voice trembling with a mix of rage and fear. "If you think you can blackmail me, you're even dumber than I thought."

Cody smirked, leaning back slightly in the dock, his sudden calmness a stark contrast to his earlier agitation. "It's not blackmail, Chloe. It's leverage. And right now, I've got more than you do."

Victoria Hunt's icy gaze silenced their exchange. "Enough," she hissed, her tone commanding. "Mr Lane, if you truly intend to change your plea and cooperate with the prosecution, understand that it will not absolve you of your actions. The court takes a dim view of opportunistic deals, and they will scrutinise your motives closely."

Before Cody could respond, the doors to the courtroom opened, and the usher stepped inside, signalling the start of the proceedings. The defendants were instructed to stand as the judge entered.

"All rise," the usher called, and the murmur of the courtroom hushed as everyone stood.

High Court Judge Sir Thomas Harvey entered, his robe pristine and his demeanour exuding authority. His sharp eyes swept across the room before he took his seat.

"Court is now in session," he intoned, his voice steady and commanding. "This is the case of Regina v Chloe Smith, Cody Lane, Kylie Morgan, Manic Radio Group Ltd, and others. Now, as this is a Crown Court case, and there is a jury to be sworn in, we will begin with an explanation for the public gallery, which I can see is stuffed to the gunnels with the media."

Chloe turned to see that half of Manic's news personnel, along with ITV, Sky, BBC, written media and representatives from the various community radio stations in the West Midlands, several of which were owned by Woody Bones and his community radio network, had crammed into the public gallery. The media circus surrounding the trial was in full swing, with journalists eagerly scribbling notes, cameras clicking just outside the courtroom doors, and whispers spreading like wildfire as they awaited the opening statements.

Then there were several colleagues from Manic, including not just from the former Dudley and current Birmingham hub, but the Olympic Park hub in London, the Huddersfield, Cardiff, Manchester Piccadilly, Dundee and Exeter hubs, and also the Speke hub, which was the network centre of the Manic Radio Group's operations which not just covered the North West of England, but also controlled the network for Northern Ireland and the Republic of Ireland. Chloe recognised many of them—presenters, producers, and executives—all of whom had been complicit, either directly or indirectly, in maintaining the toxic culture at Manic. Their presence served as a reminder of just how deeply the rot had spread within the organisation.

The fact that they were not there as witnesses for either side but as members of the public and the media only added to the tension in the room. Chloe's stomach churned as she realised the sheer weight of what was at stake—not just for her, Cody, and Kylie, but for Manic Radio as a whole. The trial wasn't just about individual guilt; it was about exposing an entire system of abuse, exploitation, and corruption.

Sir Thomas adjusted his glasses, his voice cutting through the silence like a knife. "Let it be known that this trial concerns allegations of severe criminal conduct, including rape, coercive control, conspiracy to administer harmful substances, corporate negligence, and related offences. The charges are grave, and the public interest in these proceedings is significant. However, I remind everyone present that this is a court of law, not a theatre. Decorum must be maintained at all times. Now, for the media, I must warn that there are reporting restrictions-"

Chloe watched as the journalists from Manic started jeering at the judge's mention of reporting restrictions, and she knew why, as Manic's newsroom loved to control narratives, spinning stories to fit their agenda. Sir Thomas Harvey's sharp gaze immediately shifted toward the outburst in the gallery. His voice, now carrying a distinct edge of authority, cut through the murmurs.

"This is a courtroom, not a newsroom," he said firmly. "Any further disruption will result in immediate removal from these proceedings. I will not tolerate any behaviour that undermines the integrity of this trial. That applies to all present, regardless of your affiliation."

The murmurs quickly subsided, the Manic journalists exchanging uneasy glances as they shrank into their seats. Chloe suppressed a smirk at their discomfort, though the weight of her own predicament kept her from feeling any real satisfaction.

Sir Thomas continued, his tone steady. "As I was saying, reporting restrictions are in place to ensure a fair trial. The jury is to be shielded from external influence, and any breach of these restrictions will be dealt with severely. The public's right to know must be balanced with the defendants' right to a fair hearing. Furthermore, I must advise that as I believe several of the public gallery is Manic Radio presenters, producers and support staff, your attendance is noted, and any disruption or misuse of these proceedings to further personal or corporate interests will not be tolerated."

Chloe felt a chill run down her spine at the judge's no-nonsense approach. Sir Thomas Harvey's reputation for meticulous attention to detail and firm control of the courtroom was well-known, and she realised there would be no room for theatrics or manipulation under his watchful eye.

"Right, I would like the usher to allow the jury to enter the courtroom for the swearing-in process," Sir Thomas Harvey announced, his voice echoing in the tense silence.

The usher opened a side door, and the prospective jurors began filing into the jury box. Each one looked apprehensive but composed, their eyes darting around the room as they took in the seriousness of the setting. Chloe watched them intently, her stomach churning as she imagined the power these twelve strangers would hold over her future.

As the jurors settled, Sir Thomas addressed them directly. "Ladies and gentlemen of the jury, you have been selected to serve in a trial of significant public interest. Your duty is to listen to the evidence impartially and to deliver a verdict based solely on the facts presented in this courtroom. You must set aside any personal biases or preconceived notions. If, for any reason, you feel unable to fulfil this role, now is the time to speak."

The courtroom held its breath as the judge's words lingered. A few jurors shifted in their seats, but none spoke up.

Until one stood up. "Your honour, one of the defendants is known to me," the prospective juror said, her voice hesitant but clear. She was a middle-aged woman with short, greying hair and a composed demeanour. "I attended the University of Birmingham, where Ms Chloe Smith is currently a student. We were not in the same cohort, but I recognise her from some academic events."

Sir Thomas Harvey nodded, his expression neutral. "Thank you for bringing this to the court's attention. Do you believe that this prior knowledge would impair your ability to act impartially in these proceedings?"

The woman hesitated, then shook her head. "No, Your Honour. I didn't have any personal interactions with Ms Smith, and I don't feel it would affect my judgement. But I thought it best to disclose this information."

Victoria turned to Chloe and Oliver, annoyed with their interruptions, and whispered sharply, "Ms Smith, I suggest you refrain from panicking. Her admission is a minor connection and does not automatically disqualify her unless there's a clear bias. Let me handle it."

"Oh, piss off Hunt, or I'll leak your sex tape on the cloud," Chloe muttered under her breath, her voice dripping with venom. Victoria shot her a warning glance, her patience clearly wearing thin.

Sir Thomas Harvey cleared his throat, silencing the murmurs and tension brewing among the defence team. "Thank you for your transparency, Madam Juror," he addressed the woman calmly. "Given your statement, and unless the defence or prosecution objects, I see no reason to dismiss you from this panel."

Victoria remained seated, her face impassive. Despite Chloe's whispered demands, she chose not to object, recognising that any protest would only draw unnecessary attention and irritate the judge. The prosecution likewise remained silent, clearly satisfied with the juror's honesty.

"Very well," Sir Thomas continued, "you may remain seated. Let us proceed with the swearing-in of the jury."

The jurors were sworn in one by one, the solemnity of their oaths adding to the weight of the moment. Chloe's stomach churned as each juror pledged to deliver a true verdict according to the evidence. She glanced at Cody, who was sitting rigidly, his jaw clenched, clearly debating his next move.

Once the jury was sworn in, Sir Thomas addressed them again. "Members of the jury, this trial will examine serious allegations. You will hear detailed and, at times, distressing evidence. Your role is to remain impartial, to consider only the facts presented, and to deliberate with care and integrity. The court will provide guidance at every stage of the process. Do not discuss this case with anyone outside of this courtroom or allow external information to influence your judgement. Breach of these rules may result in contempt of court proceedings."

His gaze swept over the public gallery, lingering briefly on the cluster of Manic personnel. "And for the avoidance of doubt, this directive applies equally to any individuals in attendance with vested interests in the proceedings."

A ripple of unease passed through the Manic representatives, several of whom averted their eyes under the judge's stern gaze. Chloe shifted uncomfortably, acutely aware of how much was riding on the outcome of this trial—not just for her but for the company that had nurtured and enabled her rise.

"The prosecution may now proceed with its opening statement," Sir Thomas declared, his tone brooking no delay.

****

James was sat at home, the television on ITV Central News for the lunchtime broadcast. He watched as the lead anchor introduced the story dominating the headlines.

"We begin with the high-profile trial that commenced today at Birmingham Crown Court. Three individuals, including Chloe Smith, Cody Lane, and Kylie Morgan, along with several entities linked to the Manic Radio Group, face charges including rape, coercive control, drug facilitation, and corporate negligence. The trial has already drawn significant attention, with the public gallery packed and strict reporting restrictions in place."

James felt a knot tighten in his stomach. Seeing Chloe's name, his own sister, flashed on the screen alongside such heinous charges was surreal. Lyra sat beside him, gently bouncing Cory in her arms, offering quiet support as the coverage continued.

"The Crown Prosecution Service has labelled this case a 'watershed moment,' aiming to expose not only individual crimes but a systemic culture of abuse and negligence within the broadcasting industry. Our reporter outside the court has more."

The screen cut to the familiar exterior of Birmingham Crown Court, where reporters and cameras crowded the entrance. A journalist spoke over scenes of defendants arriving under police escort.

"Today's proceedings saw the jury sworn in and the charges formally read out. The prosecution is expected to present evidence linking the defendants to a pattern of abuse facilitated by a toxic corporate culture at Manic Radio. High Court Judge Sir Thomas Harvey has warned against any attempts to disrupt or sensationalise the trial. One of the defendants, Cody Lane, has pled guilty, while his two fellow defendants, Chloe Smith, a 22 year old resident of Birmingham, and Kylie Morgan, 24, a former presenter on Manic Radio's West Midlands drive show, have pled not guilty."

"Mr Lane, an employee of Manic Radio in their Birmingham hub, has, in a surprising move, offered to provide evidence implicating the other defendants and detailing the toxic culture at Manic Radio. This unexpected development could significantly alter the course of the trial."

James leaned forward, his heart racing. Cody's decision to plead guilty and cooperate with the prosecution was a seismic shift. It confirmed what Theodore had warned—that the defence was fractured, and alliances were crumbling under the weight of the charges.

Lyra glanced at James, concern etched on her face. "That could be a game-changer, couldn't it? Cody turning on them like this?"

James nodded, his mind racing. "It could be. If he's naming names and exposing what really happened, it'll strengthen the prosecution's case. But it also means Chloe and Kylie are going to come out swinging. They'll try to discredit everyone, especially me."

Lyra placed a hand on his arm, her touch grounding him. "You've got the truth on your side, James. No matter what they throw at you, you've come too far to back down now."

The broadcast continued, showing Cody entering the courtroom flanked by police officers. His face was pale but set with determination, a stark contrast to Chloe's tense expression and Kylie's dismissive smirk as they followed behind.

"The trial is expected to last several weeks, with testimony from numerous witnesses, including former employees and associates of the defendants. The prosecution aims to demonstrate not only individual culpability but also a corporate failure to safeguard employees and prevent systemic abuse. Reporting restrictions remain in place to ensure a fair trial, but the case is already sparking widespread debate about accountability in the media industry. Fiona Baxter, ITV Central News."

The segment ended with the TV returning to the ITV Central News studio, where the host, Tamara Lee, had Woody Bones sitting next to her. "I have with me Woody Bones, a former radio station owner and community radio advocate, to discuss the wider implications of this trial for the broadcasting industry. Also joining me is Global Media's Head of Legal, James Jenkins, gentlemen, thank you for joining us."

The camera cut to Woody Bones, a familiar figure in the Midlands broadcasting scene, and James Jenkins, representing one of the largest commercial radio operators in the UK. Woody, with his characteristic bow tie and casual demeanour, sat poised yet approachable, while Jenkins exuded the polished professionalism of corporate legal expertise.

James recognised the younger of the two men from a blog that he had read entitled "The Real Brookes Babes: A Cautionary Tale" written by Carly Jenkins, an HR expert at Bauer, and her husband James Jenkins, who had been a victim of exploitation in the early 2000s while working for a similar toxic radio culture to Manic. The blog had exposed the deep-seated issues in the industry, serving as an early warning for what was now unfolding in court. James Smith recalled how reading their experiences had resonated with him during his darkest days at Manic.

The Brookes Babes were a notorious promotional stunt that encapsulated the toxic culture prevalent in radio during the early 2000s—a culture eerily similar to what James had endured at Manic. The irony, James knew, of Brookes Vibes having eventually been swallowed by Manic in mid-2010, and becoming Manic Vibes Oxfordshire earlier in 2025, added another layer of complexity to the unfolding events.

The anchor, Tamara Lee, turned to Woody first. "Mr Bones, as someone who has spent decades in the radio industry, what do you believe the trial of Chloe Smith, Cody Lane, and Kylie Morgan signifies for the broadcasting sector?"

Woody adjusted his bow tie, his tone measured but firm. "Tamara, this trial is a wake-up call. The broadcasting industry has long been plagued by a culture of exploitation and toxicity, especially in high-pressure environments like commercial radio. What's happening at Birmingham Crown Court isn't just about holding individuals accountable—it's about exposing systemic failures. Companies like Manic prioritised profit and ratings over the well-being of their employees. This trial could force the industry to take a hard look in the mirror."

Tamara nodded, turning to James Jenkins. "Mr Jenkins, your blog alongside your wife's insights at Bauer highlighted similar issues in the past. Do you believe lessons were learned, or has the industry failed to adapt?"

Jenkins leaned forward, his expression serious. "Unfortunately, Tamara, the lessons weren't fully learned. The Brookes Babes scandal in the early 2000s should have been a turning point, but many organisations treated it as an isolated incident rather than a symptom of deeper problems. What's happening at Manic now mirrors those past issues—power imbalances, a lack of oversight, and a culture where exploitation is normalised. This isn't the first scandal Manic have been involved in, as in 2018, they were embroiled in a gender pay gap controversy after revelations of significant disparities between male and female presenters came to light. Despite promises of reform, it seems the culture of accountability hasn't taken root deeply enough."

Tamara pressed further. "Do you believe the current trial will lead to lasting change, or will it become another footnote in broadcasting history?"

Jenkins sighed, his gaze steady. "That depends on the outcomes—not just in the courtroom but in the industry's willingness to change. If companies like Manic are held accountable at both a legal and public level, it could pave the way for genuine reform. At Global, we ensure that our staff are safeguarded with robust policies and systems in place to prevent any form of abuse or exploitation. It's not a perfect system, but transparency and accountability are key. If the industry collectively adopts a zero-tolerance approach, we can start to rebuild trust and ensure that what happened at Manic never happens again."

Woody Bones nodded in agreement, adding his perspective. "What's also critical, Tamara, is the role of smaller, independent stations and community radio. They often don't have the same corporate pressures, but they do face challenges in maintaining ethical standards due to limited resources. This trial should be a catalyst for the entire industry, from the top-tier players to grassroots organisations, to reassess how they operate."

Tamara turned back to the camera, her tone thoughtful. "It's clear that the implications of this trial extend far beyond the courtroom. As we await further developments, the spotlight remains firmly on the broadcasting industry's ability to confront its past and build a safer, more inclusive future. Thank you, Mr Bones and Mr Jenkins, for your insights."

The programme moved to a different segment, but James turned off the television. He leaned back on the sofa, his mind racing with the weight of what he had just watched. The trial wasn't just about justice for him, Lyra, or the others who had suffered—it was about changing the system that had allowed such suffering to happen in the first place.

****

CHAPTER 12 - Pete's Testimony
Wednesday 19th November 2025

Pete was sitting in the witness room of Birmingham Crown Court, his mind racing with memories and emotions. The sterile walls of the room seemed to amplify his unease, the faint hum of activity outside only adding to the tension. He glanced down at the plain glass of water in front of him, untouched. Despite decades behind a microphone, the thought of speaking under oath filled him with a nervous energy he hadn't felt in years.

"What you staring at, old git?" Rory Carter, one of the Manic Vibes Chester and Merseyside drive hosts, who was a defence witness, sneered. The room was stuffed to the gunnels with Court officials, legal representatives for various witnesses who were coaching their clients, several presenters, producers, support staff and management from Manic, as well as mental health professionals, IT specialists, forensic accountants and even doctors, all for the various cases in the Crown v Manic, Chloe and Kylie.

Pete knew that Rory's remark was meant to unsettle him, but he refused to rise to the bait. He had seen plenty of bravado in the radio industry, and Rory's cocky smirk was no different from the many inflated egos he'd encountered over the years. Looking at Theodore, who was chatting to one of his counterparts from a Scottish law firm, Pete saw Edgar Bones, Woody's son and owner of several Scottish community radio stations, rush past the room, obviously as there was a few minutes until Court was back in session.

Pete glanced at his watch. He had mere minutes before being called to testify. The weight of his role in this trial bore heavily on him. It wasn't just about sharing his story—it was about revealing the toxic culture that had been cultivated at Manic and holding those responsible to account. He glanced across the room at Rory, whose smug demeanour was a stark contrast to the gravity of the proceedings.

"Save the bravado for the airwaves, Carter," Pete muttered under his breath, loud enough for Rory to hear but without looking directly at him.

Rory sneered, leaning back in his chair. "Let's see if your testimony is as riveting as your oldies playlist, Pete. Maybe throw in a Cliff Richard anecdote for the jury, eh?"

As the minutes ticked, Pete noticed Toni Green, a former Manic presenter who had been finally let go a few days earlier, another suspension causing her to be dismissed from her role as a presenter at Manic Vibes from the networked evening show, a flagship programme for the station. Toni sat quietly in a corner, her face pale and eyes darting around nervously. Pete wondered if she, like him, was grappling with the enormity of what had happened at Manic. Her dismissal had been public and messy, a culmination of years of turmoil and scandal, starting from 2019, when she had joined, and had been known as Cassie Longton. Cassie's transformation into Toni Green had been emblematic of the toxic culture Manic perpetuated— a rebranding that wasn't just professional but personal, as if her identity had been entirely consumed by the station's demands. Pete couldn't help but feel a pang of sympathy for her. No one left Manic unscathed, it seemed.

The door to the witness room creaked open, and a court usher stepped inside, clipboard in hand. "Mr Peter Smith, you're up," the usher announced, her tone professional but brisk.

Pete stood, adjusting the tie that Lyra had helped him choose that morning. He glanced at Theodore, who gave him an encouraging nod. "You'll be fine," Theodore said, his voice steady. "Just tell the truth, stick to the facts, and don't let the defence rattle you."

Pete nodded, the weight of his responsibility pressing down on him as he stepped out of the room. The walk to the courtroom felt longer than it was, each step echoing in the quiet corridor. As he entered, the hum of whispered conversations in the public gallery hushed, all eyes turning toward him.

The courtroom was a mix of solemnity and tension. Chloe sat in the dock, her gaze fixed on him with a mixture of defiance and unease. Cody, now seated apart from her after his guilty plea, looked more subdued, occasionally glancing at the prosecution table. Kylie, as ever, appeared indifferent, her focus drifting lazily around the room.

"Oh, here he comes, ready to make my life hell. James has always been the golden child, hasn't he, Dad?" Chloe muttered loudly enough to carry across the courtroom, her voice dripping with sarcasm.

Pete knew that the outburst by Chloe was calculated, a last-ditch effort to unsettle him before he could speak. He paused briefly, catching her eye with a steady gaze, but didn't dignify her comment with a response. Instead, he stepped forward to the witness box, feeling the weight of decades in broadcasting bearing down on him. This wasn't a radio studio, but the stakes were far higher.

The clerk approached him, holding a Bible. "Do you swear by Almighty God that the evidence you shall give will be the truth, the whole truth, and nothing but the truth?"

Pete nodded, his voice firm despite the nerves. "I do."

As he settled into the witness box, he took a moment to scan the courtroom. The public gallery was filled to capacity, faces ranging from eager journalists to sombre members of the public. Representatives from rival radio stations and industry bodies were also present, their expressions a mix of curiosity and apprehension. He could even see a few familiar faces from his years at Manic— colleagues who had either thrived in the toxic environment or been chewed up and spat out by it.

Sir Thomas Harvey, presiding over the case, addressed him with a measured tone. "Mr Smith, thank you for joining us. You may begin by confirming your full name and professional background for the record."

Pete cleared his throat. "My name is Peter Alan Smith. I've been a radio broadcaster for over thirty years, starting out as a promo mascot at Dudley FM age 13, then as a tea boy at 16, a runner at 18 and then at 21 following my degree at Wolverhampton Polytechnic a presenter of various slots, in 1992. In 2014, Dudley FM was merged with its sister stations in the Central England area and rebranded Midlands Manic, while under the ownership of Breeze Media. I remained with the station as it evolved into part of the Manic Radio Group in 2019, the merger with Lite Group in 2022 and the rebrand of Midlands Manic this April to Manic Vibes West Midlands. I've worked across various formats, including breakfast and drivetime shows, and most recently, I was a presenter at Manic Goldies West Midlands, specialising in classic hits programming and the West Midlands Goal Zone, sponsored by... sorry, I'm used to mentioning sponsors. Old habits die hard," Pete said with a sheepish smile, eliciting a faint ripple of chuckles from the public gallery. "I believe, your Honour, you've called into the Goal Zone before, sir. I recall a lively discussion about Wolverhampton Wanderers' chances against Manchester City this past May."

The laughter from the public gallery swelled slightly, but Sir Thomas Harvey raised a hand to quell it, a faint smile betraying his otherwise composed demeanour. "Indeed, Mr Smith," he replied, his voice calm but firm. "Though my contributions to your show were decidedly less critical than your current testimony. Please, continue."

"Your Honour," Victoria Hunt, representing the defence, stood, her tone brisk but professional as she interjected. "As you have called into the witness's show, I think you ought to recluse yourself from this trial, as it could indicate bias in favour of the witness."

"Yeah," Pete heard Chloe interrupt, her voice tinged with mock indignation, "looks like Dad's got a fan in high places. No wonder James is the golden boy."

Sir Thomas Harvey's expression hardened as he turned his gaze to Chloe, his tone sharp but measured. "Ms Smith, you are a law student, correct?"

Chloe straightened slightly in her seat, caught off guard by the direct question. "Yes, Your Honour," she replied, her voice hesitant but defiant.

"Then you should be well aware that this courtroom is no place for flippant remarks or baseless accusations. Furthermore, you have not been recognised as counsel, as you have not passed Pupillage or qualified as a solicitor or barrister. Kindly keep your observations to yourself unless you are asked to speak."

Chloe sank back into her seat, her face flushed with embarrassment, while the public gallery buzzed with hushed whispers. Sir Thomas returned his attention to Victoria Hunt.

"Ms Hunt, while I appreciate your diligence, the fact that I once called into Mr Smith's radio show for a discussion

157

on football does not constitute grounds for recusal. The matters at hand are far removed from Wolves' midfield strategy," he said with a faint smirk. "Now, if we may proceed, I believe, as you are a witness for the prosecution, would the Crown like to continue their examination?"

The lead barrister for the Crown Prosecution Service, Alice Cartwright, rose to her feet, her dark robes swaying slightly as she adjusted her papers. "Thank you, Your Honour," she said, her voice calm and authoritative. Turning to Pete, she offered a reassuring nod. "Mr Smith, I'd like to begin by asking you to describe the culture at Manic Radio during your time there, particularly in the years leading up to the events detailed in this trial."

Pete took a deep breath, steadying himself. "The culture at Manic Radio, well, from what I have observed, and if I am honest, was an obsession for RAJAR ratings, for listener figures, for social media engagement. In the 6 years since Breeze Media got purchased by Manic Radio Group, the culture became increasingly aggressive. There was an atmosphere of fear and pressure, where presenters and producers were constantly pushed to do more, often at the expense of their own well-being. It wasn't just about producing good radio; it was about hitting targets at all costs. If you didn't perform or if you questioned management, you were sidelined. I was one of the few presenters Management wouldn't discipline, not because of my age, but because of my RAJAR ratings. My slots consistently brought in solid figures, which gave me a layer of protection that many of my colleagues didn't have. Prior to my leaving Manic, I had 49 consecutive quarters of excellent RAJAR ratings, the Birmingham weekday Drive show, which constantly outperformed everything that Free Radio and its successor, Hits Radio, as well as Capital, another competitor, could deliver. Those ratings were a lifeline for me, but they also created a double-edged sword—I was safe from being sidelined, but it meant I couldn't ignore the things I saw happening around me."

Alice Cartwright nodded, her gaze steady as she pressed on. "Can you elaborate on what you mean by 'the things you saw'? Specifically, how did this culture impact the employees at Manic Radio?"

Pete hesitated for a moment, gathering his thoughts. He looked briefly at Chloe, who avoided his gaze, before continuing. "The impact was... devastating. People were pushed to their limits. Presenters were expected to work long hours, often without adequate support or rest. There was rampant favouritism, and those who didn't fall in line were bullied or ostracised. I saw talented colleagues reduced to shells of themselves because they couldn't keep up with the relentless demands. There was also a complete lack of boundaries—personal relationships were openly shown... one I remember was the local Head of PR, Abdul Zahir, who was, in the break room, having sex with a producer who had come to Dudley on loan from the Cardiff hub."

Pete paused, noticing a ripple of reaction in the courtroom, from stifled gasps in the public gallery to exchanged glances among the jury. Chloe shifted uncomfortably in the dock, while Kylie remained aloof, her gaze fixed on her nails. Cody, however, appeared unusually intent, as if storing Pete's words for some scheme of his own.

"I can confirm that," Cody interrupted, his voice cutting through the tension in the courtroom. All eyes turned toward him, and he seemed to relish the attention, though his tone carried a hint of nervousness. "Abdul was one of those untouchables, wasn't he, Pete? One of the guys who could get away with anything because the bosses liked his work. They turned a blind eye to whatever he did in the office, as long as he delivered on PR."

The courtroom murmured again, and Sir Thomas Harvey rapped his gavel firmly, silencing the noise. "Mr Lane, you will have your opportunity to address the court when appropriate. For now, please refrain from unsolicited interjections."

Cody nodded, though the smirk on his face suggested he wasn't entirely cowed. Pete, however, didn't let the interruption faze him. He took a breath and continued.

"That's exactly the problem," Pete said, his voice steady. "There was a culture of enabling certain individuals—people like Abdul, and others higher up the chain—because they were seen as assets to the company. It didn't matter how they treated their colleagues or what lines they crossed. The management prioritised results over integrity, and that attitude trickled down to every level of the organisation."

"That's exactly the problem," Pete said, his voice steady. "There was a culture of enabling certain individuals—people like Abdul, and others higher up the chain—because they were seen as assets to the company. It didn't matter how they treated their colleagues or what lines they crossed. The management prioritised results over integrity, and that attitude trickled down to every level of the organisation. Staff turnover was at a high, and... well, there was a large number of people on maternity leave after Jane Spearmore, the old Regional Director, my old boss before she left in 2023, left and Cal Ellington replaced her in Dudley." Pete paused, his jaw tightening as he considered his next words. "Jane was from the old school world of radio. She understood that local connections mattered, even when corporate overlords like Lite and Manic wanted everything streamlined. Cal's different—he's a numbers man, not a radio man. I heard rumours, but I never had them confirmed, that he used to work for the Manchester hub and was a sexual predator-"

"Objection," Victoria Hunt rose swiftly, her voice cutting through Pete's testimony like a blade. "Your Honour, I object to this line of testimony. The witness is relaying hearsay and unsubstantiated allegations that are both prejudicial and irrelevant to the charges at hand."

Sir Thomas Harvey raised a hand to silence the murmurs in the courtroom, his measured tone restoring order. "Mr Smith, while I understand your testimony seeks to provide context, this court cannot entertain speculation or unverified claims. Please confine your responses to your direct knowledge and experiences."

Pete nodded, chastened but resolute. "Understood, Your Honour. My apologies."

Alice Cartwright, the Crown's barrister, resumed her questioning, steering Pete back to safer ground. "Mr Smith, thank you for clarifying. Could you instead focus on the corporate environment you directly observed and how it may have contributed to the offences being considered in this trial?"

Pete took a deep breath, his eyes briefly flickering to the jury before returning to Cartwright. "The environment at Manic was... corrosive. It wasn't just the relentless drive for ratings—it was the way management fostered a culture of fear and exploitation. There were 6 people in the Dudley hub back in 2023 who had been 'the only sane ones left standing,' as one producer put it, after a string of resignations. Those who stayed either adapted to the culture or were replaced."

"And who were these individuals who were 'the only sane ones left standing'?" Alice Cartwright asked, her tone probing yet respectful. "Were they vocal about their concerns regarding the workplace environment, or did they adapt to survive?"

Pete considered the question carefully, glancing briefly at the jury. "Those six individuals... well, they were a mix of people who either tried to keep their heads down or occasionally voiced their frustrations quietly, among trusted colleagues. Tim Young and Ellen Fisher, who, like me had joined radio during the Woody Bones era before Breeze Media, were among those who tried to advocate for a healthier work culture. Ellen originally joined Walsall Radio, one of the stations that merged into Midlands Manic, and was until earlier this year the host of East Midlands Vibes drive, with Tim her co-host. Tim had come from the Derby side of Woody Bones's network-he now, as of a couple of weeks ago, works for Boom Radio. Then there was Lyra Nott, my now daughter-in-law, she joined Northern Vibes when she graduated from Keele University in 2019-she was recruited by Manic days after the takeover from Breeze while at University."

Pete paused, gathering his thoughts as he continued, knowing the weight of his testimony could have far-reaching consequences. "Lyra moved to the Dudley hub in 2022, when Jane Spearmore was regional director and Manic had decided to locate its stations in regional hubs for efficiency and cost-cutting, in the run-up to the Lite Group merger. She worked there alongside a few other 'survivors' of the pre-Manic era—people who were trying to uphold some semblance of professionalism amidst the chaos. But the pressure was unrelenting, and the culture had already shifted drastically by then. People like Lyra, Tim, and Ellen did their best, but they were up against a tidal wave of toxicity that had been brewing since the merger."

"And for the record, where are the hubs that Manic relocated its stations to?" Alice asked, steering Pete toward a factual recitation of Manic's structural changes.

Pete straightened, his tone becoming more formal as he recalled the details. "Manic Radio operates a hub system, consolidating local stations into regional centres for operational efficiency. This is common in the industry, with Bauer and Global doing similar reorganisations. For Manic, the hubs are in Birmingham, Manchester Piccadilly, Olympic Park in London, Huddersfield, Cardiff, Speke, Dundee, and Exeter. These hubs manage the broadcasting and production for multiple regions, effectively centralising what were once local stations. There is also some satellite hubs, one in Belfast for Northern Ireland and the Republic of Ireland, one in Jersey for the Channel Islands, and one in Newport for the Isle of Wight," Pete continued, his tone steady as he detailed the logistical structure. "The consolidation of operations into these hubs was presented as a cost-saving measure, but in reality, it stripped local stations of their individuality and connection to their communities. The focus became less about serving listeners and more about maximising efficiency and revenue. Manic were able to do this following OFCOM creating Approved Areas."

"Ok, and can you explain what an Approved Area is, Mr Smith?" Alice asked, steering the testimony toward the regulatory framework that had enabled the restructuring.

Pete nodded. "An Approved Area is a regulatory term introduced by OFCOM, which is the UK's broadcasting regulator. It allows radio stations within a defined geographic area to share programming and branding while maintaining nominal local identities. It is mainly based on the ITV regions, so for Central, the East and West Midlands, which would be the approved area for consolidation. For example, the Manic stations in the East

Midlands, Manic Vibes and Manic Goldies East Midlands, are based out of One Snow Hill in Birmingham, Manic Vibes Milton Keynes is based out of the Olympic Park hub in London, and Manic Rock Scotland is based out of the Dundee hub. Essentially, it allows networks like Manic to consolidate operations across regions while retaining some semblance of local branding. In practice, however, it often leads to a homogenised output that erodes the unique character of local radio stations. Bauer operate hubs but on a smaller scale, with their Birmingham hub having Hits Radio West Midlands, the former Free Radio, and Hits Radio Stoke and South Cheshire, the former Signal Radio, broadcasting from there." Pete paused for a moment to let the jury digest the technical details. "Global, meanwhile, operates in a similar manner with their regional hubs for Capital, Heart, and Smooth stations. However, Manic took this centralisation further, with hubs handling multiple brands across vast regions, which inevitably diluted the local flavour that once defined these stations."

Pete then sighed. "In 2022, Manic also ran an experiment where they brought selected independent stations, such as Rugby Waves, a small station serving Rugby and the surrounding area, into their hub system under a voice tracking model. This meant that all shows on Rugby Waves had their shows pre-recorded, with the music inserted by algorithms. This effectively turned these stations into shells of their former selves, with little to no local input. The experiment was justified as a way to cut costs and improve consistency, but it came at the expense of the personal connection listeners had with their local stations. Rugby Waves, for example, saw a significant drop in listener engagement, and the feedback from the community was overwhelmingly negative. Furthermore, those stations didn't use little known presenters, or the presenting staff they had previously employed, but Manic, BBC, Global and Bauer personalities using pseudonyms and working either from home, or from a Manic hub. One such duo on Rugby Waves was known on air as Johnny D and Rosie M, but in fact were a well-known duo who used to present on Mercia and then later Wyvern, Free Radio and now Hits Radio. It was well known among Manic and Bauer staff, as well as the audiences it was Hits Radio West Midlands breakfast hosts John Daiezel-"

"Objection, the defence requests Mr Smith refrain from speculation about specific individuals unless this directly relates to the charges at hand," Victoria interjected, her tone sharp as she rose to her feet.

Sir Thomas raised a hand to restore order. "Ms Hunt, while I appreciate your vigilance, Mr Smith's testimony regarding the operational and cultural practices of Manic Radio is relevant for establishing context. However, Mr Smith, I remind you to limit your testimony to matters within your direct knowledge and avoid conjecture."

Pete nodded, his voice steady as he resumed. "Understood, Your Honour. To clarify, my point was that Manic's approach to centralisation and cost-cutting eroded local connections, replacing them with homogenised content. This often left listeners feeling disconnected from their stations, undermining the trust and community focus that had once been the backbone of local radio."

Alice took the opportunity to redirect the testimony. "Mr Smith, you mentioned earlier the impact of Manic's culture on its employees. Could you elaborate on how this environment may have contributed to the behaviour of individuals now facing charges in this trial?"

Pete glanced toward the defendants in the dock, noting Chloe's tense posture, Cody's smirk, and Kylie's disinterest. "The culture at Manic didn't just encourage unethical behaviour—it normalised it. Chloe, Cody, and Kylie didn't act in a vacuum. They thrived in an environment where exploitation and coercion were tacitly accepted, even rewarded. Management turned a blind eye to misconduct as long as the numbers looked good. People like Chloe were given free rein because they were considered valuable assets. There were no checks or balances, no accountability, and no safeguarding measures in place to protect employees or even audiences."

Alice pressed further. "In your professional opinion, Mr Smith, was this culture systemic?"

Pete didn't hesitate. "Absolutely. It wasn't just a few bad actors—it was a top-down issue. From regional directors to senior executives, there was a consistent failure to enforce ethical standards. Manic's obsession with profit and ratings came at the expense of human decency. The toxic culture was baked into the company's DNA, and everyone who worked there was affected by it, one way or another."

The courtroom was silent as Pete's words hung in the air. The jury seemed engaged, some scribbling notes, while others maintained steady eye contact with Pete. In the dock, Chloe's defiance faltered, her gaze dropping to the table in front of her. Cody leaned back, arms crossed, while Kylie smirked faintly, her demeanour suggesting she found the entire proceeding tiresome.

Alice stepped back slightly, her tone remaining calm yet purposeful. "Thank you, Mr Smith. I have no further questions at this time."

Sir Thomas turned to the defence. "Ms Hunt, do you wish to cross-examine the witness?"

****

CHAPTER 13 – Cross Examination
Wednesday 19th November 2025

Alice Cartwright stepped back slightly, her tone remaining calm yet purposeful. "Thank you, Mr Smith. I have no further questions at this time."

Sir Thomas Harvey turned to the defence. "Ms Hunt, do you wish to cross-examine the witness?"

Pete knew that this was the part he was dreading, as, even though Theodore had coached him what to expect, he was well aware that the defence barrister, Victoria Hunt, would do everything in her power to discredit him. Taking a steadying breath, he adjusted his posture, ready for whatever was to come.

Victoria rose gracefully from her seat, her dark robe swishing slightly as she moved to the centre of the courtroom. She projected an air of calm confidence, her piercing gaze locking onto Pete.

"Mr Smith," she began, her voice smooth but with an edge of steel, "you've painted quite the damning picture of Manic Radio—a company you were employed by for decades. Would it be fair to say, however, that you benefitted significantly from the very system you are now criticising?"

"Objection," Alice interjected firmly, rising from her seat. "The question is argumentative and designed to impugn the witness's character rather than elicit relevant testimony."

Sir Thomas glanced at Victoria, his expression measured. "Ms Hunt, please rephrase your question. This is cross-examination, not a platform for rhetoric."

Victoria offered a brief nod, her tone remaining composed. "Of course, Your Honour. Mr Smith, as a prominent figure at Manic Radio, would you agree that your position afforded you privileges and protections that were not available to many of your colleagues?"

Pete considered her words carefully, knowing the importance of his response. "I wouldn't dispute that, Ms Hunt. My longevity and ratings meant I had a level of job security that many didn't. But that doesn't absolve me from speaking out about the culture I witnessed. If anything, it gave me a responsibility to do so. Alas, I was not aware of some of the more... darker... goings on until April this year."

Victoria's lips tightened into a faint smile, her eyes narrowing as she seized on Pete's words. "Not aware, you say? Mr Smith, are we to believe that after decades within the company, you had no knowledge of the toxic environment you've described until mere months ago?"

Pete remained calm, his voice steady as he responded. "Ms Hunt, I was aware of the culture of pressure and fear, and I spoke out against it when I could. But as far as the more serious allegations—the abuse and criminal activities—we're discussing in this trial, I only became fully aware when my son, James, came forward with his experiences earlier this year."

Victoria arched an eyebrow, feigning surprise. "So, despite your seniority and long-standing relationships with colleagues, you were unaware of what you now describe as systemic issues?"

"If I am honest, I was more concerned with how Manic was eroding local radio," Pete said firmly, his voice steady despite the pointed questioning. "The centralisation of content, the loss of connection to the communities we served—those were the battles I was fighting. I was focused on preserving the integrity of the medium I love. The deeper issues, the criminal behaviours that have come to light in this trial, were deliberately hidden from me and others who were not part of the inner circle."

Victoria's gaze sharpened, and she took a step closer to the witness box. "And yet, Mr Smith, you were part of management, were you not? Surely someone of your stature would have had insight into the day-to-day operations at the stations you worked for. Isn't it convenient to claim ignorance now?"

Pete met her gaze evenly. "I was a broadcaster, not a manager, Ms Hunt. My role was to connect with listeners and deliver good radio. I wasn't privy to every meeting or decision made by management, nor was I involved in the personal lives of my colleagues... well, until my son, James, joined Manic at the end of October last year."

Victoria seized on Pete's mention of James, her tone sharpening as she pressed forward. "Ah, your son, Mr Smith. James Smith, who has been quite vocal about his experiences at Manic Radio. Would you say that your current testimony is influenced by your desire to support him, perhaps even protect him, given his prominent role in bringing these allegations to light?"

Pete didn't flinch. "Of course, I want to support my son, Ms Hunt. Any parent would. But my testimony today isn't about protecting James—it's about exposing the truth. What happened to him is part of a larger pattern of abuse and neglect within Manic Radio, and it's something the court deserves to hear about."

Victoria's lips curved into a faint smile that didn't reach her eyes. "A noble sentiment, Mr Smith. But isn't it true that your son's credibility has been called into question due to his past struggles with substance abuse and mental health issues? Could it not be argued that his allegations are influenced by his own personal grievances rather than objective truth?"

"Objection!" Alice interjected firmly. "Counsel is attempting to discredit a prosecution witness through speculative attacks on his character, rather than addressing the substance of the testimony."

"No, I'm happy to answer that," Pete interjected before Sir Thomas Harvey could rule on the objection, his voice steady but firm. "Your Honour, if I may?"

Sir Thomas raised an eyebrow but nodded. "Proceed, Mr Smith, though do be mindful of the scope of your response."

Pete turned his gaze back to Victoria Hunt, his voice calm yet resolute. "Ms Hunt, my son James has indeed faced challenges, as many people do in high-pressure environments, especially those as toxic as Manic Radio. He had, without telling anyone, been dating one of the defendants for 2 years, Kylie Morgan, and her influence on him was... well, destructive, to say the least. But those challenges don't negate the truth of what he's been through or the evidence he's brought forward. If anything, his struggles are a testament to the damage that Manic's culture has inflicted on its employees."

Victoria's expression remained controlled, though a flicker of irritation crossed her features. She leaned forward slightly, adjusting her tone to a more neutral pitch.

"Mr Smith, you mentioned Kylie Morgan's influence on your son. Are you suggesting that her actions alone were responsible for his struggles, or are you implying a broader complicity within Manic Radio?"

Sir Thomas Harvey nodded slightly, his tone firm as he ruled, "Sustained. Ms Hunt, please refrain from framing questions in a manner that distorts the witness's testimony. If you wish to explore the broader environment at Manic Radio, you may do so, but do so directly."

Victoria inclined her head, masking her irritation behind a polite smile. "Of course, Your Honour. Mr Smith, let us clarify. You have described a 'toxic culture' at Manic Radio. Can you provide specific examples of how this environment may have enabled or concealed the alleged behaviour of the defendants?"

Pete took a steadying breath, his mind briefly flickering to the many instances he had observed over the years. "Certainly. One example was the lack of accountability for individuals in senior positions. Chloe Smith, one of the defendants, was not only my daughter but someone who rose rapidly through the ranks. Normally, in radio, a presenter is not put in a timeslot like the Saturday night show, and not live on it, immediately. They usually are given graveyard shifts or pre-recorded shows to develop their skills. James was given a trial on a drive show in October, but he was accompanied by two experienced... well, if you call Al Crozier experienced... presenters, one of whom was middle management from Speke who also acted as a floating on-air manager for struggling shows. He was then assigned to series of pre-recorded shows, Ibiza Headbangers, a Manic Dance show, as well as pre-recorded Manic Rock, Manic Metal and curated playlist shows for... Manic Linkin Park, Manic David Guetta, Manic Scooter and Manic Armand Van Helden. But then Ms Morgan had managed to pull strings to get her and him on the live broadcasts from House of Manic Live."

"Manic Linkin Park?" Victoria interjected, her tone laced with a mix of incredulity and disdain. "Mr Smith, are we seriously discussing a station named after a single band?

Is this an example of the supposed innovation Manic Radio championed?"

Pete allowed himself a faint smile, meeting her gaze evenly. "Yes, Ms Hunt, Manic Linkin Park and others like it were part of their strategy—niche stations dedicated to specific artists or genres. They were gimmicks, designed to inflate streaming figures and target specific listener demographics. How it works is that people can use the Manic Prime app to listen to the main 10 Manic stations, Manic Vibes, Manic Dance, Manic Rock, Manic Metal, Manic Classical, Manic Soul, Manic Blues, Manic Hot, Manic Urban and Manic Goldies for free, or pay £4.99 for access to the on-demand, micro station and premium content like Manic Linkin Park, Manic David Guetta, and Manic Scooter." Pete paused, a hint of sarcasm creeping into his tone. "How content like Manic Linkin Park works is that they are curated playlists, which are pre-recorded with brief presenter links added, typically from existing presenters or voiceover artists contracted for multiple stations. They play, in order from oldest to most recent, that specific artists entire back catalogue, from deep cuts to greatest hits. It's a formula designed to maximise engagement and monetisation without requiring much creativity or effort. But that's precisely the issue—it prioritised marketability over meaningful content and, more importantly, over the well-being of the people creating it."

"And have you yourself presented any content for these so-called micro-stations, Mr Smith?" Victoria Hunt interjected, her tone dripping with scepticism as she circled back to Pete's testimony.

Pete nodded, his expression calm. "Yes, Ms Hunt. I've done pre-recorded segments for Manic Goldies spin-offs, such as Manic Goldies 60s, Manic Blues Brothers, Manic Rock 80s, Manic Pirate Radio and Manic Prog Classics.

These were similar in structure to the micro-stations—curated playlists with voice links recorded in advance. While they were convenient for the network and catered to niche audiences, they lacked the spontaneity and connection of live broadcasting, which is the essence of radio. Some presenters are given scripts and specific talking points to follow, but I insisted on retaining creative control over my segments."

"And why would you insist on retaining creative control, Mr Smith?" Victoria Hunt asked, her tone deceptively light, though her eyes gleamed with the intent of catching Pete off guard.

Pete straightened slightly, meeting her gaze with quiet resolve. "Because, Ms Hunt, I've always believed that authenticity is what makes radio special. A presenter's connection to the audience comes from their personality, their ability to react to the moment, and to create something that feels genuine. Scripts and pre-recorded segments strip away that authenticity, turning presenters into little more than voices reading lines. Things like the Blues Brothers, 80s Rock and Pirate Radio are a thing I loved, as I was a teen in the 1980s, and so those genres and themes resonate deeply with me. I wanted to bring a sense of personal passion and knowledge to the broadcasts. Listeners can tell when a presenter cares about the content—they can feel that energy, and it keeps them coming back. Without that connection, radio becomes sterile, just another playlist that could be generated by an algorithm."

Victoria's faint smile tightened as she absorbed Pete's response, her posture remaining composed, though there was a flicker of frustration in her eyes. She paced a step closer to the witness box, her tone cooling.

"Mr Smith, while your dedication to authenticity is commendable, would you agree that such sentiments may come across as nostalgic rather than practical in an industry that prioritises efficiency and profitability?"

"Yes, but-"

"No further questions, Your Honour," Victoria Hunt interrupted sharply, cutting Pete off before he could finish his sentence. She turned on her heel and strode back to her seat, her expression neutral but taut, as if satisfied she had made her point.

"With all due respect, Ms Hunt, if I may finish," Pete said, the irritation of being interrupted evident in his voice. Sir Thomas Harvey raised a hand to silence the courtroom's murmurs and gestured for Pete to continue.

"Thank you, Your Honour," Pete said, regaining his composure. He turned back to Victoria, his voice calm yet resolute. "Yes, Ms Hunt, the industry does prioritise efficiency and profitability, and while that may seem practical, it comes at a cost. Nostalgia, as you put it, isn't the issue—it's about recognising that stripping away the human element of radio destroys the very thing that makes it unique. Efficiency and profitability are important, but they should never come at the expense of integrity, creativity, and the well-being of the people who bring radio to life."

Pete then looked at Chloe, and sighed. "When Chloe was 18, she said that she wanted to become a radio presenter, but also a lawyer, a noble profession if I'm honest, but the reason she gave when she said she wanted to be a radio presenter was because she idolised me, her dad, someone who had dedicated his life to radio. I was proud of her ambition, but I told her from the beginning that radio was not just about glamour or fame. It was about connection, storytelling, and responsibility. I reminded her that, while the microphone gives you a voice, it also carries weight. You have to use it wisely and respectfully, because people trust you when they listen. Chloe seemed to take that to heart at first, as my wife, Sarah, gave her a position within her independent radio company, creating her own independently produced syndicated CHR show for community and small commercial radio stations," Pete continued, his voice tinged with regret. "Then she started dating Cody Lane. It was October last year when she started dating him, and... well, started taking cocaine."

Pete's voice faltered momentarily, the weight of his memories pressing heavily upon him. The courtroom remained silent, the gravity of his words settling over those present. He glanced briefly at Chloe, whose defiant posture had softened into something resembling discomfort.

"Cody was part of the culture that I've been describing— a culture that thrived on manipulation, exploitation, and indulgence. When Chloe began dating him, she changed. The enthusiasm she once had for radio, for creating something meaningful, was replaced by an obsession with power, appearances, and manipulation. I... I failed as a father."

Pete paused, his voice cracking slightly as he gathered his composure. "I failed to see the warning signs early enough. I was so consumed with my own work and my own battles with Manic's corporate machine that I didn't notice what was happening to my daughter until it was too late. She became part of the very system that I've been fighting against—one that chews people up and spits them out, leaving them broken or complicit. I... I then found out from James back in April this year that Chloe... she's always been this way—manipulative, cunning, and, dare I say, ruthless when it suited her. I ignored the signs when she was younger, thinking it was just youthful ambition. But her time at Manic amplified those traits, turned them into tools for survival in a culture that rewarded such behaviour."

"So, you're saying that you're to blame for the direction your children took?" Victoria interjected sharply, seizing on Pete's admission. Her tone was sharp, almost accusatory, as if she had found a chink in his armour. "That it was your parenting that failed to guide your children away from the very culture you now criticise?"

Pete straightened in his seat, meeting Victoria's gaze with quiet determination. His voice was steady, though tinged with a deep sadness. "Ms Hunt, as a parent, I take responsibility for my shortcomings. I should have seen the warning signs, and I should have done more to guide Chloe and James. But to lay the blame solely at my feet would ignore the systemic issues at play here. My children, like many others, were shaped by an environment that exploited their vulnerabilities. That environment was created and perpetuated by the very organisation we are discussing in this courtroom."

Victoria pressed further, her tone firm but measured. "Mr Smith, while it's commendable that you accept some responsibility, isn't it convenient to deflect blame onto an organisation when the choices made by your children were ultimately their own?"

"With all due respect, the rot in Manic-"

"I put it to you, Mr Smith, that you are using Manic Radio as a scapegoat for your own failures as a parent and your children's poor decisions. Isn't it true that Chloe and James, as adults, made their own choices, independent of any corporate culture?" Victoria Hunt's voice was razor-sharp, her words calculated to cut through Pete's measured testimony.

"James didn't deserve to get raped by his girlfriend, his sister and their cronies," Pete paused, his voice cracking with raw emotion, "and he didn't deserve to be drugged, coerced, and exploited. Those weren't choices he made, Ms Hunt. Those were things done to him. As for Chloe…" Pete took a deep breath, steadying himself before continuing, "she made choices, yes. But those choices were influenced by an organisation that encouraged and rewarded manipulation and abuse. Manic Radio created an environment where people were either predators or prey, and Chloe chose the former to survive—and thrive."

The courtroom was silent for a moment, the weight of Pete's words hanging in the air. Victoria Hunt, unperturbed, took a measured step back, her expression unreadable.

"Mr Smith," she began again, her tone softening slightly but retaining its edge, "you've spoken extensively about the culture at Manic Radio and its impact on your children. But isn't it true that you remained with the company for years, even as you claim to have witnessed its decline? Why didn't you leave if you found the environment so intolerable?"

"Because I have respect for my listeners, many of who have listened to my broadcasts since 1994, have had children, and those children have listened to my shows," Pete replied, his voice steady but firm. "Leaving Manic Radio wasn't as simple as walking away. My connection to my audience, built over decades, was something I couldn't abandon lightly. I felt a responsibility to them— to provide the familiar voice they trusted, especially in times when local radio was being eroded. For many listeners, my show wasn't just entertainment; it was a source of comfort, community, and continuity. But more than that, I stayed because I believed that, from within, I might be able to push back against the tide of corporatisation and maintain some semblance of integrity in my work, and I knew that if I had left, Manic would have filled my show with someone who could have been the next victim or perpetrator of the depraved cycle of exploitation. By staying, I could protect my team to some degree, ensure that my immediate colleagues weren't subjected to the same relentless pressure or toxicity that plagued the rest of the organisation."

Pete then sighed. "I stayed because I knew that any replacement could be someone fresh out of University, or from Bauer or Global, and forced to be a hub cum dump, be a cocaine addict, be someone who ended up potentially pregnant or fathering children who they may not have chosen to have, or worse, someone who ended up as part of the legal cases we are hearing today. I knew I had a responsibility to ensure that didn't happen, at least not on my watch, in my studio."

Victoria paused for a moment, her expression unreadable, before stepping forward again. "Mr Smith, I understand your sense of duty to your audience and your colleagues, but do you not see how remaining in such an environment could be perceived as tacit approval of its practices? By staying, were you not complicit in perpetuating the very culture you now criticise?"

Pete's jaw tightened, but his voice remained steady. "Ms Hunt, I stayed because walking away would have done nothing to change the system. I stayed to protect the people I worked with, to be a voice of reason in an unreasonable world. Was it enough? Clearly not. But to call my presence complicity ignores the efforts I made to push back against the toxicity and to shield those I could from its worst excesses."

Victoria's eyes narrowed slightly, as though she was searching for a weak point in Pete's resolve. "And yet, Mr Smith, you benefited from this environment. You had a stable career, high ratings, and a level of security others at Manic Radio could only dream of. Can you truly claim to have been an outsider to the culture you describe?"

Pete leaned forward slightly, his gaze unflinching. "Ms Hunt, I'm not here to claim sainthood. I know I had privileges others didn't, and I'll carry the guilt of that disparity for the rest of my life. But those privileges didn't blind me to what was happening around me. They gave me a platform to speak out, and they gave me the strength to stand here today and tell the truth."

Sir Thomas Harvey, who had been observing the exchange with his usual composed demeanour, raised a hand. "Ms Hunt, I believe you've explored this line of questioning thoroughly. Do you have any further points to address?"

Victoria hesitated for a brief moment, her gaze flicking toward Chloe in the dock before returning to Pete. "No further questions, Your Honour."

Sir Thomas nodded and turned to Pete. "Mr Smith, you are excused. Thank you for your testimony."

****

CHAPTER 14 – Lyra Takes The Stand
Friday 21st November 2025

James could see Lyra struggling, her seven-month-pregnant body making her feel more cumbersome than usual as they woke to the sound of Cory's cries at six in the morning. The crisp November air seeped through the cracks in the old windows of their Pensnett home, which they shared with James's parents. James pulled himself from the warmth of the duvet, shivering slightly as he reached for his dressing gown.

"I've got her," he murmured, placing a gentle hand on Lyra's shoulder.

Lyra nodded sleepily, her hand instinctively resting on her swollen belly as she turned onto her side. "Thank you," she whispered, her voice heavy with exhaustion. "James, I... I don't feel too well."

James froze mid-step, his heart skipping a beat. He turned back to Lyra, crouching beside the bed. "What do you mean? Is it the baby?" His voice was calm but tinged with worry, his eyes scanning her face for signs of distress.

Lyra shook her head slowly. "It... its normal, with the pregnancy, I think. After all, I've got two months left to go before our little one joins us. You see, giving birth, and with it being less than 5 degrees Celsius, my immune system might just be acting up," she explained, her voice faint but steady. "But it's nothing to worry about, I promise."

James exhaled slowly, his tension easing slightly. "Alright. Just rest, okay? I'll take care of Cory and get you some tea. If it gets worse, though, we're calling the midwife."

Lyra gave him a small smile. "Deal."

James walked to the corner of the room where Cory's cot was set up. He lifted his crying daughter gently, rocking her in his arms as her cries softened into hiccups. "Just think Cory, only 2 months until your little brother is born, and you'll be a big sister," James murmured softly, planting a kiss on Cory's forehead. She responded with a small coo, her tiny fingers curling around the edge of his t-shirt.

"You know, Cory, you, your new mum Lyra, your little brother and your granddad Pete and Granny Sarah are the only things keeping me going right now," James whispered, his voice low as if confiding in his infant daughter. "With everything happening in court, the media, and all the chaos surrounding Manic… it's you lot that keep me grounded."

He carried Cory into the living room, as his bedroom was off that room in Pete and Sarah's Pensnett home, careful not to wake anyone else. The house was still and quiet, save for the faint hum of the central heating kicking in. James settled Cory into her bouncer, her little hands reaching for the colourful toys dangling from the frame.

As James busied himself with making tea and preparing Cory's breakfast, his mind drifted to the upcoming day. Lyra was scheduled to give her testimony at Birmingham Crown Court. She'd been dreading it, not just because of the stress it would place on her physically, but because of the emotional toll it would inevitably take. Her testimony would be pivotal—both in corroborating James's experiences and in exposing the broader culture of abuse and negligence at Manic Radio.

James couldn't shake the nagging feeling that Lyra wasn't up to it. Her pregnancy, the strain of caring for Cory, and the relentless media attention had left her drained. He was deeply worried about her health, but he also knew how much she wanted to stand by him and contribute to the fight for justice.

****

"Mrs Smith, you were a former presenter at Manic Radio, primarily on the Manic Vibes Stoke & Cheshire regional show, correct?" Alice Cartwright, the Crown's barrister asked. Her tone was polite but professional, her sharp gaze fixed on Lyra as she adjusted her position in the witness box.

Lyra, seated with an air of quiet strength despite her obvious discomfort, nodded. "Yes, that's correct. I joined Manic Radio in 2019 and worked there until April 2025. I was slated to join Bauer Media in May 2025, but Manic-"

"Objection, the witness is veering into testimony outside the scope of the question," interrupted Marcus Blake, one of the defence barristers representing Manic Radio.

"Objection sustained," Sir Thomas Harvey interjected, his voice firm but measured. "Mrs Smith, please confine your responses to answering the specific question posed. Ms Cartwright, you may proceed."

Alice gave a small nod of acknowledgment to the judge before turning her attention back to Lyra. "Thank you, Your Honour. Mrs Smith, during your time at Manic Radio, can you describe the workplace culture you experienced, particularly in relation to how employees were treated?"

Lyra hesitated for a moment, her hands resting protectively on her belly. "The culture at Manic Radio was... difficult, to say the least. There was a constant pressure to deliver high ratings, which often meant cutting corners, both in terms of ethics and employee well-being. It wasn't uncommon for presenters to work excessive hours, sometimes without adequate breaks. There was also a pervasive sense of fear—fear of being sidelined, demoted, or even ostracised if you didn't conform to management's demands."

Alice nodded encouragingly. "And were you personally subjected to any behaviours or practices that you would consider inappropriate or harmful during your time there?"

Lyra's jaw tightened, her gaze steady as she met Cartwright's eyes. "Yes. On several occasions, I was subjected to coercion and manipulation by management and colleagues alike. There was a specific incident where I was pressured to attend after-work events that were less about networking and more about maintaining appearances. These events often devolved into situations where boundaries were blurred, and I felt unsafe. One manager in particular—Cal Ellington—made it clear that my career progression depended on my willingness to 'play along.'"

"Right. Now, I would like to take you back to the afternoon of the 15th of April 2025," Cartwright continued, her tone measured as she guided Lyra through her testimony. "On that day, there was an incident involving James Smith at the One Snow Hill hub in Birmingham. Were you present?"

Lyra nodded slowly, her expression grave. "Yes, I was. I was due to start my drivetime show on Manic Vibes Stoke & Cheshire and was heading to the Urban studio to speak with James. I had arrived early as I had been doing a voice tracked session for Manic Dua Lipa, a curated playlist station. I was there from 11am to 8pm, as the voice tracked session lasted two hours due to a technical problem. You see, we had only moved into the One Snow Hill hub the previous day from the original Dudley studios, and the new setup had multiple teething issues. I was on a break between the voice tracked shows and my regular slot of 4pm to 7pm on Manic Vibes Stoke & Cheshire, so I decided to check in on James. He had been struggling with the toxic culture at the station, and I was concerned about him."

Cartwright stepped closer to the jury, ensuring they were following every word. "And what did you witness when you arrived at the Urban studio?"

Lyra's voice wavered slightly, but she steadied herself. "When I entered the studio, I saw James and Cody Lane. Cody was in a state of partial undress, and it was immediately clear that James was being coerced into... into an inappropriate situation. The atmosphere was oppressive. James looked terrified and humiliated. It was clear this wasn't consensual—it was exploitation."

Tuesday 15th April 2025

The sterile hum of the One Snow Hill hub was interrupted by the faint murmur of voices spilling through the thin walls of Studio 3. Lyra, clutching her reusable water bottle and a folder of prep notes, paused outside the door. She recognised Cody Lane's voice—low, smug, and unmistakably condescending. Her instincts kicked in, and unease settled in her chest.

Inside, the sight confirmed her worst fears. Cody Lane stood leaning against the control desk, his shirt partially unbuttoned, while James knelt on the floor, his head bowed and his expression blank. The tension in the room was suffocating, the power dynamic glaringly clear.

Cody's face twisted into a smug grin as he noticed Lyra's arrival.

"What the fuck is going on?"

Lyra's voice cut through the oppressive silence like a whip. The sharp edge in her tone jolted both James and Cody, freezing them in place. For a moment, the sterile recording booth felt smaller, the air heavier, as Lyra's gaze moved between the two of them.

Cody, ever the chameleon, straightened up with a forced grin, pulling up his jeans as though nothing had happened. "Lyra! Didn't know you'd be dropping by. Reevesy wanted to give me a blowjob, so I happily complied," he said, his voice laced with a veneer of nonchalance that failed to mask the underlying tension.

Lyra stepped further into the room, her fists clenched at her sides. She ignored Cody's smug explanation, her attention fully on James. He looked utterly defeated, his shoulders slumped, and his gaze fixed on the floor as if willing himself to disappear. The sight of him like this— broken, humiliated—ignited a fire in her.

"Didn't you, Reevesy?" Cody then said a bit more forcefully, hinting to James that if he didn't comply, he'd make things even worse for him later. James swallowed hard; his throat dry as sandpaper. His body stiffened, a mixture of fear and disgust coursing through him.

"That... that's right, Cody. It's because I love having your cock in my mouth," James choked out, his voice barely above a whisper, each word laced with humiliation. He couldn't bring himself to look at Lyra, knowing her sharp eyes were dissecting the scene in front of her. "After all, you're more of a man than I am. Can you... fuck me again?"

"That... that's right, Cody. It's because I love having your cock in my mouth," James choked out, his voice barely above a whisper, each word laced with humiliation. He couldn't bring himself to look at Lyra, knowing her sharp eyes were dissecting the scene in front of her. "After all, you're more of a man than I am. Can you... fuck me again?"

Lyra's eyes narrowed, her disgust evident. The confidence Cody usually exuded faltered for a brief moment under her icy stare. She crossed her arms, her stance unyielding, and exhaled slowly, as if trying to rein in her fury.

"This stops now," she said coldly, her voice cutting through the tense silence.

Cody smirked, though it was less convincing than usual. "Come on, Lyra, don't be such a buzzkill. It's just a bit of fun—consenting adults and all that. Isn't that right, Reevesy?" He threw a glance at James, whose face was a mask of shame and resignation.

James didn't respond, his silence speaking louder than any words could.

Lyra stepped forward, her presence commanding the room. She stood between James and Cody, her eyes locked on the latter. "Fun? This looks more like exploitation to me. You think I'm blind, Cody? Or stupid? Do you know who you're messing with?" Her tone was low but dangerous, her words laced with barely restrained anger.

Cody raised his hands in mock surrender, attempting a chuckle that fell flat. "Relax, Lyra. No need to get all heroic. Reevesy and I have an understanding."

Lyra's glare hardened. "The only thing I understand is that you're a predator who's gotten too comfortable in this toxic pit of a station. Get out of here before I make a call that will end your cushy little job in the newsroom."

Cody chuckled at that. "Really, Nott? Reevesy's my brother-in-law, and he's fully consenting, so if I want to let him suck me off or fuck his arse because he's a needy bitch who lives for this kind of humiliation, I will. Anyway, why are you so uptight? Is it because you're still a virgin? Reevesy, fuck this stuck-up bitch, and I'll tell Kylie that you might even be eligible for redemption."

Lyra didn't flinch, her piercing glare firmly locked onto Cody. The words he spewed, drenched in malice and arrogance, seemed to roll off her as she stood her ground, unshaken.

"That's enough," she said sharply, her voice carrying an edge that silenced Cody's smug retorts. "You think you can keep hiding behind this station's toxicity? Not on my watch."

Lyra noticed James glancing at her, and that he was trying to hide the strength that she was showing from her, the focus she had on Cody and his exploitative behaviour, and the sense of dignity she seemed determined to restore in the room. Cody, sensing his usual power over James was slipping under Lyra's unwavering glare, scowled, his confidence fracturing.

Cody's bravado faltered, his grin shrinking into a thin line as he realised Lyra wasn't going to back down. "Fine," he muttered, adjusting his jeans and heading for the door. He turned briefly, his expression a mix of irritation and defiance. "Reevesy, don't forget who keeps you relevant around here." With that, he disappeared into the hallway, leaving an oppressive silence in his wake.

Friday 21st November 2025

"Mrs Smith, you intervened in what you believed to be an act of exploitation involving your now-husband, James Smith, and the defendant, Cody Lane. Is that correct?" Alice Cartwright asked, her tone calm but pressing.

Lyra nodded, her face resolute but tinged with emotion. "Yes, that's correct. It was clear to me that James was not in a position to consent. Cody had been manipulating him for months, using his authority and James's vulnerabilities to coerce him into these situations."

Cartwright paused, letting the gravity of Lyra's words settle over the courtroom. The jurors leaned slightly forward, their focus unwavering. "Mrs Smith, what was James's reaction after Cody left the room?"

Lyra swallowed hard, her hand instinctively resting on her belly for comfort. "James was... broken. He couldn't even look at me. He kept apologising, saying it was his fault, that he deserved it. He was shaking so badly I thought he might collapse. It took me hours to convince him that he wasn't to blame and to get him to open up about what had been happening."

Cartwright nodded sympathetically. "Thank you, Mrs Smith. Now, could you describe how this incident—and others like it—reflect the broader workplace culture at Manic Radio?"

Lyra took a deep breath, her voice firm despite the emotion threatening to break through. "Manic Radio thrived on a culture of fear, coercion, and exploitation. It wasn't just Cody. There were others—managers, presenters, producers—who used their positions to manipulate and harm those they saw as weaker or more vulnerable. The toxic environment was systemic, and it allowed people like Cody to act with impunity. Anyone who tried to speak out was silenced or driven out."

Alice turned to address the judge, her tone calm but firm. "Your Honour, Mrs Smith's testimony is essential to illustrate the broader culture at Manic Radio, which is directly relevant to understanding the environment in which the alleged offences occurred. It is not about assigning guilt by association but about providing context for the systemic issues. Furthermore, my next question will link the cases against Ms Chloe Smith and Ms Kylie Morgan, that's if the Court would allow it."

Sir Thomas Harvey: "Ms Cartwright, you may continue your line of questioning, provided it remains relevant and does not stray into speculative territory. The court will permit Mrs Smith to comment on the workplace culture only insofar as it provides context for the charges faced by Ms Chloe Smith and Ms Kylie Morgan."

Alice nodded, her expression composed. "Thank you, Your Honour."

Turning back to Lyra, she continued. "Mrs Smith, on the 16th of April 2025, you received several messages from Ms Morgan, which form part of Exhibits 14 and 15. Could you please describe the content of those messages for the court?"

Lyra looked at the relevant exhibits that had been passed to her by the usher, her hand trembling slightly as she scanned the familiar screenshots.

The first one, from the 'Gals and Geezers' group chat, were a mix of photographs and videos of the events of the evening of the 15th of April, after Lyra had tried to get Pete to allow James to come back to the family home. There were photos, a few with Kylie at the centre of most of them. There were selfies of Kylie posing with her clique, bottles of champagne in hand, accompanied by captions like "Another night of chaos! ✹💧 " and "Who needs rules when you're on top?". Lyra's jaw tightened when she noticed James in the background of one of the photos, tied up, with the breasts of his sister, Chloe, in his mouth, and her husband, Cody, behind him, making James appear utterly powerless and humiliated. The image was a brutal confirmation of everything James had told her that day—about the toxic culture, the manipulation, and the exploitation that thrived unchecked at Manic Radio. Lyra's chest tightened as she struggled to process the sheer depravity on display. This wasn't just workplace banter; this was abuse.

"This first one is from a conversation called Gals and Geezers," Alice said, looking at Lyra. "Could you explain to the court what the concept of the Gals and Geezers group is."

Lyra cleared her throat, steadying herself as she prepared to address the courtroom. "The Gals and Geezers group chat was a WhatsApp group that included a mix of presenters, producers, and other staff from Manic Radio. Its sole purpose is to share nudes, sex photos and other such explicit content among staff, often involving deeply inappropriate and exploitative images. Its membership was confined to those... under 30... like me. It wasn't a admit by choice kind of group chat, where you could actively choose to join or leave; it was an unspoken rule that if you were under 30 and part of Manic, you were automatically added to it by senior staff or peers. This group operated as part of the broader toxic culture at Manic Radio, where boundaries were non-existent, and exploitation was normalised."

The jury exchanged uneasy glances, the weight of Lyra's testimony settling heavily in the courtroom. Alice allowed a moment for the information to sink in before continuing.

"And can you tell me who the Admin was for that group?" Alice asked, and Lyra turned the page to the settings of the Gals and Geezers WhatsApp group chat, which had been provided as evidence. She glanced at the familiar details, her expression darkening as she prepared to respond.

"The admin of the group," Lyra said, her voice steady despite the tension in the room, "was Nathaniel "Nate" King, a senior IT Technician at the Speke hub. You can see on the screenshot that the phone number for him is his Manic issued phone number, not a mobile phone one but a 0151 number registered to the Liverpool hub of Manic Radio." Lyra paused, her voice calm but carrying the weight of her words. "The other admins are Felix Trent and Eve MacDonald, two IT officers who work at the Olympic Park hub in London."

"LIAR!" A voice from the public gallery interrupted Lyra's testimony, loud and aggressive. Lyra looked up at the public gallery to see Eve MacDonald, a 25 year old junior IT officer, standing with a furious expression, pointing at Lyra. The sudden outburst caused a murmur to ripple through the courtroom. Judge Sir Thomas Harvey immediately banged his gavel, his stern voice cutting through the noise.

"Order in the court!" he commanded. "Ms MacDonald, you are here as an observer, not a participant. Any further disruptions, and you will be removed. Do I make myself clear?"

Eve hesitated, her face flushing red, before nodding stiffly and sitting down. The judge turned his attention back to Lyra, his expression softening slightly. "Mrs Smith, please continue."

Lyra took a steadying breath, her hands clasped tightly together to stop them from trembling. "As I was saying, the group's admins were Nate King, Felix Trent, and Eve MacDonald. They were responsible for maintaining the group and, in many cases, encouraging the sharing of explicit content. It was an open secret that joining this group was seen as part of fitting in at Manic. If you didn't engage, you risked being ostracised or targeted."

Lyra shifted slightly in her seat, her posture still poised despite the tension in the courtroom. "The Gals and Geezers group was marketed internally as a 'youth-centric' space," she explained, her voice tinged with disgust. "Manic Radio's culture idolised youth, image, and so-called 'edginess.' Being under 30 was seen as a status symbol at the station, something to be flaunted. The group operated under the pretence of being a casual chat, but in reality, it was a platform for harassment, exploitation, and maintaining a hierarchy that celebrated inappropriate behaviour."

Alice nodded, allowing the jury to absorb Lyra's testimony before proceeding. "You've mentioned explicit content being shared in this group. Can you describe its nature and frequency, particularly how it relates to the culture at Manic Radio?"

Lyra hesitated, her hands tightening over her belly as she prepared to delve into uncomfortable territory. "The content shared in the group ranged from suggestive photos to outright explicit images and videos. It wasn't uncommon for presenters and producers to post intimate or compromising pictures of themselves or others. Often, these were shared without consent. It reinforced a toxic environment where boundaries didn't exist, and people were objectified for entertainment."

Alice's voice softened slightly, but her focus remained unwavering. "Were you ever pressured to contribute to this group yourself, Mrs Smith?"

Lyra nodded, her gaze steady. "Yes. On several occasions, colleagues suggested I should 'loosen up' and share something to 'prove I was part of the team'. One person, Al Crozier, even tried to grope me, to which my former boyfriend, Si Wilcox, found out and, as he's a professional wrestler who now works in Florida as part of the WWE developmental program... well, kind of suplexed him onto a table at a bar where many Manic employees had gathered for drinks."

The courtroom buzzed softly as Lyra's revelation settled over the jury and gallery. Alice, mindful of the judge's earlier instructions to remain within the bounds of relevancy, carefully steered the questioning back to the charges against Chloe Smith and Kylie Morgan.

"Thank you, Mrs Smith," Alice said, her tone measured. "Now, focusing on the rest of the messages. Would you read out the message from Ishal Kabul."

Lyra knew that message by heart, as she had reread it numerous times since it had been shared in the chat. She took a deep breath and glanced at the evidence exhibit in front of her before reciting the message.

"Nott finally got fucked by the cum dump yesterday. I've seen the CCTV. She's got massive tits, ain't she?"

The tension in the courtroom was palpable as Lyra read out the message. The crude and invasive nature of the statement caused several jurors to shift uncomfortably in their seats. Sir Thomas Harvey's face remained impassive, but the tightness in his jaw betrayed his disapproval.

"And the response from Mr Lane?" Alice Cartwright prompted, her voice steady but pointed as she guided Lyra to continue.

Lyra hesitated for a moment, her voice faltering slightly as she read Cody Lane's response from the exhibit. "'Double F's for a guess,'" she recited quietly, her cheeks flushing with a mix of anger and humiliation. "And then Felix wrote 'Reevesy could bury his cock in her tits and they'd still be sticking out. After all, he's 10 inches, isn't he? He's probably ruined her pussy for the rest of us.'. That was then followed by Penny L... I mean, Penny O'Rourke as she is now, as she got married in June before she gave birth to her and James's baby, Alfie James O'Rourke, in July 2025." Lyra paused, collecting herself before continuing, her tone laced with both frustration and determination. "Penny's message said, 'You know, she'd be the fourth one that Reevesy's got preggers since he started here.'"

The courtroom remained silent as Lyra's words hung in the air, the jurors visibly uncomfortable with the explicit and deeply invasive nature of the comments. Alice gave Lyra a moment to compose herself before proceeding.

"I will now play a video, for the jury, of the next message of the conversation, a video posted by Ms Chloe Smith in that chat."

The court grew still as Alice signalled to the usher to prepare the exhibit. A large screen to the side of the courtroom lit up, the courtroom atmosphere tense with anticipation. Lyra's hands clutched the edge of the witness stand, her knuckles white as she braced herself for the evidence that was about to play.

"Your Honour," Alice said, turning to Sir Thomas. "With your permission, we will now play Exhibit 16, a video shared by Ms Chloe Smith in the 'Gals and Geezers' chat on the 16th of April 2025."

The judge gave a solemn nod. "Proceed."

The video began to play. The grainy footage depicted James in what was clearly a degrading and coerced act, of him giving a blowjob worn by his sister, Chloe. Chloe's mocking voice could be heard faintly in the background, making crude comments as James's humiliation unfolded.

The courtroom was silent save for the audio from the video. Several jurors turned pale, their discomfort evident as they watched. Lyra kept her gaze fixed ahead, refusing to look at the screen but not shying away from the moment. She owed it to James—and to herself—to stay strong.

"You're a right whore, big bro," Chloe's voice mocked on the video, her tone dripping with malice. "You love it, don't you? Always knew you'd end up like this. And you know what? So does Kylie. She's already got plans for you tonight."

The video then showed Chloe's hand on James's head, forcing him to choke on the strap-on, her laughter echoing cruelly through the room as James's muffled protests were audible. The video cut off abruptly, leaving the courtroom in a heavy silence. The visceral nature of the evidence left a palpable unease among the jurors, and even some members of the public gallery looked visibly shaken.

Alice turned to face the jury, her expression grave. "Ladies and gentlemen of the jury, this video demonstrates the abusive power dynamics at play and the toxic culture at Manic Radio, where individuals like Ms Chloe Smith and Ms Kylie Morgan felt emboldened to exploit others without fear of consequences."

196

She turned her attention back to Lyra, who had taken a moment to collect herself, her face pale but resolute. "Mrs Smith, following this incident, you received a telephone call from Ms Morgan, correct?"

Lyra nodded, her voice steady but her expression strained. "Yes, that's correct. It was later that day, around noon. Kylie called me after the messages and video were shared in the group chat."

Alice Cartwright stepped closer to the witness stand, ensuring the jury could see Lyra's resolute composure despite the subject matter. "What was the nature of that call, Mrs Smith?"

Lyra hesitated briefly, her hands tightening over her belly. "Kylie was... mocking, as usual. She said she'd seen the messages and the video, and she made it clear she approved of what had happened. But then she turned her attention to me. She said that James was, and I quote, 'a perfect little puppet' and that if I wanted him released from their games, I'd have to make some sacrifices."

Alice raised her eyebrows, her tone calm but probing. "Sacrifices? Could you clarify what she meant by that?"

"That I become the hub cum dump. That I let everyone have a turn with me—male or female, presenter, or producer, doesn't matter. Full access, no limits."

****

CHAPTER 15 – Answering to the Defence

Saturday 22nd November 2025

Lyra was sat, eating a cheese sandwich, the hunger that her pregnancy brought overriding her nerves. The witness room was quiet save for the soft hum of the vending machine in the corner. She knew she had to keep her energy up, especially with how emotionally and physically draining the morning session had been. She knew that she had to go back on the witness stand for the cross examination, and that she would have to be prepared for whatever tricks the defence barristers might throw her way. The calm of the witness room provided a brief reprieve, but the looming pressure of her testimony weighed heavily on her. She placed the sandwich down carefully on its wrapper, wiping her hands on a napkin, and took a sip of water.

The door opened quietly, and Theodore, her elder brother, stepped in, his face a mixture of concern and encouragement. "I've chatted to James... he's taking Cory to Sarehole Mill for the afternoon," he said softly, and Lyra knew that her 3 month old stepdaughter was in good hands.

Sarehole Mill, Lyra remembered from her GCSE English, was the inspiration for J.R.R. Tolkien's The Shire in The Lord of the Rings. She smiled faintly, imagining James wandering around the mill's serene grounds with little Cory in her pram, giving her a much-needed escape from the intensity of their current lives.

"That's good," she replied, her voice quiet but steady. "She deserves a bit of peace, even if we can't seem to find any ourselves."

Theodore nodded, sitting down across from her and smoothing his tailored suit. His presence was calming, a reminder of the support she had in her corner. "How are you holding up?" he asked, his tone carefully neutral.

Lyra sighed, running a hand over her rounded belly. "I'm doing the best I can, Theo. It's just… it's all so much. The things they said in that chat, the video, the messages—it's vile. And now I have to go back in there and let them pick me apart."

Theodore reached out, resting a comforting hand on hers. "Remember, Lyra, you're not the one on trial. You're here to tell the truth, to stand up for James and expose what's been going on. They'll try to rattle you, but you've got this."

Lyra nodded, drawing strength from his words. "I know. It's just hard... I just know that the Defence will bring up how I volunteered to become the "hub cum dump" in those messages. Even though I was trying to shield James and get him out of their sick games, I know they'll twist it to make me look complicit."

Theodore's expression hardened, his usual calm demeanour tinged with anger. "Lyra, listen to me. The defence barristers will do everything they can to undermine you, but they can't erase the truth. The messages show coercion, manipulation, and abuse—not your complicity. You were protecting James, and that's clear to anyone with a shred of humanity."

Lyra took a deep breath, feeling the weight of his words settle over her. "Thanks, Theo. I just need to focus on the facts, don't I?"

"Exactly," Theodore said, giving her hand a reassuring squeeze. "Stick to what you know, stay composed, and don't let them bait you into reacting emotionally. You're stronger than you realise."

The door opened again, and a court usher appeared, clipboard in hand. "Mrs Lyra Smith, we're ready for you in court," she announced, her voice professional yet kind.

Lyra stood, smoothing her maternity dress and giving Theodore a small smile. "Wish me luck."

"You don't need it, Lyly," Theodore replied, using his childhood nickname for her. "You've got the truth on your side. Go show them that."

Lyra nodded, her resolve solidifying as she followed the usher out of the witness room. The corridor was quiet, save for the distant hum of voices from the courtroom. She took a deep breath, steadying herself as they approached the heavy wooden doors. The usher pushed them open, and Lyra stepped into the courtroom, her eyes briefly scanning the room before settling on the witness stand.

The air in the courtroom was tense, the weight of the trial palpable. The jury watched her closely, their expressions a mix of curiosity and empathy. Chloe and Kylie sat in the dock, their demeanours as contrasting as ever—Chloe stiff and pale, while Kylie looked smugly disinterested, lazily twirling a strand of hair between her fingers. Cody, seated apart from them, avoided her gaze, his expression a mask of feigned indifference.

Sir Thomas Harvey, presiding with his usual composed authority, gestured for Lyra to take her seat in the witness box. She climbed the steps carefully, her hand instinctively resting on her belly as she sat down. The clerk approached, holding out the Bible.

"Do you swear by Almighty God that the evidence you shall give will be the truth, the whole truth, and nothing but the truth?" the clerk asked.

Lyra nodded firmly, her voice steady as she replied. "I do."

Alice Cartwright, the Crown's barrister, gave Lyra a reassuring nod before returning to her seat. Sir Thomas turned to the defence table. "Ms Hunt, you may proceed with your cross-examination."

Victoria Hunt, representing Chloe and Kylie, rose gracefully, her sharp eyes fixed on Lyra as she approached the centre of the courtroom. Her voice was smooth, but there was a steely edge to her tone.

"Mrs Smith," Victoria began, her words measured, "let me take you to the middle of the morning on 29th October 2024, when you first met James Smith, his first day at Manic Radio."

Lyra took a steadying breath, her eyes fixed on the barrister. "Yes, I remember that day," she replied, her voice calm but resolute. "It was the Dudley hub back then, at The Waterfront in Brierley Hill. James was dating Kylie Morgan then."

Victoria's lips curled into a small smile as she clasped her hands behind her back, pacing deliberately. "Indeed, he was. And you, Mrs Smith, were working as a presenter at the same hub, were you not?"

"That's correct," Lyra said, keeping her tone even.

"Now, can you name who was in the break room that day when Mr Smith joined the team?" Victoria's voice was calm, but there was an undertone suggesting she was building toward something.

Lyra paused, recalling the scene with precision. "Yes, I can. Kylie Morgan, Cody Lane, Al Crozier, and a few others whose shifts overlapped. It was a busy hub; there were always people coming and going. At the time we had breakfast shows on Derbyshire Delight, Mid Wales Manic, Warwickshire Stars, Northants Now, Midlands Manic, Northern Vibes and East Midlands Vibes and drivetime shows on Midlands Manic, which was presented by Pete Smith, my show with Al Crozier on Northern Vibes and Tim Young and Ellen Fisher's show on East Midlands Vibes. The break room was a common area where presenters and producers mingled between shifts."

Victoria nodded, her expression neutral, though her eyes gleamed with calculation. "Quite the bustling environment. And yet, amidst this, you claim to have noticed James Smith immediately, even though you were surrounded by other colleagues. Is that correct?"

Lyra met her gaze without flinching. "Yes, I noticed him... because, in retrospect, Kylie was controlling him. She had persuaded him to go public with their relationship after hiding it for 2 years. It wasn't difficult to see that he was nervous, almost out of place, while Kylie thrived in the spotlight, revelling in the attention of their newly revealed 'power couple' status. Plus, he was the son of Pete Smith, a colleague who in the 2 years prior to James joining Manic, I had looked up to as someone who was more sensible than most of the new recruits that Manic brought in."

Victoria raised a brow, her lips curving into a faint smile. "Interesting. So, you were not only observant of Mr Smith's nervousness but also attuned to Miss Morgan's behaviour. Would you say, Mrs Smith, that you were already forming opinions about their relationship dynamic on that very first day?"

Lyra straightened her back slightly, sensing the line of questioning but refusing to be rattled. "I wouldn't call them 'opinions' at the time. It was more an observation. I noticed dynamics between colleagues—it's natural in a workplace like ours, especially one as high-pressure as Manic."

Victoria tilted her head. "High-pressure, you say? Could you elaborate on that?"

Lyra nodded, keeping her tone measured. "Yes, high-pressure. Manic Radio had a culture where image and branding were everything. Presenters were expected to maintain a public persona, both on and off-air, and there was a lot of scrutiny—whether that was from management, listeners, or peers. It wasn't always conducive to a healthy work environment. There was an unofficial work uniform we had to wear, one which I didn't abide by as I didn't believe in making myself look like I was for rent."

Lyra noted the sniggers from the public gallery at her remark, but she maintained her composure, ignoring the distraction. Victoria's smile faltered slightly, but she pressed on, her voice sharpening.

"Mrs Smith, your choice of words is… vivid. Can you describe the alleged uniform that you referred to? Specifically, what made it seem inappropriate or, as you put it, akin to being 'for rent'?"

Lyra met Victoria's gaze with quiet determination. "Certainly. For women, the expectation was to wear tight, short dresses or skirts paired with high heels. The outfits were often chosen more for their visual appeal on social media posts and promotional appearances than for professionalism or comfort. It was unspoken, but clear: the more you conformed to the 'Manic look,' the better your chances of being favoured for opportunities. Don't get me wrong, there was no official dress code, and Pete was one of those who wore a shirt and tie to work, Tim a polo shirt and smart jeans and Ellen a blazer and pencil skirt. But for many of us women, there was a pressure to present ourselves in a way that aligned with the image Manic wanted to project—youthful, attractive, and marketable. It was less about professionalism and more about appearances."

"But is it not true," Victoria said, and Lyra noticed that she paused for effect, her tone shifting to one of faux sympathy, "that all three media groups, Manic, Bauer and Global, have similar expectations for their on-air talent? Would you not agree that the demand for presenters to maintain a certain aesthetic is an industry standard, not something unique to Manic Radio?"

"Depends on if you call crotchless panties or strap-on dildos part of that aesthetic," Lyra said sharply, her voice tinged with a mix of frustration and resolve. The courtroom fell silent, the weight of her words hanging in the air like a thundercloud. Even Sir Thomas Harvey glanced up sharply, his otherwise impassive expression betraying a flicker of surprise.

Victoria blinked, momentarily thrown off her polished facade, before quickly regaining her composure. "Mrs Smith," she began, her voice measured but with a noticeable edge, "that is quite the accusation. Are you implying that Manic Radio encouraged or endorsed such... inappropriate attire?"

Lyra held her ground, her voice steady and clear. "I'm not implying anything, Ms Hunt. I'm stating what I observed and experienced. During a team-building weekend in Birmingham in late 2022, several female presenters, including myself, were sent 'costumes' for a themed event. The outfits were not only demeaning but also explicitly sexualised. I refused to wear mine. Others felt pressured to conform because they feared being ostracised or overlooked for opportunities. Instead, I just wore a short skirt and a thin t-shirt just to avoid being too ostracised."

"And she looked hot as fuck," Abdul Zahir, who was sat in the public gallery, blurted out before being swiftly silenced by a sharp glare from Sir Thomas Harvey and a stern rebuke. "Order in the court!" Sir Thomas demanded, rapping his gavel against the bench. "One more outburst like that, and you will be removed."

The interruption briefly shifted the tension in the room, but Lyra remained focused, her expression unyielding. Victoria exhaled audibly, recalibrating her approach.

"Mrs Smith," Victoria resumed, her tone now clipped, "while I appreciate your candour, your statements paint a picture that may be seen as subjective interpretation rather than objective fact. Can you provide documented evidence or corroboration to support these claims of coercion and inappropriate expectations?"

"And get treated like a grass? If I had reported it to HR, then I would have been blacklisted or driven out like so many others. Because of Manic, because of Kylie, I lost the job I had been given at Hits Radio before I even started."

"Ah, yes, the claim that Manic Radio interfered with your career progression," Victoria interrupted, her voice dripping with scepticism. "Mrs Smith, would you agree that claims of this nature are easy to make but difficult to prove? After all, it is not unusual for employers, especially in competitive industries, to receive feedback about prospective hires. Is it not possible that Bauer

Media made their decision based on factors entirely unrelated to your time at Manic? Do you have any proof, Mrs Smith, that the withdrawal of Bauer Media's offer was directly influenced by Manic Radio or any of the individuals you have accused of interference?"

"Yes, I did a GDPR request to Bauer Media and obtained copies of correspondence related to my job offer," Lyra said firmly, her voice steady. "Among the documents was an email sent by Kylie to Bauer Media's Talent Acquisition team. In that email, she referred to me as 'a risk' and shared fabricated allegations about my character and conduct during my time at Manic. This email directly influenced Bauer's decision to withdraw their offer. I have submitted this email as evidence to the court."

"Yes, the redacted email that someone using a Manic Radio email address," Victoria paused, the courtroom's air thick with anticipation as she adjusted her stance and continued. "The email in question, Mrs Smith, has been submitted as evidence. However, as you are aware, the sender's identity remains redacted. Are you asking the court to take your word that the author of this email was indeed Miss Morgan?"

"Well, I'm sure that the Compliance Officer at Bauer could happily testify-"

"Mrs Smith," Victoria interrupted sharply, cutting off Lyra's response, "the court is not here to speculate about potential witnesses. It is here to deal in evidence and facts. If the Compliance Officer at Bauer Media has not been called to testify, then we must proceed with the evidence before us. Now, this email—redacted as it is—contains allegations that you engaged in inappropriate conduct at Manic Radio. Is it not possible, Mrs Smith, that such allegations could stem from multiple sources, not solely Miss Morgan?"

"Objection, your honour," Alice Cartwright, the Crown's Barrister, said. "Mr Brant, the Assistant Compliance Officer who provided the information to Mrs Smith is scheduled to testify later in these proceedings and will confirm the origin of the email. Counsel for the defence is pre-empting testimony that is yet to be given. Furthermore, the unredacted email is under exhibit 143."

Sir Thomas adjusted his glasses and turned to Victoria Hunt. "Ms Hunt, the Crown's objection is sustained. I remind you to base your questioning on the evidence already presented or the witness testimony given thus far. You may proceed, but tread carefully."

Victoria nodded, her face composed but her frustration evident in the slight tightening of her jaw. "Understood, Your Honour." She took a step back and smoothed her robe, recalibrating her strategy.

"Mrs Smith," Victoria began again, her tone now more deliberate, "I would like to take you back now to the 15th of April 2025. You and Mr Smith had sexual intercourse for the first time, correct?"

Lyra's expression didn't falter as she met Victoria Hunt's gaze head-on. "Yes, that is correct," she replied evenly, her tone calm despite the deeply personal nature of the question.

Victoria clasped her hands behind her back, her pacing deliberate. "And this occurred, according to your earlier statement, in a recording booth at the One Snow Hill hub in Birmingham during a highly inappropriate set of circumstances?"

"That is also correct," Lyra said, her voice unwavering. "Though I would like to clarify-"

"Is it not the fact that you, jealous of my client, partook in sexual intercourse with Mr Smith not because you wanted to help him but because you sought to manipulate him, control him, and tarnish my client's reputation in the process?" Victoria interrupted, her voice laced with accusatory fervour. "After all, you married Mr Smith within 3 months of the alleged event, and that that sexual intercourse was only to take advantage of Manic's policy where they would provide a cash payout to each expectant mother, so long as conception of a child was at an approved event or on company property?"

Lyra raised her chin slightly, her gaze steady and unwavering despite the offensive insinuation. "No, Ms Hunt," she replied firmly, her voice cutting through the tension in the courtroom. "That is categorically untrue. My actions were neither motivated by jealousy nor manipulation. My decision to have sexual intercourse with James that day was not calculated or premeditated— it was an emotional reaction to months of witnessing his degradation and abuse at the hands of your client and others. It was borne out of care, not malice or self-interest."

"I put it to you, Mrs Smith, that you took advantage of Mr Smith's vulnerable state to manipulate him for your own gain," Victoria said, her voice rising slightly as she pressed her point. "You capitalised on his isolation, his fragile emotional condition, and his estrangement from his father to insert yourself into his life. Would you not agree, Mrs Smith, that such actions are not the actions of a supportive colleague but rather of someone seeking personal advantage?"

Lyra's face remained calm, her resolve unshaken. "No, I do not agree," she said firmly, her voice carrying a quiet strength that filled the courtroom. "James was in a deeply vulnerable state because of the actions of your client and others. I stepped in to help him, to offer him a way out of the toxic and abusive environment that he had been trapped in. My actions were motivated by compassion and concern for his well-being, not by self-interest."

Victoria tilted her head slightly, her expression sceptical. "Compassion and concern, you say? Yet your actions resulted in a relationship that escalated to marriage within mere months. A cynic might say, Mrs Smith, that such rapid developments suggest ulterior motives—financial gain, perhaps, given your knowledge of Manic's policy on payouts for expectant mothers."

"Objection, your Honour, my learned friend is leading the witness and making baseless accusations without evidence," Alice interjected, her voice sharp but composed. "The witness has already addressed the motivations for her actions. Counsel for the defence is attempting to cast aspersions rather than focus on the facts."

Sir Thomas adjusted his glasses once again, his tone firm but measured. "Ms Hunt, you are cautioned to avoid conjecture and to focus your questioning on substantiated matters. The objection is sustained. Please rephrase or move on."

Victoria nodded curtly, though her lips tightened ever so slightly. "As Your Honour pleases." She paused, gathering herself before continuing in a more measured tone.

"Mrs Smith, let us return to the specific policies at Manic Radio. You have testified that you were aware of the company's payout policy for expectant mothers under certain conditions. Do you deny that this policy influenced your actions at all?"

Lyra met her gaze steadily. "Yes, I am denying it," she said firmly. "While I was aware of the policy, it had no bearing on my actions or my relationship with James. I admit that, when he joined that I had a crush-"

"Ah ha, so your interest in Mr Smith predated his alleged victimisation, and thus your actions may have been driven by personal desires rather than altruism?" Victoria interjected sharply, seizing on Lyra's words. "And you claimed you were in a relationship with a Si Wilcox at the time back in October 2024, and that when Mr Wilcox and you split up in January 2025, you turned your desires full focus onto Mr Smith, exploiting his vulnerability to initiate a relationship for your own personal gain?"

Lyra sighed, gathering her composure as she prepared to counter Victoria's accusations. Her voice was steady, though tinged with quiet frustration. "Ms Hunt, I won't deny that I found James attractive when he joined Manic Radio, nor will I deny that my relationship with Si Wilcox ended around the time you mentioned. However, my actions towards James were not driven by any ulterior motives or personal agenda. When I stepped in to support him, it was because I saw someone in need of help—a colleague being degraded and manipulated in ways that no one should endure. My personal feelings did not cloud my judgement or my intentions."

Victoria's sharp gaze remained fixed on Lyra, but her tone softened slightly, becoming more probing than accusatory. "Mrs Smith, you've painted yourself as a protector, someone acting out of altruism. Yet, in doing so, you entered into an intimate relationship with Mr Smith—someone who, by your own admission, was in a vulnerable state. Do you not see how that might be construed as an imbalance of power, as a decision that could be seen as exploitative, even if unintended?"

Lyra paused, choosing her words carefully. "I understand how it might appear from the outside, Ms Hunt. But the reality was very different. James and I connected as equals, as two people seeking to find solace and support in each other during a difficult time. Our relationship wasn't about power or exploitation; it was about mutual understanding and care. I did not manipulate him, nor did I take advantage of his vulnerability. If anything, I gave him the strength to regain control of his own life."

Victoria tilted her head, a faint smirk playing on her lips as she sat at her position in the defence's table. "You paint a rather idealised picture, Mrs Smith. However, the court must consider all possibilities. Now, let me take you to the 16th of April. You alleged that the WhatsApp messages from the Manic Radio group chat escalated into targeted harassment against both you and James Smith, culminating in deeply inappropriate and degrading comments. Can you clarify exactly how these messages impacted your decision-making and mental state during that day?"

Lyra exhaled, her hand resting protectively over her belly as she steadied herself. "Yes, I can," she said firmly. "The messages weren't just cruel—they were a calculated form of humiliation designed to isolate James and control him further. The things said in that group chat—insinuations, slurs, and threats—weren't just words. They were part of a larger culture at Manic Radio, a culture that thrived on degrading and exploiting individuals for entertainment and control."

"Are you sure it was not just the usual banter between work colleagues, Mrs Smith?" Victoria Hunt interrupted, her tone pointed but maintaining an air of feigned neutrality. "After all, workplaces often have camaraderie that includes playful teasing. Are you not over-exaggerating the severity of these interactions?"

Lyra's expression hardened, her voice unwavering as she replied. "No, Ms Hunt, it was not 'playful teasing' or 'camaraderie.' What I witnessed and experienced was systematic humiliation and targeted abuse. These were not harmless jokes or banter—they were designed to degrade, isolate, and control. There is no workplace camaraderie in spreading private, intimate images and making vile comments about a colleague's body or personal life. The messages went beyond professional boundaries and into the realm of abuse."

"And this alleged hub cum dump role you volunteered for, I put it to you, Mrs Smith, that as you had lost your virginity with Mr Smith, you wanted to, so to speak, put yourself on the market for other Manic employees. After all, you had the WhatsApp messages indicating your willingness to participate in such activities, did you not?"

Lyra's face flushed with a mix of frustration and anger, but she maintained her composure. Her voice was resolute as she replied, "No, Ms Hunt. The messages you are referring to were sent in a moment of desperation when I was trying to protect James. I never had any intention of becoming what you so crudely describe as 'on the market.' My actions were calculated to create an opportunity to extract James from a deeply toxic and abusive environment. Those messages were manipulated and taken out of context by people who wanted to humiliate and control me."

Victoria raised an eyebrow, her lips curling into a sceptical smirk. "So, Mrs Smith, you are claiming that your own words, written willingly in a group chat, were merely part of some grand plan to save Mr Smith? Forgive me if that seems rather implausible."

Lyra leaned forward slightly, her voice steady but tinged with defiance. "What I am claiming, Ms Hunt, is that the environment at Manic Radio was so oppressive, so toxic, that I felt I had no other choice. I made those statements because I believed it was the only way to shield James and gain leverage over those who were exploiting him. It was a calculated risk, not an indication of my personal desires or character. The reality of what James endured, and what I witnessed, goes far beyond anything that can be reduced to your cynical interpretation of my actions."

The courtroom was silent for a moment, the tension thick in the air. Even the jury seemed captivated by Lyra's composed but passionate defence of her actions. Victoria, undeterred, adjusted her posture and moved on.

"Mrs Smith, let us address another aspect of your testimony. You have stated that the culture at Manic Radio was uniquely toxic and abusive. Yet you chose to remain there for several years. Can you explain why you continued to work in an environment you now describe as so unbearable?"

Lyra took a deep breath, her eyes briefly flicking to the jury before returning to Victoria. "I stayed because I believed that, despite its flaws, Manic Radio had potential. I loved my work, my listeners, and the idea of connecting with people through radio. Furthermore, there wasn't any positions open at Bauer or Global, and the BBC wasn't hiring as they are currently having cuts to their budgets thanks to the previous Conservative government's austerity measures. Leaving a job without a clear alternative wasn't feasible, especially in a competitive industry like broadcasting. But over time, the environment at Manic became increasingly toxic—particularly after the restructuring in 2022, when the culture shifted from one of teamwork and creativity to one driven by manipulation, exploitation, and branding above all else."

"At the time, Tom Green, the mid-morning presenter on Hits Radio, was considering leaving, and I had applied to Bauer to replace him," Lyra continued, her tone steady but tinged with frustration. "I saw an opportunity to move to a station with a better reputation for professionalism and support for its employees. A close friend of mine works for Bauer at Hits Radio and had told me about openings, so I applied. When I was offered the position, it felt like a lifeline—an escape from the toxic environment at Manic. But, as I've already stated, that opportunity was taken from me due to interference from Kylie Morgan and others at Manic. Their deliberate actions ensured I couldn't leave, trapping me in an environment that was actively harming not just me but many others, including James."

Victoria's eyes narrowed slightly, sensing that Lyra's steadfast testimony was resonating with the jury. "Mrs Smith," she said, her voice softening slightly, as if attempting to feign understanding, "you've painted a compelling picture of systemic toxicity at Manic Radio. However, would you not agree that some level of competition, banter, and pressure is inherent to any high-performing workplace, especially in an industry as fast-paced as broadcasting?"

Lyra shook her head, her expression resolute. "There's a difference between professional competition and targeted humiliation, Ms Hunt. A difference between healthy workplace camaraderie and an environment that actively degrades and manipulates its employees. What happened at Manic Radio wasn't pressure to perform—it was abuse disguised as workplace culture."

Victoria paused, letting the courtroom settle before speaking again. "Mrs Smith, one final question. You've spoken extensively about James Smith's suffering and the actions you took to support him. But isn't it true that, by entering into a romantic relationship with him while he was in such a vulnerable state, you may have inadvertently perpetuated the very imbalance of power you claim to have opposed?"

Lyra met Victoria's gaze head-on, her voice unwavering. "No, Ms Hunt. Our relationship wasn't about power. It was about mutual support. James and I found strength in each other during a time when both of us were being targeted by the toxic environment you're defending. If anything, our relationship was a step towards reclaiming the autonomy and dignity that Manic Radio tried so hard to strip away from us."

Victoria's expression tightened slightly, her composure slipping for just a moment before she turned back to her table. "No further questions, Your Honour."

Sir Thomas Harvey nodded and turned his attention to Lyra. "Mrs Smith, you may step down."

Lyra exhaled deeply, feeling the tension in her body begin to ease as she stood. She avoided looking at Kylie and Chloe as she made her way back to the witness room, her mind replaying the exchange in the courtroom. Theodore was waiting for her, his expression a mix of pride and concern.

"You held your ground, Lyly," he said quietly, giving her hand a reassuring squeeze. "No one could have done better."

Lyra managed a small smile, though her exhaustion was evident. "Thanks, Theo. I just hope the jury sees through their games."

As she sat back down in the witness room, she felt the weight of the trial settle over her once more. But for the first time in weeks, she allowed herself a flicker of hope.

The truth was out there now, and with every word spoken in that courtroom, she felt one step closer to justice—not just for James, but for everyone who had suffered under Manic's toxic reign.

****

CHAPTER 16 - A Weekend of Reflection

Saturday 22nd November 2025

James noticed his dad was being elusive, especially after the postman had come with the post and Pete had put the letter into his coat pocket without opening it. Pete had been unusually quiet all morning, busying himself with small tasks around the house—tidying the living room, reorganising the books on the shelf, and tinkering with the old radio that sat in the corner. James, seated at the kitchen table with a lukewarm cup of tea, watched his father's movements with a growing sense of unease.

"Dad, are you alright?" James asked cautiously, his voice breaking the silence that had settled over the room.

Pete paused mid-motion, the screwdriver in his hand hovering over the radio. He glanced at James briefly before resuming his work. "I'm fine, lad," he replied, his tone light but unconvincing.

James wasn't buying it. "You've been fidgeting all morning. What was in that letter?"

Pete sighed, setting down the screwdriver and rubbing the back of his neck. "It's nothing to worry about. Just some paperwork I need to deal with."

James raised an eyebrow. "Paperwork that's making you avoid eye contact and rearrange books that haven't been touched in years?"

Pete's lips twitched into a faint smile at his son's persistence, but it quickly faded. He reached into his coat pocket and chuckled before withdrawing it without bringing anything from the pocket.

"Let's just say, I'm under strict orders to not say anything until the 1st of next year. Orders not from the Police... but... well, I can't say... all I can say is that I'll be taking your mum down to London for the New Year... for a very important meeting. Anyway, fancy listening to what mess Manic make of the Goldies West Midlands footie phone-in that used to be mine until earlier this month?"

"You mean your Wolves love-in where Villa fans used to call in to shout how you were that 'gold and black, you'd be giving penalties to Wolves for a simple tackle in a Derby? Oh, didn't you see on Instagram... it's been cancelled. Replaced with a network 100 Classic Hits Countdown," James said, pulling the post up on his phone. He scrolled to find the Instagram post from the official Manic Goldies account, showing a flashy graphic announcing the "Top 100 Classic Hits Countdown with Pete Smith".

James watched as his dad's face went from curious to furious as Pete read the post. His eyebrows knitted together, and his jaw tightened as he set the phone down on the kitchen counter with a sharp exhale.

"Unbelievable," Pete muttered, his voice thick with irritation. "They didn't even tell me they were using my name for that nonsense. I handed in my resignation to avoid being part of their corporate circus, and now they're dragging my name back into it without a word... unless they've used one of my banked voice tracked shows?"

James knew that, even though he had been suspended by Manic between April and October, and had not had his own contract renewed, Manic were still airing shows that he had voice tracked, with no obvious edits that he could discern. It was one of the many ways Manic continued to wield control over its former employees, even after they had left the network.

Looking elsewhere on the Manic Prime app, James had a feeling that his links for Manic Linkin Park, one of the curated micro-stations dedicated to a specific artist, were still live, ones that he had recorded the previous December and had been inserted a few weeks after they had been recorded. Loading up the specific station, James waited for In the End to finish, as he knew that he had delivered a 2 minute link for Crawling. As the last haunting notes of In the End faded out, James listened intently, leaning forward slightly as his own voice, recorded nearly a year ago, filled the room.

"You're listening to Manic Linkin Park, the station dedicated to all things Chester, Mike, and the gang. That was In the End, one of the most iconic tracks of the early 2000s. Now, one of the things I like about the album Hybrid Theory, which this track was from, is how raw and emotional it is. It really captures that mix of angst and hope, which resonated with so many people at the time. Up next, its track number 9 from the same album, with A Place for My Head. One thing people don't know about that track is how it almost didn't make the cut for the album. Mike Shinoda once said in an interview that they fought hard to include it because it encapsulated their sound so perfectly. Anyway, here it is: A Place for My Head on Manic Linkin Park, where the music never stops."

The sound of the 2000 track filled the kitchen, but James wasn't listening to the song anymore. His jaw tightened as he replayed the implications of what he'd just heard. "The music never stops" felt less like a tagline and more like a sinister mantra. Manic Radio, it seemed, had no intention of letting go of its former talent, even when their voices were no longer willingly part of the network.

James then turned to Manic Dua Lipa, where he had the feeling Lyra had voice-tracked a segment before her departure. As he queued up the station on Manic Prime, James braced himself for the next unsettling discovery. Sure enough, as "Levitating" faded out, Lyra's familiar voice chimed in, bright and engaging despite the fact it had been recorded months ago.

"That was Levitating, a track that keeps reminding us why Dua Lipa is the queen of modern pop. We're going through every track Dua has done, no matter the album, here on Manic Dua Lipa, and up next off Future Nostalgia is Pretty Please, a track which was inspired by Dua's desire to capture vulnerability and sensuality in a way that feels raw and honest. It's one of those songs that really showcases her growth as an artist. Stick around, because we've got more hits and deep cuts coming your way on Manic Dua Lipa."

James let out a frustrated sigh, rubbing his temples as the track began to play. Lyra's voice sounded so upbeat and professional, a reminder of the passion and dedication she had poured into her work—even as the toxicity of Manic Radio loomed in the background. The fact that her voice, too, was being used without her consent only deepened his anger.

"They're still using her voice, too," James muttered, glancing at Pete, whose expression darkened further. "It's like they're determined to squeeze every last drop out of us, even when we're gone."

Pete leaned back against the kitchen counter, his arms crossed as he stared at the floor. "It's not just exploitation; it's control," he said bitterly. "They want to keep their grip on us, to remind us that even when we leave, we're still part of their machine."

James nodded, feeling the weight of his father's words. "Do you think it's deliberate? Like they're trying to undermine us, keep us tied to them so we can't move on?"

Pete sighed heavily, running a hand through his greying hair. "I don't know if it's a deliberate scheme or just their standard way of operating. Either way, it's a reminder of why I left, why you left, and why Lyra was desperate to get out. Manic doesn't care about people—just their image and profits."

James clenched his fists, his anger bubbling just beneath the surface. "There has to be something we can do. This isn't just unethical—it's borderline illegal. Using someone's voice without their consent, continuing to profit off them after they've left... there has to be a way to fight back."

"Look at your contract, James. It's in there, or should be," Pete said, his tone weary but resolute. "Manic's contracts are watertight when it comes to intellectual property and perpetuity clauses. They own everything we did while we were on their payroll—our voice tracks, our branding, even our ideas, if they can spin it that way. It's why they can keep airing your voice and Lyra's without so much as a phone call."

James's jaw tightened, his frustration growing. "But surely there's a limit? They can't just keep using us like this forever, can they?"

Pete shrugged, his expression a mix of resignation and anger. "Legally, maybe they can. Morally? It's despicable. But when has morality ever stopped Manic? They thrive on exploitation—it's their business model. Anyway, you've got a Zoom call with your little lad, haven't you?"

James sighed, as he knew that he was due to contact his son, Alfie, the child he fathered with Penny O'Rourke, who was only 3 months old and Cory's half sibling, however Penny had sent him a message the previous evening which had soured the mood.

"I did, but Penny sent me a WhatsApp. Apparently, a solicitor has advised her that while I'm involved as a witness next week in the cases against Chloe, Manic, Kylie and several others, I'm best off 'not contacting Alfie directly to avoid any potential complications with the ongoing proceedings.'" James's voice was heavy with frustration as he set his phone down on the table. "It's like they're trying to control every aspect of my life—even my relationship with my own son."

Pete frowned deeply, the lines on his face etched with concern. "That sounds like something her solicitor cooked up to play it safe, but it's bloody unfair to you and Alfie. You've got every right to stay in touch with him. Don't let the trial silence you as a father."

James sighed, rubbing the back of his neck. "I get that they're trying to avoid anything that could be spun by the defence, but it feels like another way for Manic's toxicity to bleed into my personal life. First, they tried to control my career, and now it's spilling over into my family."

Pete moved closer, placing a reassuring hand on James's shoulder. "You're fighting the good fight, lad. It's not going to be easy, but you're doing what's right for Alfie, Cory, and every other poor soul who's been dragged through Manic's mess. Don't let their games get into your head."

James nodded, grateful for his father's words but still feeling the weight of the situation pressing down on him. "I just want this to be over, Dad. For all of us. I want to move on, build a life for my kids where none of this hangs over their heads. Instead, I'm going to take Cory down to Merry Hill. I know she's only 3 months, but I was going to buy her a toy, and I thought I'd see if Mum or you fancy coming."

Pete gave James a small smile, his eyes softening. "That sounds like a plan, son. And don't underestimate how much just getting out of the house can do for you, too. Sometimes a bit of normality is exactly what you need to keep going. Why not take your mum, as I've got some... paperwork... to do about that letter I've had come in the mail." Pete's voice trailed off as he patted his coat pocket, a shadow of contemplation flickering across his face.

James nodded, sensing there was more to the letter than his father was letting on but deciding not to press further. "Alright, I'll see if Mum fancies a trip out. Maybe I can pick up something nice for Lyra while we're there too."

Pete's face softened further at the mention of Lyra, and he gave a small nod. "That'd be good, lad. She's been through hell these past few months. A little surprise might remind her that there's more to life than courtrooms and testimonies."

James smiled faintly. "Yeah. She deserves that—and so much more."

****

After James left with Sarah, Pete knew that Lyra was with her brother, Theodore, having some brother-sister time, the 27 year old that was his daughter-in-law and the soon-to-be mother of James's third child. Pete felt the silence of the house settle over him like a heavy blanket. With the letter still in his coat pocket, he sat at the kitchen table, staring at it as if it were a ticking time bomb.

The truth was, he knew that two of his friends in the radio industry had received the same letters in the past, and that he had back in 2019, but had responded in the negative. Now, the letter was back, and he suspected it carried the same proposition. The thought of reopening that chapter of his career, especially after all that had happened with Manic, left him conflicted.

Pete reached into his pocket and pulled out the envelope, his hands slightly trembling as he opened it. The letterhead was unmistakable—HM Government, Cabinet Office, Honours and Appointments Secretariat. Pete knew that he had had the same letter 6 years earlier, and that, as he was at the time an active broadcaster, instead of his current position as a soon to be programme director for Woody Bones's community radio network, he had chosen to decline the offer.

Honours and Appointments Secretariat

Cabinet Office

70 Whitehall, London SW1A 2AS

21 November 2025

Dear Mr Smith,

Following a recent review of the forthcoming New Year Honours List, I am delighted to inform you that you have been recommended for appointment as an Officer of the Most Excellent Order of the British Empire (OBE). This recognition reflects your outstanding contributions to the field of broadcasting, including your decades-long dedication to engaging, informative, and entertaining radio programming.

Should you choose to accept this honour, your name will be included in the New Year Honours List, due for publication on 1 January 2026. We kindly request that you keep this correspondence strictly confidential until that date.

To proceed, we ask that you complete the enclosed Acceptance Form and return it to the address provided by 5 December 2025. If you prefer to decline the honour, we ask that you notify us in writing by the same date.

We understand that this decision is deeply personal, and we respect the diverse perspectives individuals bring to such recognition. Should you have any questions, please do not hesitate to contact the Honours and Appointments Secretariat.

Yours sincerely,

Eleanor Cartwright

Secretary, New Year Honours Committee

Pete sat in silence, the letter resting on the table in front of him. His heart felt heavy, not with dread, but with the weight of the decision before him. The words on the page stirred a mix of emotions—pride, disbelief, and a deep sense of responsibility.

The irony that his close friends and fellow Midlanders, Les Ross and Carl Chinn, two of Birmingham's most recognisable broadcasting and academic figures, had also received honours, albeit MBEs instead of OBEs, was not lost on Pete. Both had graciously accepted their awards, Les for his illustrious broadcasting career and Carl for his dedication to the city's history and culture. Pete had always admired them, not just for their accolades but for the authenticity they brought to their respective fields.

He thought about the last six years since he declined the honour in 2019, a time when Breeze Media, the company that had brought Woody Bones' ILR radio network in 2010, was being brought out by Manic Radio in 2019. The culture at Manic had shifted rapidly in the years that followed, growing more corporate and exploitative with each passing day.

Pete had stayed on as long as he could, trying to maintain the values and integrity that had made local radio special, but the toxic environment eventually forced his hand. Now, the offer of an OBE felt like a bittersweet validation of his career—a recognition of all he had fought for, but also a stark reminder of how far the industry had fallen.

The other letter Pete had was from RAJAR, the Radio Audience Joint Research organisation, notifying him that he had gained another quarter of #1 in the Birmingham Drive slot before his resignation in early November.

Despite Manic Radio's toxic culture, Pete had managed to maintain the loyalty of his audience, a testament to his authenticity and connection with listeners. It was a small but meaningful reminder that his work had made a difference.

Pete leaned back in his chair, his gaze fixed on the letters. The OBE offer was an honour, one that he knew would mean a great deal to his family, especially James. After everything they had been through with Manic, this recognition felt like a glimmer of hope—an acknowledgment that their efforts hadn't been in vain. But accepting it also felt complicated.

Did he want his name associated with an industry that had caused his family so much pain? Could he reconcile the honour with the dark memories of his years at Manic?

He folded the letter carefully and slipped it back into the envelope, deciding he needed time to think.

James was wandering through Merry Hill shopping centre with his mum, Sarah, and baby Cory nestled in her pram. The bustle of the weekend crowd provided a welcome distraction from the weight of the trial. As they browsed the aisles of a toy shop, Sarah held up a soft teddy bear for Cory to inspect, earning a delighted giggle from the baby.

"She's already got a whole zoo of toys at home, Mum," James teased, though he couldn't help smiling at Cory's enthusiasm.

Sarah chuckled, placing the teddy bear back on the shelf. "You can never have too many cuddly friends, James. Especially for little ones like her."

James sighed, leaning against the pram handle. "I just want her to have a normal childhood, Mum. Something far removed from all this Manic mess."

Sarah placed a comforting hand on his arm. "She will, love. You and Lyra are building a good life for her, and that's what matters. The court case will pass, and you'll come out stronger on the other side."

James nodded, though the doubt lingered at the back of his mind. His phone buzzed in his pocket, and he pulled it out to find a message from Lyra.

Lyra: *Just finished catching up with Theo. He's as opinionated as ever but insists we'll be fine. How's Cory enjoying her shopping trip?*

James smiled at the message, typing a quick reply.

James: *She's in heaven—Mum's already picked out three toys for her. We're at Merry Hill. Let me know if there's anything you need me to grab for you or the baby.*

Lyra's reply came almost instantly.

Lyra: *A bath soak. Something indulgent. It's been a long week, and I could do with a little pampering.* 😊

James tucked his phone away, making a mental note to stop by a shop with bath products before they left. The thought of doing something small to brighten Lyra's day brought a flicker of warmth to his chest. Amidst the chaos of their lives, moments like this reminded him of what truly mattered.

As they wandered into another aisle, James spotted a bright pink pram toy that caught Cory's eye. He picked it up, holding it out for her to see. "What do you think, little one? Fancy adding this to your collection?"

Cory let out a delighted squeal, reaching out for the toy with tiny hands. James laughed, handing it to Sarah, who added it to their growing pile of purchases.

"She's got good taste," Sarah remarked with a grin. "Just like her dad."

****

CHAPTER 17 - Nerves
Monday 24th November 2025

James knew that it was his big day, that he would be required to testify in the cases of Manic's various companies, as well as his sister Chloe and his ex-girlfriend, Kylie. Sitting in the witness room, he knew that his mother, Sarah, was in the public gallery, as she had not been called by either side as a witness to the proceedings, and that as his dad and Lyra had already given their testimony, they would be at home looking after Cory.

Looking at the 1990s designed room in Birmingham Crown Court, James couldn't help but notice how dated and sterile it felt, with its grey walls and blue upholstery. The room had a faint hum of the fluorescent lights, and the occasional echo of footsteps from the corridor outside was the only sound. He fidgeted with the cuffs of his shirt, his nerves prickling as he mentally prepared for the daunting task ahead.

Looking round, he could see both several more witnesses for the prosecution like he was, as well as several manic presenters who were witnesses for the defence, and he shuddered as he spotted some familiar faces. These were people who had once been colleagues, even friends, but now they sat on the opposing side, ready to challenge his account of events.

Suddenly a woman he recognised ran into the witness room, completely out of breath, her hair dishevelled, and her face flushed. The woman, though flustered, immediately caught James's attention.

"James, is that you?"

James immediately felt guilt, as it was Lorna Perkins, someone who he had first met when he had stolen money from the student union bar till at university, had hired her when she was a prostitute, and had used her services. Later, she had resurfaced as a newsroom colleague at Manic. Their relationship had grown more complicated over time, culminating in the coercive situations she had been a part of during his darkest moments at Manic.

The irony that the first time the two had had to face each other outside the toxic environment of Manic Radio was here, at Birmingham Crown Court, was not lost on James. He felt a knot tighten in his stomach as he met Lorna's gaze. She looked frazzled but determined, her expression a mix of apprehension and something he couldn't quite place—regret, perhaps?

"Lorna," James said, his voice low and hesitant. "I didn't expect to see you here."

She let out a breathless chuckle, brushing a stray lock of hair from her face. "Nor did I, to be honest. But here we are. It's not exactly a reunion, is it?"

James swallowed hard, unsure of how to respond. The weight of their shared past loomed large between them, the unspoken words filling the sterile room.

"So, you got out I see?" James then said, sighing. "Where are you working now?"

Lorna hesitated for a moment, her eyes darting around the room before settling on James. "No, I'm still at Manic, still stuck in the newsroom at Manic Midlands. It's... complicated. After everything that's come out, it's not exactly a fun place to work anymore, but I didn't have the luxury of just walking away like you did." Her voice was tinged with bitterness, but there was also a trace of resignation. "Anyway, there's been some news there... Manic's sacked its CEO."

James's eyebrows shot up at Lorna's revelation. "They sacked the CEO?" he repeated, his voice a mix of surprise and curiosity. He hadn't expected such a dramatic shift, especially in the midst of the legal storm engulfing the company.

Lorna nodded, crossing her arms as if bracing herself. "Yes, effective immediately. The board announced it this morning. Apparently, the OFCOM investigation and everything that's come out during this trial was the last straw. They're trying to salvage the company's reputation, or whatever's left of it."

James let out a low whistle. "I didn't think they'd actually do it. I figured they'd try to protect him until the bitter end. Who's taking over?"

"Some Bernard guy, I don't know. Also, the owner is selling up. It was on BBC News this morning. Apparently Global are circling like sharks looking to buy Manic."

James felt a chill run through him at Lorna's words. Global Media, the behemoth of British commercial radio, known for its aggressive acquisitions and monopolistic tendencies, was circling Manic like a vulture over a dying carcass. The idea of Global taking over filled him with an unsettling mix of dread and resignation.

The fact that Global, a few days earlier, had made all its regional presenters redundant as the Media Act 2024, which Bauer had took advantage of the previous year when they made Greatest Hits Radio one national station, allowed them to automate most of their services, didn't fill James with confidence either. The prospect of Manic falling into Global's hands and undergoing the same corporate sterilisation and homogenisation made his stomach churn.

Loading up the BBC News app and heading into the Business section, James felt even more dread when he read the article.

Adam Banks to resign as CEO of Manic Radio Group, Ralph Bernard to Replace

In an early morning press release by Manic Radio Group, the company announced the immediate resignation of Adam Banks as Chief Executive Officer amid mounting scandals and the ongoing fallout from the trial at Birmingham Crown Court. Ralph Bernard, a veteran of the UK radio industry and former CEO of GWR Group, has been appointed as interim CEO, effective immediately.

The announcement comes as OFCOM's investigation into Manic Radio Group intensifies and shocking revelations continue to emerge during the trial of several key figures associated with the company. Insiders suggest that the decision to replace Banks was made under significant pressure from the board of directors and investors, eager to distance the company from its tarnished leadership.

In a related development, industry sources have revealed that Global Media, the largest commercial radio group in the UK, is in advanced discussions to acquire Manic Radio Group. If successful, the acquisition would consolidate Global's dominance over the UK radio market. However, such a move is expected to face scrutiny from the Competition and Markets Authority, given concerns over media plurality and monopolistic practices.

The trial continues to expose systemic issues within Manic Radio Group, including allegations of abuse, exploitation, and widespread misconduct. Former employees and whistleblowers have testified to a culture of coercion and control, with Banks and other executives at the centre of the controversy.

Manic Radio Group has not commented on the ongoing trial but stated that the leadership change is part of a broader effort to rebuild trust and integrity within the organisation. Meanwhile, Bernard is expected to oversee a major restructuring of the company and address its deeply entrenched problems.

James knew that Adam Banks was a former Brookes Vibes promotions manager who had risen through the ranks of Manic's predecessors. A former GWR Group employee, Banks had created i the 2000s a promotional group called the Brookes Babes, which became infamous for its ethically dubious stunts. Seeing his name in this context sent a shiver down James's spine. Banks's leadership style, deeply rooted in exploitation and profit over integrity, had clearly metastasised throughout the company.

Before James could fully digest the article, a court usher appeared at the door. The man, dressed in a dark suit, clipboard in hand, cleared his throat. "Mr James Smith?"

James stood, his legs feeling unsteady. "Yes, that's me."

"You're up next. Please follow me." The usher's tone was polite but firm, a subtle reminder of the gravity of the situation.

James nodded, giving Lorna a brief glance. "Good luck," she said softly, her earlier sharpness replaced with a trace of empathy.

"Thanks," James replied, his voice barely audible. He followed the usher down the sterile corridor, each step echoing ominously. The sound of his shoes against the tiled floor seemed louder than it should have been, mirroring the thundering of his heart.

As they approached the courtroom, James caught sight of Sarah through the open doors to the public gallery. She gave him a small, reassuring smile, her hands clasped tightly in her lap. James took a deep breath, straightening his posture as he stepped into the courtroom.

The room was a mixture of modern efficiency and traditional gravitas. The judge, wearing a wig and robes, presided from the bench. To one side, the prosecution team sat with their neatly organised files, their demeanours focused but calm. On the opposite side, the defence barristers whispered among themselves, occasionally glancing towards James with assessing eyes. Chloe and Kylie sat behind their legal team, their expressions unreadable.

James felt the weight of every eye in the courtroom as he made his way to the witness stand. The clerk approached with a Bible in hand, her voice steady as she asked, "Do you swear by Almighty God that the evidence you shall give will be the truth, the whole truth, and nothing but the truth?"

James nodded, his voice clear despite the nerves simmering beneath the surface. "I do."

As he settled into the witness box, the Crown's barrister, Alice Cartwright, stood and approached. Her professional demeanour exuded calm authority, and her eyes met James's with a reassuring steadiness.

"Mr Smith," she began, her tone firm but supportive, "can you confirm your position at Manic Radio Group prior to your departure?"

James straightened slightly, his hands gripping the edges of the witness box. "I was a presenter on a number of Manic's stations, such as Manic Dance, Manic Rock, Manic's micro stations and latterly Manic Urban. I joined in late 2024 and was suspended in April 2025, shortly before leaving the company."

Tuesday 29th October 2024

It was 6am, and James knew that the reason for his early arrival at the Waterfront hub in Dudley of Manic Radio's network was due to his induction schedule. The early morning air was brisk as he stepped into the 1990s building. The hub buzzed with a unique blend of energy: producers juggling schedules and a faint hum of technology permeating the air.

James was greeted at reception by Cal Ellington, the Central Regional Director for Manic, a tall man in his late 20s, early 30s, with a confident stride and a sharp suit. Cal's handshake was firm but brief, and his expression was a mix of professionalism and mild impatience.

"James, welcome to the team," Cal said, his tone clipped. "You're in for a busy day. Kylie is ready and waiting for you in the Warwickshire Stars studio, as I've decided that you'll be sitting in for the latter half of the breakfast show she and Tina do."

James nodded, trying to conceal the nervous excitement bubbling within him. He had spent weeks preparing for this moment, but the reality of stepping into Manic Radio's hub, surrounded by the relentless pace and curated chaos, was daunting. Cal's brisk tone left little room for pleasantries.

"Follow me," Cal instructed, leading James through a maze of corridors. The fluorescent lights buzzed softly overhead, casting a sterile glow that contrasted with the vibrant branding plastered on the walls—Manic's signature blue and orange, punctuated with motivational slogans like "Feel the Beat, Own the Airwaves" and "Your Vibe, Our Mission."

They entered the Warwickshire Stars studio, where Kylie Morgan and Tina Reynolds were in the middle of a lively segment. Kylie, with her signature blonde waves and infectious energy, was seated at the main mic, while Tina, a brunette with a sharp wit and warm smile, handled the side desk. The duo's chemistry was undeniable, their banter flowing effortlessly as they transitioned between a Top 40 hit and a quirky listener poll about favourite childhood snacks.

James knew that his girlfriend, Kylie, was already a seasoned presenter, but seeing her in action was a different experience entirely. Her confidence and charisma seemed amplified under the studio lights, and for a moment, James felt a pang of intimidation.

"Anyway, Kyles, I was thinking," Tina said, and James knew from listening to Manic's Birmingham and the Black Country station, Midlands Manic, that it would be time for the half hourly reminder of the £500k Money Drop, , which was Manic's signature listener competition. The station's branding often revolved around such grandiose promotions, and the giveaway was heavily promoted during every show. "What would you do with half a million?"

"Easy," Kylie said, her voice light and playful as she leaned into the mic. "I'd buy a villa in Ibiza, right on the beach, and throw a massive party. Of course, being a Manic host, I'm blocked from entering the competition, but hey, a girl can dream, right?" Her laugh was infectious, and James noticed the way the producer in the adjacent booth gave her a thumbs-up.

"Good answer," Tina replied with a grin. "I'd probably go for something more sensible, like paying off my mortgage. But knowing you, Kyles, that villa would turn into the next big party destination faster than you can say 'DJ set.' Anyway, to enter the Money Drop, just text DROP to 87106 or hop onto our website at manicradioplays.co.uk and click through to enter online. Entries cost £3, but there's also a free entry route, by calling 0330 880 3601, which is included in most phone plans. So, there's your chance, folks—£500,000 up for grabs, and with just a few taps or clicks, you could be in with a shot."

Kylie flashed a grin, seamlessly adding, "Its a network competition across all Manic Radio stations, as well as all Manic Dance, Manic Metal, Manic Goldies, Manic Rock, and Manic Soul shows—so the competition is definitely heating up! Lines close next Friday at 3pm, and Dr Manic from Manic Dance will phone one lucky winner live on-air to make their dreams come true."

James noticed how Kylie and Tina hit the spots flawlessly, weaving the promotional content into their banter as though it were a natural extension of the conversation. The balance between entertainment and advertisement was a skill honed to perfection, a testament to their professionalism and experience. Yet, as James observed, he couldn't shake the feeling that this seamlessness was a performance in itself—every word, every laugh, meticulously engineered to fit Manic's hyper-polished brand.

Cal leaned in toward James, his voice low so as not to interrupt the broadcast. "This is what you'll be doing soon enough," he said, gesturing towards Kylie. "She's *one of the best in the game—knows how to hit the marks and keep listeners engaged. Watch closely, and you'll learn a thing or two."*

James nodded, though a flicker of doubt crept into his mind. He wondered whether he could truly replicate the effortless charm and energy that Kylie exuded. The room seemed to pulse with a vibrancy he wasn't sure he could match.

Monday 24th November 2025

"Cal told me to remain in the studio and watch the rest of the show," James recounted, his voice steady as he addressed the courtroom. "It was surreal, seeing the high-energy pace up close. Kylie and Tina switched between banter, ads, and music seamlessly, all while juggling messages from listeners and cues from the producer. I was struck by how… polished everything was. It wasn't just a show; it was a well-oiled machine."

Alice Cartwright nodded, encouraging James to continue. "And how did you feel in that moment, Mr Smith? Did it meet your expectations, or were there aspects that surprised you?"

James hesitated, choosing his words carefully. "It met my expectations in terms of the professionalism on display, but what surprised me was how rehearsed everything felt. Even the off-the-cuff comments seemed carefully curated. It wasn't the free-flowing, spontaneous atmosphere I had imagined radio would be. Everything was about maintaining the Manic brand. It felt less personal, more… corporate."

There was a faint murmur in the courtroom, an undercurrent of intrigue at James's candid response.

"And how did your induction proceed after the show ended?" Cartwright prompted.

"After the show, Kylie introduced me to the team," James replied. "Everyone was friendly enough, but there was an undertone I couldn't quite place. It was like everyone was performing, not just on air but off it too. The conversations were light, superficial, and there was this constant focus on appearances—how we looked, how we sounded, and how we could be packaged for the audience. But then Dad appeared around lunchtime for work."

Tuesday 29th October 2024

James leaned back in the break room's sofa, his arm slung casually around Kylie's shoulder, her head resting against him. The hum of conversation and bursts of laughter surrounded them, a constant background buzz that felt more like a student union than a workplace. He hadn't even been at Manic for 12 hours, and already, it felt like he was part of a whole new world.

In his pocket was his Manic Radio ID card, which had been printed while he was doing some of the compliance modules earlier in the day. It bore his photo, freshly taken that morning, along with the words Manic Dance Presenter - James Smith.

He was aware of Pete, his dad, sitting at the corner of one of the tables, nursing a mug of tea that James guessed had gone cold about twenty minutes ago. Pete didn't quite fit in here. The break room's chaotic energy clashed with his old-school sense of professionalism. James could see it in the way Pete kept glancing around, like he was searching for a quiet corner that didn't exist. Still, he stayed, watching but not engaging, a silent observer in a room full of noise.

James felt Kylie shift slightly in his lap, drawing his attention back to her. Her lipstick was a little smudged, probably his fault, but she didn't seem to care. She was scrolling through her phone with one hand, the other resting casually on his shoulder. Her confidence was magnetic, and James found himself admiring the way she owned the room without even trying.

"Oi, Morgan," Al Crozier shouted from his perch on the arm of the sofa. His perfectly styled hair and pristine trainers made him look more like a model than a radio presenter. "Save some for the air, yeah? Jimmy Reeves, the next Manic heartthrob, turning our humble Dudley studio into a scene straight out of Love Island."

"Well, I ain't on 'til brekkie, babes," Kylie said with a grin, "And Jimmy here's got a couple of hours until he's in your show, so we're just... making the most of the break." She glanced up at James, who chuckled, unbothered by the attention. The fact that both Al and Kylie used James's on-air name for effect felt weirdly comfortable, as if it were a glove that fit perfectly, but James couldn't help but notice his dad's disapproving glance from across the room. Pete shifted uncomfortably, clearly not on board with the overt displays of affection and the lively chatter that bordered on unprofessionalism.

"Alright, let's get a bit of decorum here, yeah?" Pete said, forcing a smile and trying to keep his tone light. "This is a break room, not the Love Island villa."

"Come on, old man, we're twentysomethings, not 'hot chocolate and biscuits, bed by 9," Cody Lane, the newsreader on Midlands Manic and the rest of the Dudley hub stations, piped up from across the room, grinning cheekily. Cody was dressed in his usual trendy streetwear, effortlessly fitting in with the rest of the young crowd. He leaned back in his chair, one foot propped up on the edge

of the table, clearly enjoying the shift from news bulletins to banter. "Anyway, Crozier, looking forward to the weekend mate?"

James was curious about where this conversation would go, but he felt his dad's disapproving eyes linger on him and Kylie. Pete's discomfort was almost palpable, a silent tension that contrasted with the boisterous energy of the break room. James knew this wasn't his dad's world. It was a far cry from the community-focused, authentic radio Pete had built his career on. This was glossy, loud, and unapologetically performative.

And James loved it.

Al looked up from his phone, catching Cody's eye with a grin that was half mischief, half swagger. "Oh, mate, the weekend's gonna be legendary. Pussy as far as the eye can see... I mean, it's going to be good fun. I'm going up to Liverpool to see Toni, maybe have a night with her and some of her mates from Hits Radio... few drinks, bit of blow, you know the drill." Al shot a sideways glance at Pete, whose expression was a blend of discomfort and disapproval.

"Ah, right, you and Toni, between you and Kylie and James, you've got the 'power couple' slots sorted, haven't you?" Pete said, trying to inject some humour to lighten his growing discomfort. "I guess we're living in the age of 'Insta love' now."

James flashed Pete a sheepish grin, though he didn't seem remotely phased by Pete's disapproval. "It's all part of the game, Dad. You know that. People want a bit of 'real life' from their presenters, yeah?"

Kylie chimed in, still lounging comfortably in James's lap. "Yeah, it's all about that relatability. Listeners don't just want voices—they want to know we're like them, having a laugh, living a bit, y'know? Makes us seem... accessible."

James watched his dad's discomfort and chuckled, as he knew the older man was of the generation who had listened to Ed Doolan on commercial radio, a veteran Australian broadcaster who became a local legend in Birmingham for his no-nonsense, community-driven style. This slick, hyper-branded, influencer-esque approach was entirely alien to Pete's sensibilities, and James could see it written all over his face.

"Hey guys!" Liam Price, one of the Mid Wales Manic breakfast hosts, shouted as he pulled out one of his earbuds, "Manic Dance have announced they're dropping a F1 related track in the next 10 minutes on the Lunchtime EDM show. They've given a clue too... '33'."

James instantly knew what Liam was talking about, having been a DJ in Ibiza as well as the student union at Wolverhampton University. He leaned forward, the energy of the conversation pulling him in. "I know what it is. It's '33 Max Verstappen' by Carte Blanq and Maxx Power, came out last year. Capital would never touch that track in a million years. It goes 'Tu-tu-tu-du, Max Verstappen' for most the song. It's as popular in Holland as Kernkraft 400 is in Germany. It's a big track in the Euro scene, especially after the F1 hype around Verstappen - I mean, he's a triple F1 Champion, his team boss is the husband of Geri Horner, for god's sake. It's not just an F1 track, it's a cultural moment."

Monday 24th November 2025

"Objection, Your Honour," interrupted Victoria Hunt, the defence barrister. Her voice carried the practiced cadence of someone who wielded objections as a scalpel, sharp and precise. "The witness appears to be editorialising. His testimony is straying into subjective commentary rather than sticking to factual events. While fascinating, it is not directly relevant to the proceedings."

"With all respect, Your Honour," Alice Cartwright, the Crown's barrister, quickly interjected before Sir Thomas Harvey could respond. Her tone was measured, professional, but firm. "The witness's testimony, while occasionally anecdotal, is contextualising the culture at Manic Radio. It highlights the atmosphere in which the alleged misconduct occurred. It is crucial for the court to understand this context to fully appreciate the pressures and dynamics faced by employees, particularly the claimant, at the time in question."

Sir Thomas Harvey adjusted his glasses, his expression neutral as he considered the arguments. "Ms Cartwright," he said, his voice even, "I appreciate the need for context. However, I would remind the witness to refrain from veering into unnecessary commentary or personal evaluations. Mr Smith, please limit your responses to factual recounting of events and their direct impact on the matters at hand."

James nodded, swallowing hard. "Understood, Your Honour."

Alice gave James a reassuring nod before resuming her questioning. "Mr Smith, let us focus on your interactions with senior staff and colleagues during your induction period. Did anything stand out to you as unusual or concerning?"

James took a steadying breath, his gaze fixed on Alice. "Yes," he said, his voice firm but measured. "There was a heavy emphasis on maintaining the 'Manic image.' It wasn't just about doing a good job or connecting with listeners—it was about how we looked, acted, and projected ourselves as part of the brand. That pressure was clear from the very first day."

"And did this pressure manifest in any specific instructions or behaviours from senior staff?" Alice asked, her tone probing but not leading.

"Absolutely," James replied. "Cal Ellington, the regional director, was very clear about what was expected. He told me that everything I did—on and off-air—needed to align with the brand. He even hinted that keeping up appearances was more important than the quality of the content we produced. That was reinforced by my colleagues' behaviour, which often felt performative, like they were trying to outdo each other in being the most 'Manic.'"

Alice nodded thoughtfully, glancing at her notes before continuing. "You mentioned earlier that your father, Pete Smith, joined you during lunch on your first day. Did his presence shed any light on the cultural differences you were beginning to notice?"

James allowed himself a small smile, the memory of his father's discomfort momentarily easing his nerves. "Yes, it did. My dad's an old-school broadcaster—he believes in authenticity, connecting with listeners in a real and meaningful way. Watching him in that break room, surrounded by this hyper-competitive, image-driven culture, it was clear how out of place he felt. He even tried to inject some of his usual humour to lighten the mood, but it just highlighted the gap between his values and the environment at Manic."

Alice Cartwright's tone remained calm as she shifted her focus. "Mr Smith, I'd like to draw your attention to the 2nd and 3rd of November 2024, during the weekend you spent in Liverpool. Can you describe the circumstances of that trip and its relevance to your testimony today?"

James felt the room grow heavier with expectation. The events of that weekend were etched into his memory, both for their chaotic nature and the revelations they had sparked.

"That weekend was a weekend planned by Al Crozier and Toni Green. Basically, most weekends, presenters, producers and sales staff meet up with crews from the other hubs for a massive social, often including DJs and presenters from the network's flagship stations like Manic Dance and the local CHR stations. Folks from rival networks like Bauer's Hits Radio and Global's Capital also show up, especially if the weekend is hosted in major cities like Liverpool, Manchester, or London."

James paused, glancing briefly at the defence barrister, who appeared poised to object. Taking a breath, he continued, carefully choosing his words. "It was an unofficial tradition—these weekends weren't part of any formal Manic activity, but they were well-known across the company. The Liverpool weekend was particularly intense. There were parties in private venues, and the atmosphere was... unrestrained. Heavy drinking, drug use, and some questionable behaviour were not just common but expected. I... admit... I partook in all of the above."

Alice raised her hand slightly to acknowledge the tension in the room, allowing James a moment before continuing. "Mr Smith, while the details of your participation are noted, could you clarify whether any senior staff were present during these gatherings, and if so, what their involvement or stance appeared to be?"

"Not really. It was more of a free-for-all," James said carefully. "Senior staff weren't there as official representatives, but there were plenty of people who had managerial roles or who were closely connected to them. What stood out to me was the way these weekends fed into the overall culture at Manic—this sense that anything went, as long as it didn't become public. The senior staff I knew about would never officially acknowledge these parties, but there was no real effort to discourage them either. In fact, there were times when it felt like some of the higher-ups quietly encouraged the atmosphere, knowing it kept employees loyal to the brand and eager to outdo each other in being 'Manic enough.'"

"Objection, the witness is editorialising again," Victoria Hunt interjected sharply. "We're here to discuss relevant events, not conjecture on senior staff motivations."

Alice nodded slightly in acknowledgment of the objection but responded with a measured tone. "Your Honour, I'm simply establishing the broader cultural environment at Manic Radio, which directly relates to the claims of coercion and exploitation within the company. The witness's observations of unofficial gatherings and their impact on the workplace atmosphere are highly pertinent."

Sir Thomas Harvey raised a hand for silence, adjusting his glasses as he turned to James. "Mr Smith, please keep your responses grounded in direct experiences and observations. While some context is helpful, we need to focus on factual events. Carry on, Ms Cartwright."

Alice gave a small nod. "Mr Smith, were there any particular incidents or behaviours during that weekend which made you feel uncomfortable or pressured to conform?"

James hesitated for a moment before answering. "Yes. There was one night when we were all at this club that had been rented out. I saw people—presenters and producers—pressured into drinking more than they wanted or taking part in activities they weren't comfortable with. It was all done in this... light-hearted way, like it was just banter. But you could tell some of them didn't feel like they could say no. The unwritten rule was that if you didn't join in, you'd be seen as not being a team player, not being 'Manic enough.'"

Alice pressed on. "And how did that influence your approach to your work at Manic after that weekend?"

James took a deep breath. "It made me feel like I had to play along, to fit in. The culture of these weekends seeped back into the studio and the day-to-day environment. People who participated—who drank the most, partied the hardest—they were often the ones who got the better shifts or were in the inner circle. It was clear that going along with the culture wasn't just a personal choice. It affected your career."

****

CHAPTER 18 - Flashbacks
Saturday 11th January 2025

It had been over a week since James had been kicked out, and while his life was still a tangled mess, the initial shock had begun to wear off. The frigid air of that January morning, the weight of his belongings on his back, and the crushing sense of betrayal from his family—those memories were vivid, but now they felt more like a distant nightmare. Yet, the consequences lingered, and he knew that his struggle was far from over.

The fact that he was now Kylie's plaything, the contract that he had signed forcing him to become the plaything of every Manic presenter, producer, newsreader and even salesperson at the Dudley hub, as well as whatever other personnel came from whatever hub in the country to work in Dudley, weighed on him heavily. The contract itself was legally binding, leaving him no clear route of escape. It was a masterclass in manipulation, and Kylie had exploited every loophole, every clause, to ensure James's compliance.

He was sat in Studio 4 of the Waterfront hub, the Warwickshire Stars studio, which was being decommissioned ahead of the April 2025 relaunch of it being part of Manic Vibes West Midlands, an engineer in front of him, the engineer's hand on his head, forcing James to orally service him.

James knew that, as it was a Saturday, and the only show broadcast from Dudley was on the national Manic Rock station, as well as Ibiza Belters, a new live show on the CHR network which replaced his old voice-tracked Ibiza Headbanger show on Manic Dance, most of the staff were absent, and the building was eerily quiet apart from the low hum of studio equipment and the occasional footsteps echoing through the corridors. The operations of

Warwickshire Stars, James knew, was going to be the first show broadcast from One Snow Hill, its sole Breakfast show the only one of that station, with everything else being networked from Speke, with Midlands Manic, the station his dad broadcast on, being the last to move as part of the phased relocation plan. The move to One Snow Hill symbolised Manic Radio's relentless push toward centralisation, efficiency, and profitability, often at the expense of individuality and humanity—a recurring theme in James's now turbulent existence.

As the engineer's hand tightened its grip on his head, James fought to suppress his growing sense of degradation. His body obeyed the demands placed on him, but his mind wandered, searching desperately for some sense of escape or solace. He clung to fleeting thoughts of resilience and redemption, however faint they seemed.

When the ordeal was over, James wiped his face with trembling hands and sat back against the studio wall, his breath coming in shallow gasps. The engineer muttered a curt, "Good lad," before zipping up his trousers and leaving the room without a backward glance. The door clicked shut, leaving James alone with his thoughts and the silent equipment.

Hearing the squeak of trainers in the corridor, James instantly knew who was the only other member of presentation staff at Manic, his sister Chloe's fiancé, Cody Lane, James knew that Cody would happily force him to not just provide oral sex, but be a literal cum dump, his anus being filled by Cody's smaller erection and his mouth being required to clean the newsreader.

That personal connection made the situation even worse, a cruel reminder of how twisted his world had become. Cody's smug expression, his cocky demeanour, and the power he so gleefully wielded over James had made every encounter with him unbearable.

The door creaked open, and Cody stepped inside, a smirk plastered across his face. He was dressed casually in a hoodie and joggers, the very image of someone who knew he was in control. He leaned against the doorframe, crossing his arms as he surveyed James.

"Well, well, Reevesy," Cody drawled, his voice dripping with condescension. "Didn't think I'd catch you slacking off in here. But I suppose it's fitting—you've found your place, haven't you?"

James didn't respond, keeping his gaze fixed on the floor. His body tensed, every muscle screaming for him to do something, anything, to regain control of the situation. But the contract was always there, lurking in the back of his mind, reminding him of the consequences of defiance. His father's career. His family. It was all on the line.

Cody pushed off the doorframe and sauntered over, his footsteps echoing in the small studio. "You're not going to ignore me, are you? That's not how this works." He reached down, gripping James's chin and forcing him to look up. "You're going to behave, just like Kylie told you to. Isn't that right?"

James swallowed hard, his throat dry. "Just... get it over with," he muttered, his voice barely audible.

Cody chuckled, clearly relishing the power he held. "Oh, don't worry, Reevesy. I intend to."

He released James's chin and stepped back, loosening the drawstring of his joggers. James's stomach churned, the familiar wave of shame and helplessness washing over him as he prepared for yet another degrading encounter.

253

But then, a thought struck him—small, fleeting, but enough to momentarily pierce the fog of despair.

This can't go on forever.

As Cody continued his routine of humiliation, James's mind drifted to the idea of a way out. Somewhere, deep within the labyrinth of English law, there had to be a loophole, a clause, a precedent—something that could undo the nightmare Kylie had locked him into. Contracts were binding, yes, but no contract could permit outright abuse, could it? He clung to that shred of hope like a lifeline, even as the present reality threatened to crush him.

When Cody finally left, the smug satisfaction practically radiating off him, James slumped against the wall once more. His body was exhausted, but his mind was alight. He needed a plan—one that would allow him to fight back without endangering his family or his father's livelihood.

Tuesday 4th February 2025

James was on his knees in Studio B1 of One Snow Hill, under the desk of the Warwickshire Stars breakfast show. His orders had been simple - he had to pleasure Kylie's co-host, Tina Reynolds, only using his tongue, and keep her pleasured for the entire 4 hour Breakfast show. The fact that he was being forced to be naked, wearing only a cock ring, nipple clamps and an anal plug while both Kylie and Tina were wearing their usual short skirts and crop tops meant that the humiliation was relentless, with every passing moment reinforcing James's role as nothing more than an object in the toxic web Kylie and her clique had woven. The bright lights of the studio contrasted sharply with the shadowy undercurrent of exploitation that had come to define his existence.

The Warwickshire Stars breakfast show played on, with Kylie and Tina seamlessly delivering their high-energy banter to an audience oblivious to the darkness lurking behind the scenes. Tina's polished smile and melodic laugh masked the twisted dynamic at play, while Kylie threw occasional glances under the desk, her smirk betraying her satisfaction at James's plight.

James's mind wandered as he mechanically followed the degrading commands, his body moving on autopilot. The weight of the cock ring and the sharp pinch of the nipple clamps were constant reminders of his situation, but his thoughts weren't entirely consumed by the physical discomfort. He clung to fragments of a plan—an escape from this nightmare. If he could find the right moment, the right ally, perhaps he could turn the tables.

The fact that he knew Lyra Nott, the Northern Vibes drive host, was still at Dudley, her show for Stoke and Cheshire, like his dad's, being the last two to move on the weekend prior to the rebrands of Northern Vibes to Manic Vibes Stoke and Cheshire and Midlands Manic to Manic Vibes West Midlands, meant that he was all but cut off from them.

"So, babes," James heard Tina say as the clock struck half past 6, only 30 minutes gone of the 4-hour show, her voice dripping with mockery, "Reevesy down there's got quite the tongue on him, doesn't he? Too bad he doesn't have a shred of dignity to go with it."

James could hear the pre-recorded news bulletin in the background, so he knew that the two 23 year olds were off air for a few minutes. Kylie's laugh echoed through the studio, sharp and malicious, as she leaned back in her chair and stretched her legs under the desk, brushing her foot against James's shoulder.

"Oh, Tina, you don't know the half of it," Kylie said with a grin, her voice carrying the kind of smug authority that made James's stomach churn. "Reevesy here is a natural. I mean, who wouldn't want a personal stress reliever under the desk? It's like having a little pet that knows exactly how to behave. Oh, you coming over Cody and Clo's place tonight, T? They're having a pre-wedding bash, and Reevesy is the guest of honour."

James shuddered at the thought of what his girlfriend and, the way she acted, pimp, mistress and even manager, said, that he was the guest of "honour" at his own sister's pre-wedding bash, code for him being treated like a pony ride at a private party, subjected to further degradation and humiliation. The idea of being on display at his own sister's celebration was one of the cruellest twists in his already tortured existence.

Tina's laugh sounded almost kind compared to Kylie's, but it was laced with the same venom. "Oh, I wouldn't miss it for the world. I love a good show, especially when it's Reevesy on display." Her words hit James like a slap to the face. He could hear the underlying excitement in her voice, the thrill they both derived from his suffering.

For a moment, James found himself wishing for the impossible—to be able to walk away, to escape from all of this. But the weight of the contract, of the system they had him ensnared in, left him feeling like he was sinking in quicksand. Any move to break free would be met with brutal consequences. His family. His father's career. The lie of it all was suffocating.

A sharp reminder of his position came when Kylie's foot brushed against his shoulder again, this time pressing harder, as if to emphasise her control over him. "You know, Reevesy," she purred, her voice now low and taunting, "It's not like you even have a choice in all this.

You're ours now. And tonight, you'll be putting on quite the show for all the guests at Cody and Chloe's. No escaping that."

James could feel the blood draining from his face at the thought of what awaited him. He had spent so much time replaying possible escape scenarios in his head, but none of them seemed plausible. The law was a maze, his father's name a fragile thread holding him in place. Every time he thought about rebellion, about speaking out, the reality of the consequences shattered those dreams.

As the hours dragged on in the studio, the pain of his physical discomfort faded into the background, replaced by the ceaseless churn of his mind. He began to realise the bleak truth—there was no easy way out. If he wanted to escape, it would require something far greater than just a legal loophole. He would need to take control, somehow, and it would cost him more than he was willing to admit. But for now, all he could do was endure, waiting for the right moment, the right ally, to emerge from the shadows.

The end of the show couldn't come soon enough. His body felt like it was on autopilot, moving in response to the commands that came from above him, both Kylie and Tina's voices filling the air with mockery and disdain. Yet, in the back of his mind, a single thought echoed like a mantra... that it can't go on forever.

It was a faint glimmer of hope, but in the darkness of his situation, it was the only thing that kept him going.

Friday 21st February 2025

James sat on the edge of his bed in the Priory Queensway apartment that his sister and Cody leased, the one that Kylie had moved into back in January, having given up her Great Bridge flat, Cody standing in front of him, forcing James to give his brother-in-law a blowjob. James knew that his throat was hurting, as Cody had took a pill which would maintain his erection for an extended period, prolonging James's ordeal. The metallic taste in James's mouth and the ache in his jaw were secondary to the sharp humiliation cutting into his core. Each degrading act reinforced the tightening noose of his entrapment, but there was a stubborn ember of resistance buried deep within him that refused to extinguish.

The bedroom door swung open without a knock, and Kylie stepped in, a glass of wine in one hand and her mobile in the other. She was dressed casually, but the glint in her eyes betrayed her usual appetite for control. "Ah, there's my two favourite boys," she said with a smirk, taking a leisurely sip from her glass as she observed the scene before her.

"Don't let me interrupt," she added, perching herself on the armchair in the corner. "Just here to... supervise."

James's humiliation deepened, his eyes darting downward as he focused on the floor. Cody laughed, his hand gripping the back of James's head more firmly. "Kylie, babe, he's been slacking a bit today. Think we should add something to keep him in line?"

Kylie tilted her head, pretending to consider. "Hmm, maybe. What do you think, Reevesy?" She directed her gaze at him. "Do you think you deserve a little... motivation?"

James's response was a soft, almost inaudible mumble. "No."

"No?" Kylie echoed, raising an eyebrow. She stood and walked over, placing her glass on the bedside table. "That's not the attitude we like, is it?" She crouched
258

down to his level, forcing him to meet her gaze. "You're forgetting your place again, Reevesy."

Cody laughed again, releasing James and stepping back to zip up his trousers. "He always needs reminding. Guess that's what makes this so fun."

Kylie straightened, her smirk fading into something more calculating. "Fun's all well and good, but I like efficiency too. If he's not performing, it's a waste of my time—and yours." She turned her attention back to James. "Maybe you need a reminder of just how fragile your position is."

James stiffened at her words, his body betraying the fear that coursed through him. He knew what Kylie was capable of and how far she was willing to go to maintain her control.

"Tomorrow," she continued, her tone now icy, "Kyler, Lady Ellie and some of the Stratford folks will be coming, and you will service all of them... you will make Ellie cum like the whore you are and you will let Kyler's monster cock fuck your arse. Am I clear?"

James tried to cross his head in the negative, tried to shake his head in defiance, but the weight of fear and the unyielding pressure of his situation kept him still. He swallowed hard, the taste of bile and shame lingering in his mouth as he met Kylie's gaze. There was no trace of empathy in her eyes, only the cold satisfaction of someone who knew they held all the power.

"Am I clear, Reevesy?" Kylie's voice cut through the tense silence, sharp and commanding. She stepped closer, her shadow looming over him as he sat frozen on the edge of the bed. "I won't ask again."

James forced himself to nod, a small, reluctant movement that only deepened the sense of self-loathing gnawing at him. *"Yes,"* he whispered hoarsely, his voice barely audible.

"Yes... what?" Kylie's tone was laced with mockery, daring him to utter the words she wanted to hear.

"Yes, ma'am," he croaked, the words feeling like acid on his tongue.

Kylie's smirk returned, satisfied. "Good boy," she said, patting his cheek condescendingly before turning to Cody. *"Make sure he's well-rested tonight. I want him fresh for tomorrow. No excuses."*

Cody chuckled and gave a mock salute. "You got it, babe."

With a final glance at James, Kylie grabbed her glass of wine and sauntered out of the room, her heels clicking against the hardwood floor. The sound of the door closing behind her was both a relief and a reminder of how tightly she held the reins of his life.

James sat motionless for a long moment, his mind racing as he tried to process what had just happened and what lay ahead. The walls of the room seemed to close in on him, suffocating and oppressive. His throat ached, his body was sore, and his spirit felt crushed—but the faint ember of hope he clung to refused to die out entirely.

Suddenly his sister, Chloe walked in, a strapon and no other clothes on, and James knew what she was going to expect him to do, that his own sister, who had created the contract, was going to make him service her like he had just serviced her husband, that he was nothing but her sleeve for her to fill.

And he hated it.

Grabbing the nearby bag of cocaine, James knew that he could easily end the suffering, taking more than the normal amount, that he could end his life in one simple stroke. He sat there, staring at the small plastic bag in his trembling hands. The white powder seemed to taunt him with its promise of escape—a way to silence the endless torment, the relentless humiliation, and the suffocating despair. For a brief moment, the thought of ending it all seemed almost peaceful.

But then, something deep within him stirred. It wasn't a spark of courage or rebellion—it was something quieter, almost imperceptible. A stubborn instinct for survival. A faint whisper in the back of his mind reminded him that this was what they wanted: for him to break, to give up, to surrender entirely.

He put the bag down slowly, his fingers shaking as he clenched them into fists. His breathing came in ragged gasps as he forced himself to focus on the faint glimmers of hope that still lingered somewhere deep within him. The thought of exposing Kylie and her toxic web of control was daunting, but it was the only chance he had to reclaim his life. He couldn't let them win.

Chloe, standing by the doorway with an air of smug authority, tilted her head in mock curiosity. "What's taking so long, James? Don't tell me you're thinking about backing out. You know better than that."

James forced himself to look at her, his jaw tightening. "I'm not backing out," he said quietly, his voice trembling but resolute.

She laughed, the sound cold and hollow. "Good. Because I'd hate for things to get messy." She stepped closer, her predatory gaze locking onto his. "Now, be a good boy and do as you're told."

James swallowed hard, every fibre of his being screaming at him to fight back, to say no, to run. But he knew he had to bide his time. Acting rashly would only give them more power over him. He lowered his gaze and nodded, the faint ember of resistance burning quietly within him.

****

CHAPTER 19 - Rebuttal
Tuesday 25th November 2025

It was the second day of James giving evidence, but instead of him answering questions from the Crown's barrister, he found himself facing the unyielding gaze of Victoria Hunt, the barrister for Chloe and Kylie, and Marcus Blake, who was Manic's corporate defence counsel. Both had reputations for their tenacity, and James felt a cold knot in his stomach as he stepped into the witness box. The courtroom was quiet save for the shuffle of papers and the soft murmur of voices from the gallery.

Sir Thomas Harvey, presiding, nodded for proceedings to continue. "Ms Hunt," he intoned, "you may begin your cross-examination."

Victoria rose, her expression calm but sharp as a blade. She approached the witness box slowly, her black robe flowing behind her. "Mr Smith," she began, her voice smooth, "I'd like to take you back to the 23rd of October 2022. You were a student at Wolverhampton University, am I correct?"

"That's correct," James replied, his voice steady but edged with apprehension. He knew where she was going with this. The date, the context—it was a pivotal moment in his early years, one that he couldn't deny.

Victoria clasped her hands behind her back, pacing slightly. "And it's true, is it not, that during your time as a student, you were employed by the university's student union bar? A role which required you to handle cash transactions and maintain trust with your employers?"

James nodded. "Yes, I worked there part-time."

Victoria stopped and turned to face him directly. "Would you agree that in a role like that, honesty and integrity were essential?"

"Yes, I would," James said cautiously.

Victoria allowed a brief pause, letting the tension build. "Then, Mr Smith, can you explain to the court why, on that particular date, you were caught stealing from the student union bar's till, and not by the manager, but my client, Ms Morgan?"

James felt his stomach drop. His mind raced as he tried to recall the precise details. It had been a long time ago, but that moment was etched in his memory—one of the darker chapters of his past. He shifted slightly in the witness box, his hands gripping the sides.

"Yes," he began slowly, his voice measured, "I did take money from the till that night. It was a mistake—one I deeply regret. I was young and stupid, and I wasn't thinking about the consequences."

"And can you tell me what you did with the money, please?" Victoria asked, and James knew that he had to be truthful as he was under oath. He sighed, the weight of that long-past decision pressing down on him. "I used it to... well... hire a... prostitute."

The room fell into an awkward silence. Even Sir Thomas Harvey appeared momentarily taken aback. The jury shifted slightly in their seats, some exchanging glances. Victoria Hunt maintained her composure, though there was a faint glint in her eye as she continued.

"Thank you for your honesty, Mr Smith," she said smoothly. "Now, you've mentioned that Ms Morgan was the one who caught you. Can you recall her reaction and what followed after she discovered the theft?"

James nodded, his throat dry. "She… confronted me. Told me she wouldn't report it to the manager if I promised to pay it back and never do anything like it again. I was mortified. I agreed straightaway and returned the money as soon as I could."

Victoria tilted her head slightly. "So, you're saying that Ms Morgan showed you leniency? That she kept the incident quiet and allowed you to move on with your employment?"

"Yes," James admitted, his voice quieter now. "She could have reported me, but she didn't."

Victoria took a few steps closer to the bench. "It seems, Mr Smith, that Ms Morgan acted with some degree of understanding towards you in a moment of poor judgement. Would you agree?"

"Yes," James said reluctantly.

"And it was a week after you had commenced a relationship with Ms Morgan, correct?"

"Yes," James said quietly, feeling the courtroom's focus press down on him.

Victoria's voice maintained its measured tone, but her questions grew more precise. "So, to clarify, after she discovered you stealing, Ms Morgan chose not to escalate the matter to university authorities, and shortly thereafter, you began a romantic relationship with her. Is that correct?"

"Yes," James replied.

"Thank you, Mr Smith." Victoria turned slightly, addressing the court as she paced. "It appears that Ms Morgan acted in a way that allowed Mr Smith to learn from his mistake without jeopardising his future employment. While some might question the propriety of their subsequent relationship, it's clear that Ms Morgan's actions at the time were not vindictive or malicious. Would you agree, Mr Smith?"

James felt a tightness in his chest. "I can't speak to her motives, but I'd agree that she didn't punish me harshly."

Victoria stopped pacing, her tone shifting slightly. "And when you later joined Manic Radio, Ms Morgan was already established there. As your partner at the time, she helped you acclimatise to the environment. She introduced you to colleagues, provided guidance, and supported your career development—did she not?"

"Yes," James admitted.

Victoria's voice remained smooth but began to take on a sharper edge. "So, Mr Smith, despite your allegations about Ms Morgan's later conduct, it is undeniable that she provided you with opportunities and guidance that helped you advance in your career. Without her, it's unlikely you would have had the same initial footing at Manic. Would you agree with that assessment?"

James hesitated, feeling the weight of the question. "She helped me-"

"No further questions, your honour," Victoria paused, her eyes briefly glancing at the defence table before returning to her seat. "However, my learned colleague, Mr Blake, will take it from here."

Marcus Blake rose, his approach more methodical, his tone deliberate. "Mr Smith," he began, "I want to revisit something you said yesterday. You said, and I quote, that you felt pressured to conform to a culture that prioritised image over substance. Can you clarify what you mean by that?"

James took a breath, steadying himself. "What I meant was that at Manic, everything was about appearances— how you looked, how you sounded, how you fit into the brand. It wasn't just about doing a good job on-air; it was about being marketable, about embodying the Manic image at all times."

Blake nodded, his expression impassive. "You've described this as pressure. But is it not the case in Contemporary Hit Radio stations like Manic, Bauer Media's Hits Radio and Global Media's Capital network that image and branding are fundamental to their success? Isn't it industry standard for presenters to maintain a consistent on-air persona, engage with listeners on social media, and project a certain level of professionalism and charisma?"

"Yes," James said cautiously, "but the level of control at Manic went beyond that. It wasn't just about having a public persona; it was about micromanaging every aspect of our behaviour, both on and off-air. The pressure was constant, and it made it hard to know where the job ended, and our personal lives began."

Blake clasped his hands behind his back, taking a moment before responding. "So, you're suggesting that the company's high standards for branding and image somehow crossed a line. Can you provide specific examples of how this allegedly oppressive culture manifested?"

James hesitated, his mind racing to find the right words. "There were times when we were told exactly what to wear, what to post on social media, even how to phrase certain on-air segments. If someone didn't fit the image—

if their look or attitude wasn't deemed 'Manic enough'—they risked losing opportunities. I saw colleagues passed over for shifts or sidelined because they didn't play into the brand's aesthetic."

"Ah, the alleged dress code. I have here the Manic Radio Group's Employee handbook... I assume that you received an electronic copy of this?"

James nodded, his voice steady but with a hint of caution. "Yes, I received an electronic copy during my induction at."

Blake held up a printed version of the document, flipping Manic through its pages with deliberate precision. "Then you will be familiar with it, and the fact there is no section on workplace attire, correct?"

James felt a flicker of hesitation. "That's correct," he replied carefully, "there's no official section on dress code in the handbook."

Blake nodded, his expression neutral. "So, you would agree, then, that there is no formal policy requiring presenters to wear specific types of clothing—no written rule enforcing the so-called 'Manic look.' Is that accurate?"

James took a slow breath before responding. "That's true, there was no official rule. But the expectations were made very clear. It was unspoken, yet everyone understood. If you didn't dress the part, you weren't taken as seriously. It may not have been written in the handbook, but it was very real."

Blake allowed a brief pause, then leaned slightly forward. "Unspoken expectations, you say. Do you have any documented proof of these so-called unwritten rules—

emails, memos, or communications that explicitly dictated attire?"'

James shook his head, his frustration starting to rise. "No, there were no emails or official directives. It was more about the culture—how management treated people, who they chose to promote. It became obvious what was expected if you wanted to get ahead."

"Thank you. You said as well that management encourage the drink and cocaine culture among its presenters and producers," Blake continued, his tone now sharper. "Do you have any direct evidence—such as emails, messages, or other forms of communication—indicating that management officially encouraged such behaviour?"

James took a steadying breath, knowing this was a key line of attack. "No, there wasn't anything official in writing. But-"

"So, you admit that there was no written directive from management encouraging or condoning the alleged behaviour?" Blake interjected, his voice firm and unwavering.

"Well, I put it to you, Mr Smith, that "Well, I put it to you, Mr Smith, that what you describe as 'encouragement' was nothing more than a culture of camaraderie among colleagues in a high-pressure industry. Late nights, social events, and the occasional excess are not unique to Manic Radio but are common across various industries. Would you not agree?"

James felt the weight of the courtroom pressing down on him. He straightened his posture and met Blake's gaze. "I'd agree that socialising and bonding are common in many industries. But this wasn't camaraderie. It was a toxic culture where participation in those excesses felt compulsory. If you didn't take part, you risked being ostracised or losing career opportunities. It wasn't just socialising—it was systemic pressure. And then there was the hub cum-"

"Ah, yes, the alleged 'hub cum dump' role you claim to have been pressured into," Blake interrupted smoothly, his tone sharp and sceptical. The courtroom grew tense as his words hung in the air. "Mr Smith, are you suggesting that this so-called role was an official designation or policy within Manic Radio Group?"

James took a deep breath, steadying himself. "No, it wasn't an official role. But it was an unspoken part of the toxic culture. It became a term used in group chats and among colleagues to describe how people were treated—those who had fallen out of favour either by machinations of colleagues or mismanagement by senior staff. The phrase wasn't official, but the attitude and the behaviours it represented were very real. It symbolised how people who didn't conform or who were seen as expendable were treated."

Blake adjusted his stance, his expression a mix of scepticism and disapproval. "So, Mr Smith, you're alleging that this offensive term, which you admit was never formalised, is indicative of systemic issues at Manic Radio. Yet, you've provided no written evidence, no corroborating documents, and no testimony thus far to support the existence of such a role beyond hearsay. How do you expect the court to take this claim seriously?"

"So, being raped by several of my colleagues—people I worked with, people I trusted—and being forced into situations where I was used as a... a toy for their gratification, that's not serious enough for this court to take note?" His voice trembled, but there was a defiant edge to it, a determination to be heard despite the shame and trauma tied to his words. "Having to service 20 people in one night, both male and female, not just from the Dudley hub but from the Stratford hub, the Speke hub, the Dundee hub... all coming together and treating me like I was there as a gloryhole, that I was there as an object for their amusement—that's not serious enough for this court to take note?" James's voice cracked, and the weight of his testimony hung heavy in the courtroom. His hands gripped the edges of the witness box as if anchoring himself against the tide of emotion threatening to overwhelm him. His gaze darted to his mother, Sarah, in the gallery, her face pale and lined with anguish, but her presence offered him a shred of strength.

"Did you read the report that my aunt, a General Practitioner, wrote after she gave me a thorough examination the day I managed to escape Kylie's control? Did you see her detailed notes documenting the injuries, the physical evidence of what was done to me? Or the fact that, following that, I have been attending meetings of Narcotics Anonymous to help me overcome the forced drug dependency that was part of the coercion? Is that not evidence enough of the physical and psychological toll this so-called 'culture' inflicted upon me?"

"Ah, the drug dependency... or should I say willing cocaine habit? I believe that you were, following the commencement of your employment at Manic Radio, a willing participant in the use of cocaine, Mr Smith. Is it not true that you willingly partook in this drug use during your employment with Manic, as well as at the aforementioned social gatherings?" Marcus Blake's voice was cold, his calculated tone designed to chip away at James's credibility.

James took a moment, breathing deeply before replying, his voice steady despite the emotion simmering beneath the surface. "Yes, I admit I used cocaine voluntarily at first. I was young, impressionable, and I wanted to fit in.

But what started as experimentation quickly became something far darker. It wasn't a choice anymore—it was forced on me, used as a way to control me and keep me compliant. They created the dependency and used it against me."

"Are you seriously saying that you were forced, when in fact you, like many radio presenters, not just at Manic but at Bauer or Global, chose to partake in recreational drug use? Cocaine use, while regrettable, is unfortunately not uncommon in high-pressure industries. Can you truly claim that your actions were entirely without agency?"

James gritted his teeth, his frustration evident. "I'm not denying my initial choice to try cocaine, Mr Blake. But-"

"No further questions for this witness, Your Honour," Blake cut James off abruptly, turning back to his seat with an air of finality. The courtroom fell silent, the weight of the exchange hanging heavily in the air.

Sir Thomas Harvey adjusted his glasses, his calm yet authoritative voice breaking the silence. "Mr Smith, you may step down for now. The court will reconvene after a short recess."

James nodded, his legs trembling as he stepped down from the witness box. He avoided the eyes of the defence team and instead focused on his mother in the gallery. Sarah gave him a small, encouraging smile, her face lined with worry but radiating unwavering support. He made his way out of the courtroom, each step feeling like a struggle against the emotional weight pressing down on him.

****

"We're live from Birmingham Crown Court on the sixth day of the trial involving former and current employees of

Manic Radio Group, where allegations of systemic abuse and misconduct have sent shockwaves through the broadcasting industry. Today's proceedings saw Mr James Smith, a former presenter, face rigorous cross-examination from the defence barristers representing Manic Radio and its implicated employees."

Pete was sat at the Three Towns Radio studios, one of Woody Bones's community radio network, listening to the feed that one of its sibling stations, The Gap, a Solihull based station which covered the Meriden Gap, a part of the Midlands where urban meets rural England. The Gap had an agreement with BBC Local Radio to share certain news feeds, and today, they were broadcasting live updates from Birmingham Crown Court. Pete sat back in the studio chair, his headphones on, as the familiar voice of the BBC reporter detailed the latest developments.

"Mr Smith's testimony today was particularly harrowing, with vivid accounts of coercion, drug dependency, and systemic exploitation. The defence team, led by Marcus Blake and Victoria Hunt, sought to challenge his credibility, bringing up past actions and attempting to downplay the broader cultural issues within the company. However, Mr Smith's emotional and unflinching recounting of his experiences left an indelible impression on the court."

Pete's fingers gripped the edge of the desk as he listened, his emotions a storm of anger, sadness, and helplessness. He had known James's ordeal had been brutal, but hearing it articulated so starkly in a public forum was a new kind of pain. His thoughts were interrupted by Woody Bones stepping into the studio, flyers in hand as well as a satchel. Pete had to chuckle at how the former local radio boss who had sold his original ILR network in 2010 to Breeze Media still actively went out and did promotion work for the community stations he now managed.

Woody placed the flyers on the desk, his face serious but softened by his usual air of calm. "Pete," he said, his voice low, "I've just been catching up on the court coverage. It's a bloody circus out there, but your lad… he's showing real courage."

Pete nodded, his gaze distant as he processed Woody's words. "Yeah, but at what cost, Woody? Every word he says, they twist it, dissect it. And this isn't just about him. It's about all the people who've been chewed up and spat out by Manic."

Woody pulled out a chair and sat down across from Pete, setting his satchel on the floor. "You've got every right to be angry, mate. What they've done—not just to James, but to so many others—it's despicable. But this trial, it's shining a light where it's needed. People are paying attention now."

Pete sighed heavily, running a hand through his greying hair. "I just wish it didn't have to be James up there, baring his soul like that. He's already been through so much."

Woody leaned forward, his expression earnest. "Pete, your lad's stronger than you think. I've been in this industry long enough to know when someone's got fight in them. James isn't just fighting for himself—he's fighting for everyone who's been silenced, pushed out, or broken by this system."

Pete glanced at Woody, his lips pressing into a thin line. "And what about when it's over, Woody? When the court packs up and the headlines move on? What then?"

Woody gave him a small, knowing smile. "That's where we come in, mate. You've got a new role here, a fresh start. And James? He's got people like you and Lyra in his corner. He's not alone, Pete. He'll find his way—same as you did when you walked away from Manic."

Pete nodded slowly, the weight of Woody's words sinking in. "I just hope he can see that. Right now, it feels like he's carrying the world on his shoulders."

Woody leaned back in his chair, his voice gentle but firm. "And when he can't carry it, that's when we step in, Pete. Family, friends—we're here to remind him he doesn't have to do this alone."

Pete took a deep breath, the storm inside him quieting just a little. "You're right, Woody. He'll get through this. We all will. Anyway, have you heard who's back in the radio game now?"

Woody raised an eyebrow, leaning forward with an amused curiosity. "Oh, go on, Pete. Surprise me. Who's back in the game now?"

Pete loaded on his laptop the BBC Website, where the article about Manic firing its CEO, Adam Banks, and announcing his replacement, former GWR and GCap CEO, Ralph Bernard, had been posted. He turned the screen to face Woody, a wry smile playing on his lips. "This guy. Ralph Bernard. Back in the spotlight, taking over Manic. You remember him, don't you?"

Woody let out a low whistle as he read the headline. "Ralph Bernard? Blimey, that's a name I haven't heard in a while. Last time I checked, he'd gone quiet after the GWR and GCap days. He made me an offer once for the old stations, back in 2006 before he left GCap. Remember how we used to call him the Borg, because any station he acquired was assimilated into the GWR way of doing things?"

Pete chuckled, though the laugh carried a note of bitterness. "Yeah, the Borg. And now he's stepping into Manic at the worst possible time. Feels like history repeating itself, doesn't it? One big name trying to clean up the mess another big name left behind."

Woody nodded thoughtfully, leaning back in his chair. "The man's got a reputation for being a fixer, but Manic's a whole different beast. It's not just a business mess—it's a cultural and ethical disaster. Fixing that isn't about spreadsheets and boardrooms; it's about rooting out the rot that's taken hold deep down."

****

CHAPTER 20 – Return to Family Court

Monday 15th December 2025

James sat outside Courtroom 4 of the Birmingham Civil Justice Centre, his leg bouncing nervously. Lyra, now dangerously close to her due date, sat beside him, her hand resting on his knee to still its restless movement. Theodore and Dr Patel stood a few feet away, engaged in a hushed discussion over their notes. The faint hum of activity in the courthouse buzzed around them, but for James, time seemed to have slowed to a crawl.

James knew that in the criminal trial of Kylie, Chloe, Manic and several others, that case was ongoing, and Kylie, as she was on the stand in that case, would be unable to attend the hearing today. That absence added another layer of tension to the proceedings. James's focus was divided: while this hearing concerned custody arrangements for Cory and Alfie, the spectre of Kylie's criminal trial loomed large, casting a shadow over everything.

Lyra gave his hand a gentle squeeze, pulling him out of his thoughts. "You're doing brilliantly, James. Stay focused on today. This is about Cory and Alfie, nothing else."

James nodded, trying to draw strength from her calm presence. Across the hallway, Penny O'Rourke arrived, flanked by her solicitor, Mr Adam Pearson. She looked weary but composed, her polished exterior giving little away. James couldn't help but notice the absence of her husband, Weston, yet again—a detail Dr Patel had planned to highlight.

The courtroom doors opened, and a court usher called the case. James, Lyra, and their legal team stood, straightening their posture as they prepared to step inside. The air in the courtroom felt heavy, the muted colours and simple furnishings doing little to ease the weight of the moment.

As everyone took their seats, the magistrate, Mrs Justice Harrington, entered and called the proceedings to order. She glanced at the room, her expression unreadable, before addressing the assembled parties.

"This is a continuation of the custody proceedings for Cory Morgan and Alfie O'Rourke. I understand there have been significant developments since our last hearing. I will remind all parties that this court is concerned solely with the welfare of the children involved. Let us proceed without unnecessary diversions."

Dr Patel rose, her calm and measured tone filling the room. "Your Honour, since the previous hearing, my client, Mr James Smith, has adhered fully to the interim custody arrangements for Cory Morgan. He has also maintained regular contact with Alfie O'Rourke through video calls, although these were ceased upon advice to Mrs O'Rourke by her solicitor, citing that as she was a witness in the ongoing criminal case involving her employer, Manic Vibes Ltd, the video calls posed a potential risk to her testimony being compromised. While we respect the complexities of this situation, we must emphasise that ceasing all contact between Mr Smith and Alfie, even virtually, is not in the child's best interests. My client has acted in good faith throughout and seeks to reinstate these video calls immediately."

Mrs Justice Harrington nodded, her gaze turning to Mr Adam Pearson. "Mr Pearson, what is your client's position regarding the video calls?"

Mr Pearson rose, adjusting his tie. "Your Honour, my client, Mrs Penny O'Rourke, was advised to pause the video calls as a precautionary measure due to her involvement as a witness in the aforementioned criminal trial. She has not done so out of malice but out of an abundance of caution. Mrs O'Rourke remains committed to Alfie's well-being and is open to resuming video contact once the trial has concluded and any potential risks are mitigated."

Dr Patel stood again, her voice calm but firm. "Your Honour, while we understand Mrs O'Rourke's concerns, there is no evidence to suggest that these video calls pose any genuine risk to the trial. The abrupt cessation has caused distress for my client and, more importantly, for Alfie, who has benefitted from maintaining a connection with his father. Furthermore, both I and my employer, Nott Solicitors, had monitored the three permitted calls before Mrs O'Rourke ceased them, and no content could be construed as posing any threat to the integrity of her testimony or the trial. If it would please you, I have copies of the video which, with permission, I would like to play for the court.

James knew that, on the calls, his contact with Penny was minimal, with the only topic of conversation between them the health of the four month-old Alfie. The remainder of the calls had been filled with James cooing over his son, singing nursery rhymes, and simply talking to him to build familiarity. He was acutely aware that these moments, however small, were vital in forming a bond with his child.

Mrs Justice Harrington tilted her head slightly, her thoughtful gaze sweeping over Dr Patel and Mr Pearson. "Dr Patel, I will allow the submission of the video evidence but ask that you provide an overview of its content before playing it in court. We will determine its relevance before proceeding."

Dr Patel inclined her head respectfully. "Your Honour, the videos primarily depict Mr Smith engaging with Alfie in a warm and appropriate manner. The discussions with Mrs O'Rourke are limited to updates on Alfie's health and routine. There is no mention of the ongoing criminal trial or any topics that could potentially interfere with her role as a witness."

The magistrate gave a small nod. "Very well. You may submit the videos for review. I will view a selection during a brief recess if necessary." She then turned her gaze to Mr Pearson. "Mr Pearson, I trust your client has no objections to this evidence being presented?"

James sighed, as he hoped Penny wouldn't object, but he had a slight sense that she might raise a concern, perhaps to stall proceedings or shift the focus. Penny exchanged a brief glance with Mr Pearson, who stood and addressed the magistrate with careful wording.

"Your Honour," Mr Pearson began, "while my client does not wish to impede the court's ability to assess the evidence, she does harbour concerns regarding the relevance of these videos to the matter at hand. She questions whether their inclusion genuinely advances the case for custody arrangements or merely seeks to frame my client's actions in an unfavourable light. That said, we will not object outright to the court's review."

Mrs Justice Harrington's gaze sharpened, her tone firm but not unkind. "Mr Pearson, I appreciate your client's concerns, but I remind you that the purpose of this court is to evaluate all evidence relevant to the welfare of the children. The videos are intended to demonstrate Mr Smith's relationship with Alfie, and unless there is specific, substantiated concern regarding their content, they will be considered."

Seeing Penny with Alfie in her lap, while he had Cory next to him in a pushchair, made James feel a mix of emotions—pride at finally being able to care for Cory full-time, and sadness at the distance that still separated him from Alfie. His bond with Cory had grown immensely over the past month, but the thought of Alfie being kept from him weighed heavily on his heart. He glanced down at Cory, who was dozing peacefully in the pushchair, her tiny fingers wrapped around the edge of her blanket.

Friday 14th November 2025

James carefully placed Cory on the sofa, her tiny frame wriggling as her cries quieted slightly. Helen's gentle hands moved with practised precision, unwrapping the blanket and removing Cory's soiled nappy.

"Well, it's nothing unusual for a baby this age," Helen said reassuringly, glancing up at James. "She's healthy, but it's clear she's been left in this nappy for longer than she should have been. That's something we'll document, just in case."

James nodded, his jaw tightening. "Thanks, Aunt Helen. I'll make sure she's never in this state again."

Lyra knelt beside him, her presence calming. "You're doing great, James. She's safe now, and that's what matters."

James grabbed the nappy his dad had got, seeing his daughter wiggling like a little fish out of water. He couldn't help but smile despite the tension earlier that evening. "I'll put the nappy on her," James said, his voice steadier now. His hands moved with care, guided by instinct and the knowledge he'd gained from parenting books and advice from Lyra and Sarah. He gently lifted Cory's tiny legs, sliding the fresh nappy beneath her, and secured it snugly. Cory cooed softly, her cries fading as she looked up at him with wide, curious eyes.

"You're going to be alright, Cory," James whispered as he picked her up, taking her into the bedroom he and Lyra shared, her body feeling a natural part of his arms. "When I was a toddler, your granny Sarah would sing to me a song from her favourite soap."

James opened the door with his foot, so he could keep Cory in his arms without disturbing her peaceful state. Lyra followed quietly, leaning against the doorframe as James settled into the rocking chair by the window. The soft glow of a bedside lamp cast a warm light over the room.

James began to hum, his voice soft and low, as he gently rocked Cory. "Hold me in your arms, don't let me go. I want to stay forever. Home and away, with you each day."

Seeing Cory stop wriggling, and instead rest her tiny head against his chest, James felt a warmth spread through him that he hadn't known he needed. The fact that, like when he was a toddler, the Home and Away theme song could soothe his daughter brought a bittersweet smile to his face. For a moment, the stresses of courtrooms, custody battles, and the shadows of his past faded away, leaving only the simple, profound joy of holding his child.

Lyra stepped closer, her hand resting gently on James's shoulder. "You're a natural, James," she said softly, her voice filled with warmth. "She's lucky to have you."

James glanced up at Lyra, his eyes filled with emotion. "I'm the lucky one," he murmured. "I didn't think I'd ever
282

get to experience this. Holding her, singing to her—it feels like everything I've been fighting for is worth it."

Monday 15th December 2025

"I'm going to order a 15 minute recess in the case of Mrs Penny O'Rourke versus Mr James Smith regarding Alfie O'Rourke," Mrs Justice Harrington announced, her tone calm but firm. "This will allow me to review the video submissions and consider the arguments presented thus far. In the case of Ms Kylie Morgan versus Mr James Smith, I'm going to have to order a recess of a longer period while Ms Morgan is giving evidence in the Crown Court. Mr Smith's interim custody of Cory Morgan remains in place, with supervised visitation rights for Ms Morgan to resume once her criminal trial commitments permit. Now, there was one further case, an initial custody hearing in the case of Ms Chloe Smith and Mr Peter Smith regarding Nigel Smith, however, as Ms Smith is also... in the dock... of the Crown Court and is... indisposed... I'm going to order a recess of that."

James looked at his dad, who was sat near Theodore, confused, unaware that his dad had put in a custody case for Chloe's son, as there was little to no doubt that Chloe would soon end up in prison, leaving Nigel, her two month old son, either resident of a mother and baby unit in prison, or placed with a suitable guardian.

As the court recessed, James turned to Dr Patel, who was gathering her notes. "Do you think this is going well?" he asked, his voice tinged with worry.

Dr Patel glanced at him, her expression calm but serious. "The fact that Mrs Justice Harrington is taking the time to review the videos is a positive sign. It shows she's willing to consider all aspects of your relationship with Alfie. As for the broader custody issues, we've made a strong case today. Keep your focus on the children's welfare, and the court will recognise your commitment."

"What's this about Dad and my nephew, Nigel?" James asked, his brow furrowed as he turned to Pete, who sat quietly next to Theodore. "I didn't know you'd filed for custody."

Pete chuckled. "Well, I didn't want Cory to not live near or with her cousin, so I decided to step in, given the situation with Chloe. It's not looking good for her with the Crown Court case ongoing, and someone needs to think about Nigel's future. If she's convicted, the court might not look kindly on keeping him with her, even in a mother and baby unit. Nigel needs stability, and I figured he'd be better off with family rather than being placed in care. Anyway, you and Clo used to be inseparable as kids, and with you and Lyra expecting a child any day, you having Cory as well, and potentially Alfie living here part-time, I thought it made sense to keep the family together. Lyra agreed when I floated the idea. It's not just about Nigel; it's about all of you having a support network that makes sense. Anyway, you know next door to ours is to let?"

"And Lyra and I were looking for a place of our own," James finished, his voice softening as he looked at Lyra, who smiled and nodded. "Don't tell me, Dad, you've managed to get it for Lyra and me?

Pete smiled, a twinkle in his eye as he leaned back in his chair. "Well, I might have had a word with the landlord... and as for rent... well, you know The Borg is the new Manic CEO, right?"

James raised an eyebrow at his dad, his curiosity piqued. "What does Ralph Bernard being the new CEO have to do with rent, Dad?"

Pete chuckled softly, leaning forward as if letting James in on a secret. "Well, let's just say Ralph and I go way back to the GWR days. When I heard he'd taken the reins at Manic, I decided to give him a ring. After all, he's got a bit of a mess to clean up, doesn't he? Turns out, he's giving half the CHR lot a P45 party... and wants a duo for the Manic Vibes West Midlands drive... so I may have suggested you and Lyra might be the perfect fit. I mean, who better to give the station a much-needed fresh start than a duo who've been through the fire and come out stronger? He's told me that if you're willing to come on board, then there's no commute required to do your show, as he'll be issuing you with kit to do your show from home."

"A P45 Party? As in sacking all of the CHR presenters for Manic Vibes West Midlands and starting fresh?" James asked, his voice tinged with both surprise and a hint of hope.

Pete nodded. "Exactly. And he's bringing in new Regional Directors... Phil Riley, the old Orion boss, is signing on to be the Central Regional Director... and a new CFO... Darren Singer. Woody isn't too happy about half of GWR and GCap's old management team being resurrected, but Ralph assures me this isn't about going backwards—it's about creating stability after the chaos of recent years. He's well aware of the damage done by the toxic culture and the scandals. He's determined to clean house and start fresh."

Lyra glanced at James, her brow furrowed. "But would going back to Manic really be the right thing for us, James? After everything?"

James hesitated, the weight of the question settling on him. Returning to Manic, even under new leadership, felt like a risk. But the prospect of stability, of being able to work from home and focus on his growing family, was hard to ignore. He looked at Lyra, then at his dad. "I'll think about it," he said finally, his voice steady. "But first, let's get through today."

As the recess came to an end, the courtroom filled once more. Mrs Justice Harrington returned, her expression composed as she addressed the parties. "Having reviewed the video submissions, I find no evidence to suggest that the content of these calls poses any risk to Mrs O'Rourke's role as a witness in the criminal trial. On the contrary, the videos demonstrate a positive and nurturing relationship between Mr Smith and Alfie. I therefore order the immediate resumption of supervised video calls between Mr Smith and Alfie, with arrangements to be made for in-person contact as soon as practicable."

James felt a wave of relief wash over him, a weight lifting from his shoulders. He glanced at Lyra, who gave him a reassuring smile, her hand finding his once more.

Mrs Justice Harrington continued, turning to address Penny directly. "Mrs O'Rourke, I understand the complexities of your current situation, but I urge you to prioritise Alfie's welfare above all else. This court will not look favourably on any further actions that unnecessarily restrict his contact with his father."

Penny nodded, her expression carefully neutral, but James could see the flicker of unease in her eyes.

The magistrate's gaze then shifted to Pete. "Mr Peter Smith, your application for custody of Nigel Smith will be reviewed in a subsequent hearing, given the circumstances surrounding Ms Chloe Smith's criminal case. However, the court acknowledges the preliminary evidence submitted regarding your suitability as a guardian. Arrangements will be made to expedite this process should the need arise."

Pete inclined his head respectfully. "Thank you, Your Honour."

The magistrate's tone softened slightly as she addressed the courtroom. "This has been a challenging case, and I commend all parties for their efforts to navigate these difficult circumstances. Let us remember that the welfare of the children must remain our primary focus. This court is adjourned."

As the courtroom emptied, James felt a renewed sense of purpose. The fight wasn't over but today had been a step in the right direction. He turned to Lyra, her eyes shining with quiet determination. "We're going to make this work," he said, his voice filled with conviction. "For Cory, for Alfie, and for us."

Lyra nodded, her hand resting on her growing bump. "Together, we can handle anything."

Pete clapped James on the shoulder, his voice light but firm. "You've got this, son. And remember, no matter what happens, you've got a family who's here for you."

As they left the Court, James felt a flicker of hope—a sense that, despite the darkness of the past, brighter days lay ahead.

****

CHAPTER 21 – Cory's First Christmas... With a Surprise

Thursday 25th December 2025

James woke up after a restless night, his mind swirling with a mixture of relief and anticipation. The past year had been one of upheaval, but today was different—today was Christmas, and it was Cory's first. The dim winter morning light seeped through the curtains as James stretched and rolled over to find Lyra already awake, gazing lovingly at their sleeping daughter.

"Morning," she whispered, careful not to disturb Cory, who was nestled in a cot beside their bed. "Merry Christmas."

James smiled. "Merry Christmas," he replied, his voice thick with emotion. He reached out to stroke Cory's tiny hand, marvelling at the peaceful rise and fall of her chest.

"Can you believe it? Her first Christmas," Lyra said, her voice tinged with wonder.

James sat up, his thoughts briefly drifting to how much had changed since last Christmas, when he had been dating Kylie, when he had been entangled in Manic Radio's toxic web and battling personal demons. Now, with Cory in his life and Lyra by his side, everything felt different—grounded, purposeful, and hopeful.

The irony that a week had passed since Lyra's due date was not lost on James, especially as Cory was the daughter of his and Kylie's relationship, and was 4 months old, born amid a storm of chaos and unexpected twists. Yet here she was, a beacon of hope and innocence, bringing light to a life that had been shrouded in darkness for far too long.

Suddenly James heard Lyra gasp, and he knew that a late present was coming, especially as a puddle formed beneath Lyra on the floor, soaking into the carpet. For a moment, James froze, his mind racing to connect the dots. Then it hit him.

"Your waters just broke!" he exclaimed, leaping out of bed.

Lyra nodded, her face a mixture of surprise and determination. "Looks like this Christmas is about to get even more eventful," she said with a nervous laugh, clutching her abdomen as the first wave of contractions began to ripple through her body.

James started panicking as he heard Lyra say that, as, like most fathers, he felt a surge of both excitement and dread. The thought of Lyra going into labour on Christmas Day seemed almost poetic—an unexpected gift wrapped in the chaos of the holiday.

And then he fainted.

The fact that he would be present for the birth of his and Lyra's child, one which they knew was a boy and was going to name Lionel Theodore, after James's great-granddad and Lyra's brother, meant that the emotions overwhelmed him. The voice of his mother, Sarah, jolted him into awareness. He opened his eyes to see Sarah standing over him, her expression a mixture of concern and amusement.

"You owe me a fiver, Pete. James did here what you did when he was being born," Sarah said, helping James sit up. Pete chuckled from the doorway, holding a mug of tea as if it were a lifeline.

"Like father, like son," Pete quipped. "Don't worry, James. You'll be fine. Lyra's the one doing all the hard work."

James rubbed his temples, embarrassed but grateful for the light-heartedness. "Thanks, Dad. Great timing, fainting, huh?"

"Hey, its normal that "Hey, it's normal that you're overwhelmed," Pete said, patting James on the shoulder. "You're about to meet your son. It's a big moment. Look, I'll drive you and Lyra to Russells Hall Hospital. Sarah, you stay here with Cory," Pete added, setting his mug down and springing into action with a decisiveness that belied his age.

Lyra was already sitting on the edge of the bed, breathing deeply through another contraction. "I think that's a good idea," she managed, her tone steady despite the obvious discomfort.

James shook off the lingering dizziness and knelt in front of Lyra, taking her hand. "You alright?" he asked, his voice tinged with guilt for his earlier reaction.

Lyra smiled through the pain, squeezing his hand reassuringly. "I'm fine, James. You fainting is probably the most dramatic thing that's going to happen today— apart from, you know, giving birth." Her attempt at humour eased the tension, and James found himself chuckling despite the gravity of the moment. "Just think, in a few days, we start our new job at Manic... well, for me my old job but instead of Stoke and Cheshire, it's now West Midlands Drive. And we've got the new house next door we're slowly moving into, haven't we?"

James nodded, his mind juggling the excitement of Lyra's labour, the anticipation of their new beginnings at Manic, and the thought of their homecoming to a fresh house.

291

"Yeah, it's all happening at once, isn't it? New job, new house, new baby. Talk about timing."

Pete was already halfway down the stairs, grabbing the car keys and calling over his shoulder, "Right, let's get moving! Time waits for no baby!" His tone was upbeat, but there was a sense of urgency in his movements.

Sarah was in full mum-mode, gathering Cory's essentials while soothing her with a soft lullaby. "Don't worry about a thing," she assured James and Lyra as they descended the stairs. "We'll keep things running smoothly here. You just focus on bringing that little one into the world."

The drive to Russells Hall Hospital was mercifully quick, as it was literally less than 2 minutes, the Upper Pensnett estate being literally opposite Russells Hall Hospital, separated by a main road.

The car was busy, as Pete navigated the route with the precision of someone who had made this trip countless times before, his hands steady while James was sat next to Lyra, rubbing her feet with the care and nervous energy of a man doing everything possible to help, even if it was small. Lyra alternated between grimacing through contractions and shooting him affectionate, amused glances.

"James," she murmured during a brief lull in the pain, "you're doing great, but if you rub my feet any harder, I might need a second hospital visit for bruises."

James immediately loosened his grip, looking sheepish. "Sorry! Just trying to help."

Lyra reached for his hand, squeezing it gently. "You are helping, just by being here."

****

An hour later, James had the biggest shit-eating grin on his face as he cradled his newborn son, Lionel Theodore Smith. The weight of the tiny bundle in his arms filled him with an overwhelming sense of pride, love, and responsibility. The chaos of the morning and the whirlwind of emotions that had led to this moment all faded away as he gazed into Lionel's sleepy eyes.

Lyra, lying in the hospital bed, looked exhausted but radiant. She smiled at James, her eyes shining with tears. "He's perfect," she whispered, her voice hoarse but filled with warmth.

James nodded, unable to take his eyes off his son. "He is. And you're incredible, Lyra. I don't know how you do it."

Lyra chuckled softly, reaching out to stroke Lionel's tiny hand. "I had a little help," she teased, nodding toward him.

Pete and Sarah arrived shortly after, their faces lighting up when they saw James holding Lionel. Pete clapped James on the shoulder, grinning from ear to ear. "Congratulations, son. You've got yourself a Christmas miracle."

Sarah leaned over to kiss James on the cheek before turning her attention to Lionel. "Oh, he's beautiful," she cooed, her voice thick with emotion. "Look at that little face."

James handed Lionel to Sarah, his hands trembling slightly as he released his grip. Watching his mum cradle her grandson was another layer of joy he hadn't expected. "Mum, meet your... well, with Alfie, and Cory from me and Nigel from Chloe, fourth grandchild," James said with a grin, his voice brimming with pride. "Bet you didn't expect 2025 to give you not just one but a quartet of grandchildren!" James finished, his voice filled with a mix of humour and heartfelt emotion.

Pete, who was holding Cory, chuckled lightly, glancing between James, Lyra, and Sarah. "Well, I'd say the Smith family is expanding faster than a CHR playlist during Christmas! You lot have certainly kept us on our toes this year." He smiled at Cory, who was babbling softly in his arms, seemingly oblivious to the milestone day. "Anyway, I like how you've named him after his great-granddad."

"Yeah, well... I may have promised Granddad, when he had COVID, that I'd name a son after him if I ever had one," James said, his voice tinged with sentiment as he glanced at his newborn son. "Granddad Lionel was always the fun one... although Granddad Alan did always talk about his days as a technician on Crossroads back in the day."

The room filled with soft laughter, a welcome relief from the emotional whirlwind of the day. Pete adjusted Cory in his arms, rocking her gently as he reminisced. "Your Granddad Alan could talk the hind legs off a donkey about Crossroads. Always proud of his time in television, even if it was just behind the scenes. Don't get me started on the amount of times he mentioned how Noele Gordon handled herself like royalty on set," Pete chuckled, the nostalgic warmth in his voice filling the room. "He'd be chuffed to know you're carrying on a bit of that legacy— radio's not TV, but it's close enough. Which reminds me, Sarah, why don't you give your dad a ring to say that he's got another great-grandson."

James looked at his mother, who smiled warmly and nodded, pulling out her phone. "I'll call him right away. He'll be over the moon to hear about Lionel." She stepped into the corridor for a moment, leaving the rest of the family to soak in the peaceful atmosphere of the hospital room.

Lyra, propped up against her pillows, watched the scene unfold with a mixture of joy and contentment. "James," she said softly, catching his attention, "we've got a pretty amazing support network, don't we?"

James turned to her, his face softening. "We really do. I don't think we'd have made it through this year without them." He reached out to take her hand, squeezing it gently. "And now we've got this little guy. It feels like a fresh start, Lyra. For all of us."

Pete chimed in with a grin, still rocking Cory gently. "A fresh start, indeed. And speaking of fresh starts, I reckon Lionel here might just be the good luck charm for your new gig at Manic."

James chuckled, glancing at his son, who was now dozing peacefully in Sarah's arms. "Let's hope so. I still can't believe Ralph Bernard wants us on the drive show. It feels... surreal."

Lyra raised an eyebrow playfully. "It's probably because he knows you're a stubborn git who won't let the chaos at Manic define you. Plus, you've got me to keep you in line on-air."

"True," James admitted with a laugh. "Teamwork makes the dream work, right?"

The room was filled with soft laughter and quiet conversation as the family settled into the comforting reality of their new addition. Sarah returned, her cheeks flushed with excitement. "Dad's over the moon," she announced. "He said he's already planning a trip over from Catherine-de-Barnes to meet Lionel as soon as he can."

"That's Granddad Lionel for you," Pete said, smiling. "Always ready for an adventure, even at his age."

James's phone buzzed on the bedside table, interrupting the moment. He picked it up and glanced at the screen, his expression shifting from curiosity to concern. "It's Theodore," he said, glancing at Lyra. "I'll take it outside."

He stepped into the corridor, answering the call with a quiet, "Hey, Theo. What's up?"

"James, is there any news on if my nephew has arrived yet?"

James chuckled, a mix of pride and exhaustion evident in his voice. "Yeah, Theo. He's here. Lionel Theodore Smith was born about an hour ago. Healthy, happy, and already making his mark."

There was a pause on the line, followed by a soft laugh from Theo. "You actually went through with it? Naming him after me and your great-granddad? Well, I'm honoured. Little Lionel's already got quite the legacy to live up to."

James leaned against the wall, his free hand rubbing the back of his neck. "It felt right. You've been there for Lyra and me through everything, and Granddad Lionel... well, you know how much he meant to me. Naming him after both of you was an easy decision. Well, it was doing that, or Lyra making me sleep on the sofa."

Theo laughed, his tone light but filled with genuine warmth. "I'll take that as a compliment. And trust me, I'll make sure Lionel knows his namesake expects him to grow up strong, clever, and with far better taste in football teams than his dad."

James smirked. "Oi, don't start. Lionel can choose his own team—although I'll make sure he knows where his loyalties should lie."

"Look, give me half hour and I'll bring Clarice and Ellie with me. I'm sure Clarice would love to meet her newest cousin," Theodore said with a chuckle, and James chuckled himself, as he knew that the 5 year old had already took Cory under her wing, and she would be over the moon to have another baby cousin to dote on.

"Alright, Theo," James said, his voice warm. "We'll be here. Clarice will love her cousin."

As James ended the call, he took a moment to steady himself, letting the significance of the day wash over him. It wasn't just Christmas anymore—it was a celebration of new life, family, and resilience. He slipped his phone into his pocket and re-entered the hospital room, greeted by the soft hum of quiet conversation and the warm sight of his family.

"Well, Dad, Mum, Ly, it seems a certain 5-year-old Nott wants to meet her newborn cousin," James said, watching his dad still gently rocking Cory, who was now sound asleep, her tiny chest rising and falling in perfect rhythm. Sarah was cradling Lionel, her face glowing with grandmotherly pride. Lyra was propped up on the bed, her hand resting on her belly, now noticeably smaller but still symbolic of the life she had carried for nine months.

Lyra chuckled softly at James's announcement, though she winced slightly, still adjusting to the aftermath of childbirth. "Well, it seems Lionel is already making an impression. Clarice has impeccable timing—I could use a little girl's cheerful energy right now."

Pete smiled, looking down at the sleeping Cory in his arms. "I have no doubt that Clarice will walk in here like she owns the place. That little one's got the Nott confidence for sure."

Sarah, still cradling Lionel, looked up with a knowing grin. "It's in their blood, isn't it? The Nott and Smith families—resilient and fiercely protective. Lionel and Cory are lucky to have cousins like her."

James sat on the edge of Lyra's hospital bed, reaching over to gently brush her hair back. "You doing okay, Ly? Need anything before Theo and the tornado arrive?"

"I'm fine," she replied, smiling through her exhaustion. "Just... take a photo of all of this, James. I don't want to forget a single moment."

James nodded, pulling out his phone and snapping a picture of Sarah with Lionel, Pete with Cory, and Lyra smiling despite her weariness. The image captured a moment of calm and joy—a snapshot of hope after a year of chaos.

Exactly half an hour later, Theo arrived at the hospital room, holding Clarice's hand as she practically skipped inside. Ellie, Theodore's wife, followed a minute later, muttering about extortionate parking fees and Private Finance Initiative funded NHS hospitals that have the worse parking arrangements. James chuckled, as the two lawyers started an ethical debate on private parking fines while Clarice ran straight to Lyra and exclaimed with a voice full of excitement, "Auntie Lyra! Daddy said I have a new baby cousin! Is that him?" She pointed at Sarah, who was still holding Lionel, her face lighting up at the sight of the exuberant little girl.

Lyra smiled warmly, holding out her hand to Clarice. "That's right, Clarice. This is your new cousin, Lionel. Do you want to meet him?"

Clarice nodded enthusiastically, her curls bouncing as she climbed onto the chair beside Sarah. "He's so tiny!" she whispered, her eyes wide with wonder as she peered at Lionel, who was snugly wrapped in a blanket.

James crouched down next to her, grinning. "Tiny now, but he'll grow up fast. Just like you have. You're going to be the best big cousin to him and Cory, aren't you?"

Clarice nodded earnestly, reaching out a finger to gently touch Lionel's tiny hand. "I'll teach him all the important things," she declared. "Like how to draw ponies and make the best mud pies."

The room filled with soft laughter, the kind that comes from shared joy and relief. Ellie, finally done venting about parking fees, joined her daughter, leaning down to admire Lionel. "He's absolutely precious," she said softly, her voice filled with genuine affection. "And look at you two—already juggling parenthood like pros."

Lyra laughed, her hand resting on James's shoulder. "It's a team effort, Ellie. And we're definitely still learning."

Pete chimed in, his tone teasing. "Well, you've got me and Sarah to lean on. Between us, we've raised more than our fair share of Smiths."

Sarah gave him a knowing look. "And some Notts now too, it seems. But don't think that lets you off the hook, Pete. You're still on granddad duty."

Pete raised his hands in mock surrender, grinning. "Wouldn't have it any other way."

Clarice, still transfixed by Lionel, looked up at James. "Uncle James, can I hold him? I'll be super careful."

James glanced at Sarah, who nodded with a smile. "Alright, but you'll need to sit really still, okay?" he said.

With great care, Sarah handed Lionel to James, who then guided Clarice into a secure seated position before placing Lionel gently in her arms. Clarice's face lit up as she cradled him, her expression a mix of pride and awe. "Hi, Lionel," she whispered. "I'm your cousin Clarice. I'm going to teach you everything."

Lyra, watching the scene unfold, leaned against James. "This is what it's all about, isn't it?" she murmured. "Family."

James nodded, his heart full as he looked at the room—Lyra by his side, Cory snoozing in Pete's arms, Clarice bonding with Lionel, and their parents and friends all gathered in support. For the first time in what felt like forever, he allowed himself to believe that everything was going to be okay.

Theodore, observing quietly from the corner, finally spoke up, his voice calm but purposeful. "James, you've been through hell this past year. But standing here now, seeing all of this, I hope you realise—you've won. This is your life, your family, your legacy. No one can take that from you."

James looked at his brother-in-law, his eyes brimming with gratitude. "Thanks, Theo. That means a lot. And you're right—this is what matters."

As the room buzzed with soft conversation and laughter, James felt a sense of peace settle over him. He knew challenges lay ahead, but for now, in this moment, surrounded by the people he loved, he allowed himself to simply be.

This was Christmas—messy, chaotic, and absolutely perfect.

****

CHAPTER 22 – Epilogue
Monday 26th January 2025

Although James had been assured that his and Lyra's new Drivetime show for Manic Vibes West Midlands would primarily be broadcast from their new home studio, he found himself in the familiar surroundings of a professional studio at the newly revamped One Snow Hill headquarters, albeit on his own, with Lyra at home, looking after Lionel and Cory.

The reason, however, was simple - the Jury in the cases against his sister, Chloe, his ex-girlfriend, Kylie, Manic Radio Group Ltd, Manic Vibes Ltd, Manic Ventures Ltd and Manic Properties Ltd for the whole sex, cocaine, hub cum dump and financial scandals were due, any minute to deliver their verdict. James had volunteered to step into the studio to help cover breaking news for the station, knowing that the outcome of the trial would be a major moment not just for the Midlands but for the entire radio industry. The tension in the air was palpable, even through the glass of the studio's soundproof walls.

The fact it was Studio C3, the same studio, 9 months earlier, that Lyra had encouraged him to take a stand against the abusive culture of Manic Radio, made the moment all the more poignant. James sat at the console, his fingers lightly resting on the faders, waiting for the news bulletin feed to begin. The faint hum of the equipment was accompanied by the sound of his breathing, steady but laced with anticipation.

The irony that, in the control room was not just his producer, a former Hits Radio producer named Alan Jenson, but most of Manic's new regional management, mainly plucked from News UK, Bauer and Global after Ralph Bernard, the recently installed CEO, issued P45s to most of the old guard at Manic, restructuring the company

302

from its toxic roots up, was not lost on James. The new leadership team had promised a fresh start, with a focus on accountability, transparency, and a departure from the toxic culture that had plagued the network for years. But James knew that no amount of rebranding or executive reshuffling could erase the scars left behind. He was living proof of that.

Then there was, thanks to the changes, the glossy high value competitions, like the £500k Money Drop, a weekly cash giveaway, had been scrapped in favour of GWR style competitions, with premium rate phone lines and cheesy slogans like "Cash for Your Cravings" or "Win Big with a Simple Call." It felt like a step back in time, a return to the gimmicks of early 2000s commercial radio. The changes had been divisive, but they symbolised the new management's attempt to strip away the excesses of the previous regime and restore a sense of normalcy. James, however, couldn't shake the feeling that this was just window dressing, a way to mask deeper systemic issues.

He knew half of HR, Legal, the Board and even the Regional Director roles had been exterminated, with a mix of Bauer, Global and BBC alumni brought in to clean up the mess, and that, as well as each show having their normal producer, an executive producer, one who reported directly to the Board, was installed, meaning that every move within the studios was closely monitored. This additional layer of oversight was intended to prevent a repeat of the scandals that had engulfed Manic Radio over the past year. For James, the constant presence of authority figures was both a comfort and a reminder of how much the industry had changed—and how much he had changed with it.

Looking at the clock, he saw it was coming up to 4pm, and with Lyra at home ready to present from Pensnett while he was in the studio, he sighed.

"3 minutes until we go on the air," Alan said, and James nodded, taking a deep breath as he adjusted his headphones and straightened in his chair. The countdown clock on the wall ticked down relentlessly, each second a reminder of the magnitude of what was about to unfold.

"Ready, Reevesy?" Alan asked, his tone professional and James shuddered, the name he was called bringing back the horror of his time as the so-called "hub cum dump". James knew that Alan didn't mean it, but the memories of the nickname caused him to freeze.

Tuesday 15th April 2025

"And for God's sake," Kylie added, her voice turning sharp again, "don't embarrass me. If Lyra catches wind of anything... well, let's just say you won't like what happens. Now, Lane is next on your list to service, and he wants your arse. Make sure that he puts the cock ring, anal plug and nipple clamps back on you as last time you forgot to remind him, he had to pay me extra as an apology. Now, he's outside, so when I go out, you will make sure to accept his cum, to accept his abuse, and to do so without a single complaint, or else we're done. And remember... Reevesy... I'm still within the time to get an abortion if you don't comply."

James knew that last bit stung, as Kylie was pregnant with his child—a fact that should have been a source of hope or at least grounding. Instead, it had become another weapon in Kylie's arsenal of manipulation. The mention of abortion twisted his insides, not because of his own feelings about parenthood, but because of how coldly and calculatedly Kylie wielded it as leverage.

"Understood," James whispered, the words barely audible. Each syllable felt like another brick in the wall of his growing resentment, but he knew better than to push

back. Kylie thrived on dominance, and resistance only fuelled her cruelty.

She stared at him for a moment longer, her eyes narrowing as if searching for a crack in his compliance. Satisfied, she turned on her heel and swept out of the booth, her trainers squeaking slightly on the polished floor. James's head dropped again; his gaze fixed on the control panel in front of him. The room fell silent except for the faint hum of equipment, a sound that had once been comforting but now felt suffocating.

A soft knock on the door broke his trance, and James knew without looking who it was. Cody Lane, his brother-in-law, the man who his sister, Chloe, had recently married and entrapped with her own pregnancy. The fact that, unlike James, Cody, being a newsreader within Manic and a willing participant in James's degradation, had a life that appeared stable and put-together made the situation all the more humiliating for James. Cody was a rising star in Manic's newsroom, someone who seemed to navigate the same corporate swamp with ease and confidence that James had long since lost. The power dynamic between them had shifted drastically over the past few months, and Cody exploited it without hesitation.

The door creaked open, and Cody stepped in, a smug grin plastered across his face. His Linkin Park t-shirt, ripped denim shorts and expensive trainers, part of the unofficial uniform that male Manic staff wore to blend with the edgy branding, seemed to mock James's dishevelled appearance. Cody leaned casually against the doorframe, his eyes scanning James with a predatory gleam.

"Alright, Reevesy," Cody drawled, his voice dripping with faux camaraderie that barely masked his cruelty. "Kylie said you'd be ready for me. Let's not waste time, yeah? I've got to prep for the 4pm bulletin, so get those jeans *down, get that arse plug out of your arse and lube my cock up with your mouth."*

The scene felt unreal, surreal even. James sat frozen for a moment, staring at the console in front of him, the blinking lights of the equipment providing no solace. He could barely stomach Cody's smug voice, and the bile rising in his throat was only partly due to the humiliation.

Cody stepped further into the booth, closing the door behind him with a deliberate slowness that only added to James's dread. His grin widened as he leaned back against the door, arms crossed. "What's the hold-up, mate? Don't tell me you're losing your edge now. You're the one who wanted to be a star, yeah? This is part of the package."

James clenched his jaw, fighting back the surge of anger and shame that threatened to overwhelm him. He knew better than to protest. Any resistance would only bring more cruelty, more degradation. Manic wasn't just a station; it was a machine that consumed people like him, grinding them down to nothing more than tools for the brand. And Cody, despite his polished exterior, was just another cog in the machine—one who enjoyed his role a little too much.

Monday 26th January 2025

James knew that he was in the same studio, the same studio where those horrors had unfolded, but everything about today felt different. The toxic culture that had once permeated every corner of Manic Radio had been brought to its knees. The trials, the investigations, and the relentless media scrutiny had exposed the rot at the heart of the organisation, forcing change that was long overdue. James wasn't just sitting in Studio C3; he was reclaiming it.

He glanced at the clock again—less than a minute to air. His breathing steadied as Alan's voice came through his headphones, crisp and professional. "We're live in 30 seconds, James. You've got this."

James nodded, adjusting the mic and taking one last deep breath. This wasn't just another broadcast. This was the culmination of months of pain, struggle, and resilience. The verdicts would mark the end of one chapter and the beginning of another—not just for him, but for everyone affected by the toxic culture that had thrived at Manic Radio for so long.

And then 4pm struck.

"James and Lyra at Drive, today's best mix, today's best variety, Manic Vibes Midlands," the sweeper faded out, leaving James alone with the microphone and a deep, steady breath. His voice, calm but filled with a hint of gravitas, broke the silence.

"James and Lyra at Drive, today's best mix, today's best variety, Manic Vibes Midlands," the sweeper played, cutting through the tension in Studio C3. James could hear Lyra's voice as she introduced the show and threw it to the newsroom for the half hourly standard news update.

"In breaking news this afternoon," began the smooth, professional voice of the newsroom presenter, Sam Holloway, "the jury in the high-profile trial of Kylie Morgan, Chloe Smith, and several entities connected to the Manic Radio Group has reached a verdict. The verdicts will be announced shortly at Birmingham Crown Court, where our correspondent, Harriet Steele, is on the scene. We'll bring you updates in the next bulletin. In other news, a death in Wombourne ..." Sam continued, her voice fading into the background as James stared intently at the console in front of him. His heart thudded in his chest as he tried to process the moment. The courtroom, the verdicts, and the faces of everyone involved flashed through his mind in a chaotic blur.

Lyra's voice cut through the haze, calm and measured as always. "Thanks, Sam. Now, we've got an artist double play, and James, this is one you loved back in your gap year in Ibiza, isn't it?"

James shook his head to bring him back to reality, and looked on the Zetta screen, seeing that the network pushed playlist was showing that Aviici's Levels and Hey Brother were about to play. He smiled faintly, his voice steady but tinged with a bittersweet edge as he replied, "Yeah, Lyra, these tracks always bring back memories. Let's get into it—Aviici with Levels to start us off."

The familiar opening chords filled Studio C3, a wave of electronic nostalgia washing over James as he leaned back in his chair. His hands instinctively moved to the faders, adjusting the levels with precision honed from years behind the console. As the music played, he took a moment to centre himself, the memories of the past juxtaposed against the hope he carried for the future.

As the show went on, James got through the first half hour of his three hour shift with a mix of professionalism and focus. Every so often, his eyes flicked to the news feed, half-expecting the notification that the verdicts had been announced. The combination of routine radio work and the looming significance of the trial results created a surreal atmosphere—one moment he was joking with Lyra about the weekend weather, and the next he was reliving the trauma that had brought him to this point.

By time the 5pm news came on, James was nervous, as the half past 4 news had said that the Jury were still deliberating on final details, prolonging the anticipation.

Sam Holloway's voice once again filled the airwaves as James and Lyra prepared to hand over to the newsroom for the 5pm bulletin.

"This is Manic Vibes Midlands," Sam began, her tone even and controlled, though James could sense a subtle urgency beneath her professionalism. "Breaking news just in: the jury at Birmingham Crown Court has reached a verdict in the trial involving Kylie Morgan, Chloe Smith, and several entities connected to the Manic Radio Group. Our correspondent Harriet Steele is outside the courthouse with the latest. Harriet?"

James's grip tightened on the edge of the console as Harriet's voice came through, clear yet charged with the weight of the moment.

"Thank you, Sam. The atmosphere here at Birmingham Crown Court is electric, as months of testimony, cross-examinations, and damning evidence have led to this moment. The jury have delivered their verdicts on charges ranging from coercion and abuse to financial misconduct and conspiracy to pervert the course of justice. The presiding judge, Sir Thomas Harvey, is currently addressing the court, and we expect the official verdicts to be read momentarily."

There was a brief pause, the silence on air filled by the faint sound of shuffling papers and murmurs from the courtroom in the background. James's heart raced as he glanced at the clock. Every second felt like an eternity.

"Sam, I can confirm," Harriet continued, her voice steady but laced with tension, "that the first verdicts have just been announced. Kylie Morgan has been found guilty on multiple counts, including coercion, sexual assault, and conspiracy to pervert the course of justice. Chloe Smith has also been found guilty on charges of coercion and facilitating abuse within the organisation. Both women face significant custodial sentences, with sentencing to be confirmed at a later date."

The studio fell silent as Harriet's words hung in the air, the gravity of the verdicts sinking in. James felt a mix of emotions—relief, vindication, and a simmering anger at the suffering that had brought them to this point.

"Furthermore," Harriet continued, "the Manic Radio Group and its associated entities, including Manic Vibes Ltd, have been found guilty of enabling a culture of systemic abuse, negligence, and financial misconduct. The judge has ordered a comprehensive restructuring of the organisation and imposed substantial financial penalties. This ruling marks a seismic moment for the broadcasting industry, as one of its most prominent players is held accountable for its actions. I have with me Ralph Bernard, the CEO of Manic Radio, who was appointed while the trial was ongoing to clean up the organisation. Mr Bernard, what is your immediate reaction to the verdicts?"

James leaned closer to the console, his fingers hovering over the faders, as Ralph Bernard's voice came through the speakers.

"This is a pivotal day for Manic Radio and the broadcasting industry as a whole," Bernard began, his tone measured but resolute. "The verdicts handed down today reflect a reckoning with a culture that should never have been allowed to take root. On behalf of the current leadership team, I want to make it absolutely clear that the behaviours and practices described during this trial have no place at Manic or in any professional workplace. We will comply fully with the court's orders and continue to take decisive action to rebuild trust—not just with our staff but with our listeners and the wider community."

Harriet pressed further. "Mr Bernard, can you elaborate on the steps Manic will take to implement these changes? How will you ensure that this culture is eradicated permanently?"

"We've already begun to take significant steps," Bernard replied. "As many of you know, we've overhauled our leadership team, brought in independent oversight, and established new protocols for safeguarding and employee well-being. This isn't just about compliance; it's about creating a workplace where every individual feels valued and protected. Today's verdict reinforces our commitment to these changes, and we will work tirelessly to ensure that Manic becomes a model for accountability and integrity."

As Harriet thanked Bernard and the feed returned to the studio, James exhaled deeply, the tension in his shoulders easing slightly. Lyra's voice came through his earpiece, warm and steady as always.

"Well, James, that's certainly a lot to take in. How are you feeling about it all?"

James hesitated for a moment, his emotions swirling. Finally, he spoke, his voice calm but weighted with emotion. "Lyra, it's a lot to process. This verdict isn't just about justice—it's about closure. For me, for everyone who was affected by what happened at Manic, and for the industry as a whole. It's a step forward, but there's still so much work to be done. We can't forget what led us here, but we can use this moment to make sure it never happens again."

****

Books by Thomas Brant

Broadcasting Boundaries Series

BROADCASTING BOUNDARIES
BROADCASTING CHAOS
BROADCASTING DISRUPTION